PAUL IS MISSING

Kirk House Publishers

PAUL IS MISSING

DONNA CRAMER

First Edition
Printed in the United States of America

Paperback ISBN: 978-1-959681-71-7
eBook ISBN: 978-1-959681-72-4
Hardcover ISBN: 978-1-959681-73-1
LCCN: 2024915983

Cover design and interior design by Ann Aubitz
Headshot by Jim Cramer

Published by
Kirk House Publishers
1250 E 115th Street
Burnsville, MN 55337
612-781-2815
Kirkhousepublishers.com

CHAPTER 1

BRYNN GLANCED OVER HER SHOULDER as she heard her son Paul happily chortle in the stroller. She laughed as she realized he was trying with everything he had to reach the shoes boxed carefully on the shelf. Brynn returned to the heels she was trying on for her husband's cousin's wedding. She gazed at the shoes in the adjacent mirror. She wanted something attractive to give her some height without looking like stripper heels.

"No, no, Paul!" she suddenly heard a voice yell loudly. "Brynn, for God's sake, aren't you watching him at all!"

Brynn turned quickly to see her mother-in-law pulling a shoe strap from Paul's mouth. Marge snatched the shoe from him abruptly, scaring him at the very least, possibly hurting his mouth as she yanked the shoe back aggressively.

"No, Paul," she said forcefully.

Brynn rolled her eyes. He was seven months old; he had grabbed an attractive item. It wasn't like she would teach him a lesson. Paul looked at her, stunned for one second, then let loose with a roof-raising cry. Brynn immediately bent down to comfort him as everyone in the store looked over to see what all the commotion was about.

"Shh, Paul, it's ok, baby, you're fine," Brynn soothed.

"Hey, little man, what's going down?" Eric questioned loudly as he entered the aisle. He saw his son in distress, his wife with one shoe on and one shoe off, and his mother standing over both with her hands on her hips and a disapproving frown.

"She wasn't watching him at all," said Marge. "He was chewing on a shoe. Paul could have been seriously hurt."

Eric rolled his eyes. "I'm sure he's fine, Mother. Why weren't you helping Brynn? I thought you were going to watch Paul so Brynn could find the shoes she needs?"

"She said she was fine, so I stepped over one aisle to see if they had the inserts I needed." Marge looked at her daughter-in-law sourly.

There was no love lost between Marge and Brynn. There never had been. Brynn knew that Marge didn't think she was good enough for Eric. Brynn and her mother had struggled greatly while she was growing up, but she'd made it to college on scholarships. While there, she'd met Eric, who had just started his first year at law school adjacent to the undergraduate campus. Eric and Brynn had dated through all three years of his law school classes. They had planned to marry as soon as she had finished her senior year, but plans had abruptly changed when Paul was conceived the summer before. They had married. As Marge often reminded her, Eric's recently deceased father, George, had paid for the wedding. Brynn's mother had no money to afford a wedding. When Brynn expressed hurt at her mother-in-law's comments, Eric would only snort and say, "Big deal. They can well afford it. She likes to create drama. Don't let her see that it bothers you; she'll stop. She only wants a reaction."

Marge seemed to disapprove of everything that Brynn did. She didn't like the way she handled the baby. Brynn didn't watch him closely enough. She hadn't finished college. The list went on and on.

"Is she going to live off you forever?" Marge had said in an angry manner to Eric one time when Brynn had left the room but had still been close enough to overhear.

"She's my wife, Mother," Eric had said, nonplussed. "She is raising our son. She'll finish her degree soon enough. I'm making enough money to support us, and it is none of your business."

Marge's digs never seemed to get to Eric, but they always cut Brynn to the quick. The disapproval was constant. Brynn was sure that her mother-in-law probably took issue with how she breathed!

Paul was settling down now, lying comfortably draped over Brynn's shoulder.

"Did you find any shoes?" Eric inquired. "Baby, those look hot!" Eric pointed down at the black patent heels splayed on the ground at Brynn's feet.

Marge sighed disapprovingly and trilled out, "It's a wedding, not a sleazy nightclub. Brynn, don't forget you'll be in a church."

"I think she knows that, Mother," Eric said, shaking his head.

"They fit well. I think I'll get them," Brynn said, looking at Eric.

"Great," he enthused.

Marge shook her head and walked away, mumbling about finding those inserts.

"Ignore her. I often do," Eric said, bending to kiss Brynn. Brynn smiled, grateful for his support.

"Hey, my little reindeer, Paulie-Wallie, are you feeling better now?" Eric inquired gently, rubbing his son's back. Paul had a bright red birthmark on the tip of his nose, so they often called him Little Reindeer or Rudolph. The doctor said it would fade in time or might even disappear completely. Neither Eric nor Brynn worried about it.

"What a shame he is disfigured like that," Marge would often say.

Eric snapped the last time she said this, "He isn't disfigured, Mother, and even if he were, we would still love him. He's our son. Don't make a problem where there isn't one."

"Oh, look, there's Steven," Eric said heartily as he waved at a young man standing at the end of the aisle in the shoe store. The man looked toward Eric and Brynn. He whispered something to the woman he was with before patting her on the behind and walking quickly toward Eric.

Brynn rolled her eyes. Ugh, Steven, she had never liked him—she had always found him inappropriate and rude.

"Hey, man, good to see you, Eric. It's been a while."

Steven simply nodded at Brynn and smiled warmly at Marge, who had returned clutching her inserts.

"I heard you had a kid. Man, does he ever look like you! He has the same eyes and hair. It looks like he's going to be a big one, too, huh?"

Eric was not only tall but also had a sturdy, muscular build.

"Linebacker material," his high school coach had always said. Brynn remembered Eric telling her he had played high school football but had been too busy with his studies to play in college.

"Well, at least we know Brynn didn't cheat on you. There is absolutely no doubt that the kid is yours looking like that," Steven said, winking.

Brynn grimaced, remembering all too well why she disliked Steven so much.

"What the hell does that mean, Steven?" Eric questioned, seeming offended at his comment.

Steven held up a hand. "No offense, man. I didn't mean anything by it. I was trying to be funny."

Brynn shook her head and looked at her mother-in-law. Marge looked confused.

Steven! Brynn thought. He had always been the king of inappropriate comments. He had almost caused Eric and Brynn to break up not once but twice. He had continually insulted Brynn when she came over to visit Eric, was constantly making jokes about Eric getting lucky, and generally made Brynn feel that he considered her nothing more than a whore who was there to service Eric sexually. Brynn was unsure whether Eric participated in this inappropriate banter when she was not around. Eric had reassured Brynn that he found Steven's words offensive as well. The last time Brynn had seen Steven was at a club she had been to with Eric. It was a popular spot with everyone on the nearby college campus. Steven had pulled a chair up to the table where Brynn and Eric sat to join them, even though they were clearly on a date.

Steven had started his usual banter. "All set with some pussy tonight, huh, Eric?"

"Meow!" he had added, giving Brynn a lascivious glance.

"Yeah, Steven, maybe you should sit somewhere else," Eric had replied curtly.

The following week, Eric moved out of the room he had shared with Steven, and Brynn had not seen him since.

"No offense," Steven repeated, shaking his head and walking away. "Good-looking kid, Eric, old pal. "Congrats, Brynn," he said as he walked away.

Marge looked from Brynn to Eric and then hissed in a voice that was too loud if it was meant to be quiet.

"Eric, what in the world was that man talking about? Is there a question about Paul's paternity? Brynn, is there something I should know about?"

Eric sighed, "No, Mother. Steven is simply weird. He has always been like that. He thinks he's being funny, but he's not."

"But Brynn," Marge said and then hesitated.

Brynn sighed. Marge was not going to let this go.

"Brynn, were people questioning whether Eric was Paul's father? Why would that man say such a thing?"

Before Brynn could answer, Eric snatched Paul from Brynn's arms.

"Look at the baby, Mother. Look at my baby."

Eric held Paul directly in front of Marge's face.

"Does he look like me, Mother? You tell me."

"Yes, Eric, yes, he looks exactly like you."

Brynn shook her head as she gazed at Paul herself. How often had she called Paul mini-Eric because they looked so much alike? More times than she could count.

"Don't make a problem where there isn't one, Mother," Eric said, handing Paul back to Brynn.

"Brynn, are we done in this store? Mother, have you found everything you need?"

Both women nodded.

"Then, let's go," Eric said abruptly.

Brynn glanced at the other end of the aisle, where the woman and Steven were still standing and looking their way. Brynn caught Steven's eye as he stared at her and at Eric's back as he walked away. Brynn shuddered as Steven continued to stare unflinchingly. She pressed Paul more tightly into her chest and hurried her steps to catch up with the retreating Eric and Marge.

CHAPTER 2

GAIL SMILED AS SHE LOOKED AT HER DAUGHTER Alison and her soon-to-be-husband Jared standing before the judge. They would be husband and wife in seconds and spend the rest of their lives together. Time whirled by so fast. It seemed like only yesterday that she had been young and pregnant with her own baby, Alison. Gail could see herself washing the dishes in the small trailer Cecil had purchased for them all those years ago. As much as her mother had not wanted her to marry Cecil, Gail was sure she had made the right decision. In her mind, she saw Cecil entering the trailer, humming.

"How are you doing, Mom?" he inquired with a huge grin. He crossed over to her, enveloping her in a hug and touching her still mostly flat belly. "God has blessed us so much, Gail. A feeling came over me while I was working today, and then I heard a voice say, 'It's a boy.' God is telling us that we are having a boy. Have you told your mama yet?"

"No, I thought I would wait, and we could tell her together."

"That is a great idea, Gail. I know she's not sold on me being your husband, but we'll show her. We are going to have the sweetest life!"

Gail nodded and whispered, "I love you."

She threw her arms around her husband's neck. All that mattered was their happiness and the growing life inside her belly.

"Oh, Cecil, we will have a beautiful life and a beautiful family."

"You know it, honey," Cecil said, smiling. "God has blessed us. I can't wait until we have a whole bunch of kids running around here."

Gail nodded.

CHAPTER 3

6 MONTHS PRIOR

BRYNN REFLECTED ON THE BEAUTIFUL CEREMONY as she collapsed into the plush green chair in the bridal suite. Everyone had a wonderful time. Eric was in the bathroom. She hoped he wasn't throwing up. He certainly had a lot to drink, but why not? After all, it was his wedding. He was celebrating. *He was drinking for both of us*, Brynn thought with a smile. No one had said anything to her about the fact that she had not been drinking. *Maybe they thought* her *ever-present glass of water was vodka, or maybe they already knew*, Brynn thought. Her dress, with its billowing flow below her waist, hid the baby bump well. Brynn didn't care if anyone knew. She was so happy to be with Eric, and their love had made a baby. It didn't matter that it was a little earlier than they had planned. They were a family now, and that was all that mattered. Marge, Eric's mother, hadn't been that bad today. She had been gracious and kind to Brynn without making any snide comments. Maybe she would be more accepting of her now that they were family. She and Eric were happy. They were going to have a beautiful life.

CHAPTER 4

JUNE 2001

GAIL CONTINUED RUMINATING as the judge pronounced Jared and Alison husband and wife. Everything was finally going to work out. She knew it. The young teenage Alison had carried so much anger around on her shoulders. She always disagreed with her dad and forever challenged him about his staunch religious beliefs. Then Jared and his parents moved into the trailer next door to Gail and Cecil's. Alison had still been pugnacious at first, but Gail saw a gradual softening of Alison's attitude the longer she hung around Jared. She hadn't wanted them to rush into marriage, but now it seemed God had a different plan. Gail could so vividly recall every argument she ever had with Alison.

"I'm getting out, you know. I am leaving all this behind. Watch me," Alison had retorted more than once, glaring at her mother with her hands on her hips.

Gail nodded, holding her hands up to placate her daughter.

"Alison, I'm not trying to hold you back; believe it or not, neither is your father. It's just that you are so young, and so is Jared. You both have your whole lives ahead of you. You only graduated high school one month ago. Why the rush to get married? Why can't you slow down and wait a bit? Unless there is something you aren't telling me?"

"No, Mother, I am not pregnant if that is what you are trying to say. I told you and Daddy why there is a rush. Jared has already enlisted. If we marry now before he goes to his basic training, we'll be all set when he finishes. I'll be able to go with him wherever he is stationed. And if you think I should wait around here and see if someone better comes along, I will tell you right now that will not happen. The other men around here are—what can I say? —they are all gross, and they're all losers. Jared has dreams, Mama. We'll have a family. We'll have money. Maybe we will have enough money to help you and Jared's parents in a few years. Wouldn't you like to have a real house? Not live in this trailer anymore?"

"Allie, Allie, I understand that you think you love Jared."

"I don't think, Mama, I know."

"I know, but you are both so young. What if Jared gets shipped overseas?"

"He won't, Mama. It's not like there is a war going on or anything. Daddy doesn't even think I should wait to get married. He says if I love Jared, I should do it. I should marry him now."

"Oh, Alison, your father is worried that with you two spending so much time together, it will be far too easy for you to fall into sin, you know, sexual sin."

Alison looked over at her mother. She looked as if she were a million miles away. Her father, Cecil, looked very happy, talking animatedly to Jared's father. Cecil was probably just relieved that he wouldn't have to worry anymore about the premarital sex that he had been railing about for months and months. He had repeatedly brought up the topic, always droning on about how important it was to save yourself for marriage. Alison resisted the urge to snort as her father all but whispered the word "sexual." Time and again, she had to restrain herself from making the retort that sat so close to the front of her tongue. Too late! The sexual sin both her parents were so worried about had already happened two years ago, and certainly not with a partner that her parents would ever have approved of! Jared wasn't Alison's first lover, although he was the first man Alison truly loved. Alison was so happy when Jared and his parents moved into town. When Alison first saw Jared, she noticed how good-looking he was, with his sandy hair only slightly darker than her blonde hair. *Yeah, but he was probably just another loser guy who only wanted one thing;* she had thought of him at first. But as they began to talk, it became clear to her that Jared was different—much more than all those boys at school. She soon discovered that she and Jared could talk about anything, and he respected her, never trying to push himself on her. She had been ready to have sex before he had been. Jared wanted so much. He didn't want to stay here and settle for the dead-end life everyone around her seemed willing to accept. Jared had dreams. He wanted to travel, to see things, to do things. He awakened a hope in Alison that she thought had died long ago. Alison loved that she could talk to Jared about everything. They had some of their best discussions about religion. Alison had so many doubts, although she knew quite a bit about religion since she had attended church every Sunday since she had been born. Jared's parents weren't religious, but he was eager to know about all Alison knew. He was even willing to attend services with her and her mother and father. This made her dad beyond happy. Jared allowed Alison to question her beliefs. Sometimes, he would agree with her, and sometimes not, but he would never shut her down as her father so often did. If she questioned a belief with her father and he did not have the answer, he would try to silence her immediately. He would tell her not to be blasphemous and that she had to take things on faith.

"Do not question the Lord!" Cecil would shout if Alison persevered with her questions.

"Question everything!" was what Jared always said.

"How else do you learn?" Jared would repeat.

Alison knew that Jared was her person, that they were meant to be together for the rest of their lives, and that the rest of their lives were meant to start now, right now. She would let nothing, or no one, hold her back. She would have the best, the sweetest life with Jared by her side.

"Lord," Cecil prayed as they gathered around the small kitchen table. They only had a small reception for the family in her parents' trailer. "We ask for your blessing on Alison and Jared's union. We ask for your forgiveness for their sexual sin."

Alison felt Jared squeeze her hand. She didn't dare look up at him. She was afraid she would burst out laughing, and Jared probably would, too. They had been planning to get married for months, and then they discovered two weeks ago that a baby was on the way. Neither family had the money for a fancy wedding, so they had gone to the courthouse with both sets of parents in tow. Jared's mom had bought Alison a gorgeous white silk tea-length dress. It came with a tunic over it. Neither Alison nor Jared cared that she was pregnant before being married. The only person who seemed troubled by it was her father, Cecil. It didn't matter anymore now that she was Jared's wife. He would serve out his time in the military, come home, and they would have a beautiful life. All that mattered was how happy they were together and the growing life inside her.

CHAPTER 5

OCTOBER 1983

GAIL SIGHED HEAVILY as she looked at her daughter squirming in Cecil's arms in the cramped doctor's office. She shifted on the table and bit down on her lip to keep from crying out in pain. She grabbed her lower midsection. The pain was still so intense. Her body throbbed. She knew she had put off the operation as long as she could. The pain and the almost constant bleeding were becoming too much.

"It's the only answer," her doctor had said glumly.

"Gail, if you are putting this operation off because you're thinking of trying for another child, I cannot recommend against that strongly enough. You were at high risk for your first pregnancy. I can't see that working out in any way."

"God can always find a way," Cecil had grumbled miserably as he always did.

The doctor had glared at him.

"Putting this surgery off risks Gail's health and another pregnancy, well, Gail, in my opinion, it wouldn't be safe. You should be a healthy mother of one rather than deceased. You have a little one right there that needs you."

The doctor had pointed at two-year-old Alison, writhing in Cecil's arms, attempting to get down. Gail nodded and looked over at Cecil.

He had grunted, but then she watched his shoulders drop as he said,

"OK, Doctor, if you think there is no other option, we must do it. Alison needs her mama."

The doctor looked solemn but also relieved.

"I will schedule the hysterectomy at the hospital this afternoon. My office will call you with the date and instructions."

It had all happened so very quickly. Gail knew that Cecil was disappointed that there would be no more children. She knew he had wanted a whole houseful, but Cecil had been struggling to find steady work for the last few years. Gail had not been working at all, first with the baby to take care of and then with her medical issues. They could never afford more children. They were struggling to survive as they were. Maybe this was God's plan. Cecil wanted a son, and Gail could not help but feel that she had disappointed him, even though she knew he loved Alison with all his heart. Why was life working out so differently from what they had envisioned only a few short years ago? It wasn't supposed to be like this!

CHAPTER 6

OCTOBER 2001

ALISON SHIVERED, EVEN THOUGH THE DAY WAS WARM. Her mother, Gail, was fanning herself, so Alison guessed it was warm in the airport. They were surrounded by a crush of all the military families saying their goodbyes. The plane had taxied away, and the families were dispersing. Alison was still waving, staring out the airport's plate glass window.

"Allie, girl," she heard her father whisper as he touched her shoulder.

It was only then that she realized tears were rolling down her cheeks. She brushed them away and cradled her growing belly.

"He'll be home before we know it," Gail said optimistically, but Alison heard the hesitation in her voice. She knew her mother was as frightened as she was about Jared's safety in faraway Afghanistan.

"Allie, girl," her father said, clearing his throat loudly. "Jared is serving his country just like a real man should. I am so proud of both of you."

Alison nodded. When Jared had enlisted, who could have possibly known that there would be a horrific terrorist attack and that Jared would be quickly mobilized as part of the first 9,000 troops to deploy to Afghanistan.

"It will all work out, girl. Your husband will be home safe and sound in no time, and he will be welcomed home to you and the baby."

Alison nodded with a lump much too large in her throat to speak. What kind of world was her baby being born into? Alison could not help but wonder. What will happen to us? What does the future hold for our baby, Jared, and all of us?

"Come on, girl, let's get you home. You and the baby need to rest," her father said briskly.

CHAPTER 7

BRYNN SHIVERED AS SHE WATCHED THE NEWS REPORT. She bent down and kissed the sleeping Paul's soft head. It was so awful. How could this even happen, this horrific terrorist attack? She heard the door open. Eric was home from work. He entered the living room, standing behind Brynn's chair and gently touching Paul's forehead. He shook his head.

"Brynn," he said quietly, "I think you are watching the news too much."

Brynn nodded. "I know, but it's just so awful. I wish there were something we could do."

Eric nodded. "I donated to the Red Cross today in Paul's name. It's something, at least."

Brynn nodded and looked down at her sleeping son. "What kind of world is he inheriting, Eric? What does the future hold for him, for all of us?"

CHAPTER 8

TWO MONTHS LATER, DECEMBER 2001

ALISON CRADLED HER PREGNANT BELLY in both hands. She looked out the window again. Her parents would be back from the grocery store soon. They had to be. They had been gone now an hour and a half. Alison tried to breathe deeply to calm herself. She could always feel a panic attack coming on. Think of the baby, Jared's baby, she repeated. All the anxiety, the crying, the fear—it could not possibly be good for the life growing inside her. She had to be strong. This baby was all that she had left of Jared. It would be easier once the baby was here. She would be so busy caring for him. She would have less time to think. Where were her parents? Alison felt her mind begin to go down that familiar track. What if something had happened to them? What if there had been a car accident? God, she couldn't live without them! How would she survive? If they were dead or even injured, what would she do? She felt a slight pain in her stomach. What if something was wrong with the baby? She wouldn't survive if she lost anyone else! She looked at the clock on the wall above the kitchen table. Her parents should have been back by now. She felt the baby kick, a good, strong kick. At least the baby was still alive. If only Jared had been here, everything would have been better if he had been alive. Why was life working out so differently from what they had envisioned only a few short years ago? Her life wasn't supposed to be like this! She heard a car's tires scrape on the gravel outside the trailer. Her parents were home, finally!

CHAPTER 9

FOUR WEEKS LATER

ALISON GULPED IN A BREATH OF AIR. Her hands went to her belly, but then they fluttered away like butterflies as she remembered that her baby, she and Jared's baby, was gone—no more. The baby had vanished just as Jared had. Gone, gone for good, forever.

"Allie, who was on the phone?" her mother, Gail, inquired gently. She was about to comment that seeing Alison up, out of bed, and participating in life was good.

Gail shivered, remembering what had happened so recently when those military officers had shown up at their door at the end of November. Alison had been devastated when she saw those men with solemn faces and stiff military uniforms. They had told Alison that Jared, her husband of under a year, had been killed in Afghanistan. Alison nodded solemnly, saying almost nothing as the two officers spoke. They ended with, "Sorry for your loss, ma'am."

It was only after they left that Alison began to scream and shake. Her screams had been loud, long, and ear-shattering. Both Gail and Cecil had held onto their daughter for hours.

Gail tried calming Alison, saying, "Allie, the baby—think of the baby inside you. Calm down; don't upset the baby."

It had been awful, but eventually, Allie calmed down. She had been subdued for the next several weeks, refusing to eat but would try a little food when encouraged to do so for the baby.

Gail remembered well the day that Alison had said so seriously,

"If the baby is a boy, I will name him Jared after his father."

"It's a great idea, a great remembrance, Allie girl," Cecil had said seriously. "He'll be named for a hero, for a man who died with honor fighting for his country," Cecil had said proudly.

Gail believed Allie was improving, but Cecil and Gail had awoken two weeks ago to hear screaming from the bathroom. As they opened the door and saw the blood, Gail thought Alison had tried to cut her wrists as she had done that awful time in high school, but she suddenly realized that was not it.

In a voice rife with anguish, Alison said, "It's the baby, my baby."

There had been so much blood. She had miscarried and then had been so glum, but then who wouldn't be? Losing Jared and then their baby in rapid succession. It was too much.

"Who was on the phone, Allie girl?" Cecil inquired.

Alison slid down, her back touching the kitchen counter as she sank to the floor. Her mother waited for an outburst, but instead, there was only deathly quiet, and she noticed tears running silently down her daughter's face.

Finally, Alison spoke so quietly that her mother had to strain to hear.

"It was Sergeant O'Keefe. They finished the preliminary investigation. It looks like Jared was killed by friendly fire."

"Friendly fire?" her father questioned in a too-loud voice. "Friendly fire, what the hell does that mean? You mean those damn A-rabs were nice to him, and then they killed him?"

"No, Dad," Alison said in an irritated voice. "Friendly fire means the enemy didn't kill him. His own men, our soldiers, killed him."

"What! Why? How? I don't understand," Cecil said in the same too-loud voice.

"It was an accident, Dad," Alison said, now clearly perturbed by her father's obtuseness. "It was an accident; no one meant it to happen."

Alison clawed back up to standing, hanging on and leaning on the kitchen counter.

"An accident," she repeated. "He's not a hero. He's just a mistake. His life and his death mean nothing, just like my own."

Alison let out a sob and ran from the room. Gail tried to stop her, but Alison pushed her away and slammed the bedroom door. Gail tried to follow.

"Let her be. Let her go," Cecil said. "She needs time."

CHAPTER 10

TWO MONTHS LATER

ALISON WAS LYING ON THE COUCH in the trailer. They had arrived home from the hospital only two hours ago. All the windows were open, but still, it was uncomfortably warm. *We need an air conditioner*, Gail thought. They needed to find a way to afford one; even a small one would be better than nothing. Alison's wrists were carefully bandaged. She threw her arms over her head. She was so medicated, so out of it. Gail was so glad that she and Cecil had found her in time. Gail still found it hard to believe that her lovely daughter had tried to end her life once again.

"Can I get you anything, Allie girl?" Cecil gently inquired.

"A pop? Something to eat?"

God, she had lost so much weight. She looked so tiny on the couch, almost as if it would be possible for her to disappear and be completely swallowed up by the cushions.

"Nothing, Dad," Allie slurred.

"I'll get you whatever you want, darling," Cecil implored. He was about to suggest ice cream.

Instead, Allie blurted out, "A baby. I want my baby!"

"Oh, Sweetie," Gail said as she looked at Cecil.

CHAPTER 11

"LOOK AT THEM, GAIL. LOOK AT THEM," Cecil said as he gestured at the other shoppers around the store. Gail couldn't believe she had agreed to accompany him on this fool's errand. Yet here they were, walking around the store with an empty cart at the overpriced high-end food store. *Buy organic!* signs popped out all over the shelves. Gail cringed at the prices. There was nothing, not one item, that they could afford in this store, plus there were many items that she had never even heard of. And caviar—she had never even seen it before! *So now I know what it looks like,* she thought glumly. But they were not here to shop for or even look at food items. They were watching the people, the other shoppers. Cecil intended to steal a baby to give to their daughter, Alison. It was a crazy idea! Yet Cecil spoke about it constantly, always out of earshot of Alison. So many furtive conversations they had in bed at night.

"It's the only way," Cecil kept saying each night.

They had no money for adoption. Could they foster a baby? Who would give a child to Alison with her now multiple suicide attempts? The three of them lived in a rundown, much too small trailer. Didn't they do home inspections before people fostered children? They would never pass one of those! Yet Alison seemed to be getting worse with each passing day. She needed something to live for and get up for in the morning. Gail thought of Alison and shivered at the thought of losing her. Gail realized that at any moment, any day, it would be all too possible to find Alison dead. Something had to change. Cecil whispered in Gail's ear, snapping her out of her reverie.

"These people are not like us, Gail. What have any of them sacrificed for our country? Nothing! Not one thing. Alison and Jared have given everything, yet what do they have to show for it? Jared in the ground and Alison suffering every day."

Gail shook her head.

"Cecil, they're people, too. They're just like us."

"Oh, but are they? Are you sure about that, Gail? It takes a while but watch them closely. We'll come back again. You'll come with me a few more times. I've been coming here once a week for two months now."

"Cecil!" Gail retorted, "You are wasting our gas money driving for over an hour to watch mothers and children. That is just weird!"

"It takes time, Gail. This isn't easy, but I have been praying on it a lot. We are supposed to get a baby for Alison. God asks us to do hard things; you know that. Brother Mike says that all the time. God asked Abraham to sacrifice his own son. I believe we are being led by God to do this. I am sure of it, Gail. These people are different. They are not like us. They are not God-fearing. God is calling us to help Alison. No one else can or will help her. You know that. We can help Alison raise a child up right. We will teach the child to be godly and Christian." He snorted and gestured at the shoppers again, "How many of them get up on Sunday and attend Sunday service? Alison knows how to raise a baby right, and we will be right there, too, to help her every step of the way."

"Excuse me, are you buying those avocados or not?" a woman huffed in an irritated voice.

"Excuse us," Gail started to say politely, but before she could get all the words out, the woman gave both Gail and Cecil a look of disgust. She seemed to be taking in their clothes and thread-bare jackets, unlike her jacket with its fur hood. Gail looked at the purse in her cart. *I bet that's one of those designer purses*, Gail thought silently.

"If you are not buying avocados, just get out of the way. You are standing there talking, blocking traffic, and I need to get my food. I have places to be."

"Sorry, ma'am," Cecil said, but his voice was harsh, stinging, unpleasant like sour milk. "We didn't mean to bother you."

"Right," the woman said irritably, waving her hand as if she wanted to bat them away like a pesky fly. "Just move," she huffed, pulling her cart closer to the display.

Cecil whispered to Gail as they walked away, "See, not like us at all. She has no respect for people she thinks are less than her. How do you think that woman treats her kids? Also, did you see all the political bumper stickers on their cars in the parking lot? These people don't even believe in the one true president. They voted for the other guy! We would be saving a child, not harming anyone. We have to find the right family and the right time. God destined this, Gail. I know. If you're not ready, I get that. We'll go home and pray about it together. We'll come back

again. It might take some time. God will guide us, you'll see."
Cecil abandoned the empty cart in an aisle, and they walked out
of the store together. Gail shook her head. *It's wrong; it's wrong*
was beating like a refrain through her head. But it couldn't hurt
to pray with Cecil about it, could it? Maybe God did have a plan.

CHAPTER 12

GAIL FELT HER STOMACH SEIZE UP, and it felt like her heart might stop as she watched their neighbor, Betty, run out to the car. Betty had been waiting for them to pull up. Betty had agreed to look in on Alison while they went on their adventure to Total Foods. Betty had no idea what they were doing or where they had gone. But now, something had happened; something was wrong. Gail opened the car door before Cecil even stopped the car.

"Betty," Gail yelled. What had happened to Alison? What had she done? *Please be ok; please be ok,* thundered through her brain.

"We had a little incident here, but Alison's ok now."

"What!" Cecil thundered and began running for the trailer as if being chased. Gail and Betty were right behind him.

"Allie, Allie Girl," Cecil yelled with fear so very present in his voice.

"Here, Dad, I'm here," Gail heard her daughter say in a tired voice. She was sitting on the couch with a washcloth wrapped around her wrist.

"Oh, Allie, no, you didn't!" Gail said, collapsing on her knees in front of her daughter.

"She's fine, now, she's fine," Betty said soothingly.

"Not so sure about that," Cecil snapped angrily, causing Betty to back up.

"Cecil, shh!" Gail remonstrated. Lashing out at poor Betty would prove nothing.

"I'm fine, Mom and Dad," Alison said in a quivery voice. "It's not what you think—it's not. I wasn't… I didn't try to kill myself. I just —I got so upset. I didn't know what to do. Daddy, I didn't know what to do, how to make it stop!"

Gail carefully unwrapped the cloth at Alison's wrist.

"Oh, Allie," she said, both sad and relieved at what she saw there. There were no cuts but rather a bright red scrape. The skin around the wound was swollen. Alison looked down and began to cry.

"Betty, what happened?" Gail said quietly.

"Well, now, I called Alison almost an hour ago. She didn't answer the phone. I left a message and told her to call me right back. When she didn't, I came over here. The door was open, and I found Alison in the bathroom. She was running a steak knife over her wrist. I screamed. I think I scared the poor girl. I didn't mean to."

"Allie, what were you trying to do? What were you going to do if Betty hadn't come in?" Cecil questioned gently.

Alison shook her head vigorously.

"It's not what you think! Honestly, it's not what you think. I wasn't going to kill myself. I just felt so sad and so angry. I was thinking about Jared and my baby and how much I wanted them back. I got the photo album out. I wanted to see Jared's picture, and that awful letter from the Marines fell out, saying how Jared died, the friendly fire. I got so angry. I didn't know what to do. I needed something; I needed to do something!"

"Why didn't you take one of your pills, Allie Girl?" Cecil whispered.

"Because, Dad, they don't work. They aren't helping me! I needed to feel better; I didn't want to die, please believe me. I only wanted to feel better. I got out the knife and moving it over my wrist made me feel better. It helped."

"But, Allie, you could have hurt yourself accidentally."

"I know, Mom, but I just wanted to feel better. I scared Betty. I'm sorry, Betty."

"It's ok, honey," Betty said, patting her shoulder carefully.

"I'm fine now, really, Mom. I feel better—I do," Alison said, smiling weakly.

CHAPTER 13

LATER, AFTER THE DOCTOR HAD BEEN CALLED and Cecil had picked up the new medication, Alison was asleep in her bed, Gail and Cecil began to talk. Gail had been careful not to tell the doctor what Alison had done. She did not want him to suggest inpatient treatment again. The copays on their health insurance were much too high to afford. She had only told the doctor that Alison's anxiety was increasing, and the pills were not working. The doctor suggested a different prescription and a dosage increase.

"We'll see if that is effective," he had said.

He was experimenting as if Alison was some experiment! The medicine had at least made her tired, and now she appeared to be deeply asleep in her bed. Gail sighed. "I don't know if Betty will ever agree to check in on Alison again after that. She was scared. I could tell, even though she didn't say so."

Cecil shook his head.

"Alison is getting worse, Gail, not better. We need to do something soon. She needs something to live for. She's focusing too much on the past."

"I agree," Gail said wearily.

"Next week we go. We'll get everything ready this week. Then we go to that store and come home with a baby for Alison. She needs a baby now more than ever." Gail nodded. Cecil held out his hand and patted the couch next to him.

"Let's pray on it right now, Gail. We need His guidance. God will tell us what to do. He'll find the baby that is meant to be ours."

Is Cecil crazy? Gail did not like that the thought had even entered her head, but now that it had, she considered it. His idea was undoubtedly crazy. Stealing someone's child was wrong and a crime. Many mothers had been in the store that afternoon when they had gone to look for a baby. Still, Cecil had said God was telling them it was not the time.

"God wants us to return in the morning in another week," Cecil had intoned solemnly.

Gail sat silently and pondered what she had seen at Total Foods. Many of the people seemed pretentious, entitled, and unfriendly. She thought of shopping at their small, local store and how it was not uncommon to compare prices with another shopper, whether you knew them or not. People would often casually mention that there was a great deal on chicken or something else.

"Get over there quick now before they run out," someone would say.

But at Total Foods, the people seemed isolated, caught up in their thoughts or on their ever-present cellphones. Gail had noticed two women who snapped at their children, "We are not buying that. Put it back!"

Another woman had ripped a candy bar from a very young toddler's hand so quickly and viciously that the child had wailed loudly in surprise while the mother snapped, "Stop it!" and glared at the child. Could Cecil possibly be right? Were these people not like them? They seemed to have everything: money, privilege, children, but it didn't seem they appreciated any of it. Why was it fair that they had children and Alison did not? How would poor Alison ever be able to have a child? She was so very depressed, and the doctor had said that her chances of getting pregnant and carrying to term were slim. It was all too possible that she might miscarry again. Yet Alison wanted a child in the worst way. It was the only thing that she seemed to want. She had wanted Jared's baby, and, of course, that chance had ended with his death, but a baby would give Alison something, someone to live for. They were losing Alison. Gail knew it and felt her daughter slipping away more each day. If they didn't do something soon, they might lose her. Life would be unbearable for them without her. Cecil had idolized Alison since they brought her home from the hospital. He had been a good, attentive father, and the drinking that had plagued him earlier in their marriage had vanished after Alison's arrival. He quit drinking just like that. Gail felt certain that if Alison were gone, Cecil would feel no compunction to stay sober. So, Gail could lose everything after all these years. The thought was unbearable. There did not seem to be another way for Alison to get a baby. Gail had talked to a lady at church who had fostered children. She told Gail it had been an arduous process. There had been several home visits before she was approved. Gail was certain their tiny, rundown trailer would not pass any inspection. Gail kept it clean, but many items needed repair. Gail and Cecil could not afford these repairs. They couldn't set Alison up for more disappointment.

Suddenly, an idea popped into Gail's head. Maybe they could borrow a baby! They didn't have to keep the child forever. The child could stay with them for a few months, maybe a year. The baby would be well cared for. They would love him or her. Alison would have something to live for. She would get off the couch, get out of bed, and participate in life again. She might even meet someone. She would be a single mother, but there were single fathers, too, right? Alison could move on and have a real life. This baby would be a crutch, a little helper to get Alison over the rough part. If she met someone, maybe she could have her own child. The doctor had said another pregnancy for her was unlikely, not impossible, and besides, God could work miracles. Once Alison was settled and happy, they could give the baby back. Gail's thoughts soared as she perceived this brighter, happier future for all of them. Then, another thought thundered through Gail's mind. It was wrong and unfair to take another woman's child. Gail knew that even if Cecil did not. But life wasn't fair, was it? Was what had happened to Alison, to Jared fair? Why had the idea to borrow the baby popped into Gail's mind anyway? God must have placed the idea in her head in the first place. Who was she to question God? What was that Bible verse? "The ways of the Lord are inscrutable." They could keep the baby for six months or a year. Alison would heal, and they would give the baby back. There would be stories in the papers about a missing child. It would be easy to find the names and address of the parents of the child they took. They would return the baby as soon as Alison was better; maybe she would even be pregnant with her own child. Gail could envision meeting the parents of the baby they had borrowed. The parents would be ecstatic that their baby was being returned and even more appreciative of all they had. Gail could carefully explain what they had done and why. They could all become friends. Ok, it sounded fantastic, but why not? Was it wrong? Well, wasn't Alison's suffering wrong? Wasn't it wrong what Alison endured daily as she struggled to survive? Wasn't it wrong that Jared had died so tragically before he even had a chance to live? Gail opened her eyes and looked at Cecil, praying beside her on the couch. This idea of borrowing a baby? It had to have come from God. Gail could not imagine coming up with such an idea on her own, and if God wanted it done, well, who was she to say otherwise? Gail gently tapped Cecil on the knee. He stopped praying and opened his eyes.

Gail said quietly, "Cecil, we must return to that store again. We must go very soon—not wait until next week, maybe in just a few days. I was praying about it, and God wants us to do it. I know that now."

"Now you're talking," Cecil said happily. See, Gail, I knew you would come around. We'll give the right child a good life and raise him up godly."

Gail nodded. She intended to keep the borrowing part of the plan secret for now. She knew Cecil would balk at such an idea, but the way the idea had burst into her mind, it had to have come from God. And if God was willing to do this, who was she to resist? Her duty as a Christian was to follow, and she fully intended to do so.

"We'll pray every night about finding the right baby," Cecil said, reaching out a hand and grabbing Gail's knee.

Gail nodded.

CHAPTER 14

CECIL AND GAIL SAUNTERED toward the store entrance. Cecil seemed to be in a great mood, almost gleeful. Gail was nervous and uncertain. They had the used car seat strapped in the back of the car, along with toys, blankets, food, and even milk in a small cooler. Were they going to do this? Was this happening? Alison was worse than ever. She would need a lot of help caring for a baby. Gail was sure that the medication the doctor had her on now was much too strong. She shuffled around the trailer zombie-like when she was even awake. She would ask questions over and over, two times, sometimes three times, the exact same question. Gail was sure they needed to get her off that medication.

A family—two parents and an older woman with a very young boy—was entering the store directly in front of them.

Eric and Brynn, with Marge following slightly behind, walked toward the front entrance of Total Foods. Eric had his arm slung casually over Brynn's shoulder as she held a squirming Paul.

"Brynn, do you have his jacket zipped?" Marge inquired. "It's a little cold out today."

"He's all set, Mother," Eric said curtly.

No one noticed the older couple walking purposefully toward the entrance behind them. Eric was about to reach for a cart at the door when Brynn said, "Shoot, I left the list in the car!"

She thrust Paul toward Eric, and the baby's expression changed from happiness to agitation. He looked at Eric and twisted his face as if about to let out a loud cry.

"Hurry, Brynn," Eric urged. "He only wants you."

Brynn spun around, brushing past Marge and almost colliding with the older couple behind them.

"Sorry, sorry," she yelled, half running back to the parking lot.

"Where is she going?" Marge questioned, seeming annoyed.

"She forgot the grocery list, Mother."

"Oh, of course, she did," Marge wheezed. "She forgets everything. I'm surprised she hasn't misplaced the baby yet."

Cecil and Gail noticed that the family in front seemed to be arguing. They watched the young woman thrust the baby at the father. Clearly, the man was the baby's father. They looked so much alike, with the same curly hair and sturdy build. The man took the child but held him awkwardly, urging his wife to hurry back. The young woman turned and ran toward the parking lot, almost clipping Gail and Cecil but airily saying "sorry" as she sprinted past. Gail thought the older woman with the couple had an unpleasant expression on her face as if she had just taken an enormous swig of vinegar. The young boy, very handsome and with curly dark hair, looked back directly at Gail and Cecil. Improbably, he pointed at them.

"You have that puppy toy thingy?" Cecil whispered in Gail's ear.

She nodded.

"That baby is looking right at us," Cecil whispered again.

Eric pulled out a cart from the queue with such force that he hit the man's arm standing directly behind him. Cecil let out a surprised "Oh!"

Eric immediately said, "Sorry, man, sorry."

The older man only nodded.

"Excuse me," Marge said huffily to the older couple, "but other people need to get their carts, too."

"Sorry," the older woman said, looking down.

"Honestly, Eric, where is she now? What takes her so long to get back from the car? I bet she doesn't even have the list. She probably left it at home."

"She had it, Mother. I saw it in the car. She will be here any second now."

"Well, I don't think you want to spend your entire day off in a grocery store, do you, son?"

Eric sighed in frustration and turned to plunk Paul into the seat in the cart. The older woman, still behind him, visibly flinched as Eric put the child down with more force than necessary. The child's face scrunched up, and he released a giant wail.

As Cecil pulled out a cart, Gail moved closer to comfort the crying child since it seemed as if the father and the older woman (his grandmother, perhaps?) were not going to.

"Sweetie, sweetie, it's okay," Gail cooed, gently reaching out a hand toward the child. The unpleasant older woman glared at her and stepped directly in front of her, blocking her access to the baby.

"What a beautiful child," Gail gushed.

Eric and Marge ignored the stranger's comment. Marge, seemingly noticing for the first time that Paul was crying, intoned, "Paulie, baby," as she moved closer to him.

"It's okay, it's okay," Gail said quietly.

Marge watched the older couple continue into the store.

"Brynn, there you are," Marge said exasperatedly.

"What in the world took so long?"

"I guess it fell between the seats," Brynn said breathlessly.

"Paulie, baby, what's wrong?" Brynn asked as she picked up Paul, who held his hands up to her.

"Can we just start shopping before the entire day is gone?" Marge hissed quietly.

The three of them entered through the second sliding door, not noticing the older couple now standing just inside with their empty cart.

"You have him, Brynn?" Marge inquired. "How will you get your shopping done with him crying like that?"

"He'll stop in a minute, Marge. He's fine, aren't you, Paulie-Wallie?" Brynn stated, nonplussed.

"Mother, why don't you get your shopping done? I'll help Brynn with Paul."

"But I thought you said you might get an important call from work?"

"I might. I'll come find you, Mother, if we need you."

"All right," Marge sighed, giving her cart a big push as she headed down the aisle. Brynn and Eric continued into the vegetable and fruit section.

"I need a lot of things here," Brynn said pleasantly.

"Uh-huh," Eric murmured noncommittally.

Brynn began to select and bag some apples. Paul was still fussing in the cart, so Brynn reached over and grabbed him, placing him on her hip. She had her arm around him, but as she put the apples in her bag, he suddenly reared his body back.

Gail grabbed Cecil's arm, making sure he was watching. She took in a breath as the young woman almost dropped the child. Gail flinched. If the child would have hit his head on the hard floor, he could have been seriously injured.

However, the mother did not drop him; instead, she shouted, "Oh my God!" as she spilled all the apples on the floor.

"She is taking the Lord's name in vain. I don't like it!" Cecil whispered furiously.

Two shoppers drove their carts around the spilled apples. A third shopper looked at Brynn in disgust. The woman's husband approached. He seemed disgruntled and short on patience.

Staring at his phone, Eric looked up, saying, "Brynn, what the hell?"

"Whoops, I almost dropped Paul."

"Why isn't he in the cart where he should be?" Eric grumbled.

Eric said brusquely, "Brynn, I'm getting a call. Are you okay on your own? Or should I find Mother?"

Brynn rolled her eyes. "I'm fine, Eric."

Cecil moved quickly to the area where all the apples were splayed on the floor. He grabbed the bag and carefully placed the apples back in the sack. After gathering them, he handed them to the young woman, who took them without saying a word. Cecil moved away.

Eric quickly walked away. Brynn turned around to thank the man who had helped her with the apples, but he had disappeared.

"Come on," Cecil gestured to Gail. "Let's look around. I think that child is the one, though. These people are rude and disrespectful. I can almost guarantee they never attend church on Sunday. Don't even know enough to say thanks," Cecil groused.

Brynn continued to the next aisle and began to select some cereal from the shelf. She heard Paul give a chortle and saw him point at someone behind her. Brynn turned around expecting to see either Eric or Marge, but an older woman held up a small stuffed puppy and made the stuffed animal wave at Paul. He chuckled again. Brynn started to turn around to smile at the older woman, but she heard someone calling her name.

"Brynn, Brynn, where are you?"

"I'm right here, Marge," Brynn said, quickly pushing her cart toward Marge.

The older couple with the empty cart backtracked toward the fruit and vegetable aisle. Suddenly, the couple stopped, having a furtive, whispered conversation. Eric sighed as his phone rang yet again, and he looked down at it. Of course, it was Bob. Eric had known he would call. He rode all the junior partners unmercifully, and Eric was not surprised. Bob was probably calling about Eric's brief that he had left on his desk last night. Bob had already left for the day before Eric had finished and was only now probably reviewing Eric's work. *Up for some criticism yet again*, Eric thought as he clicked the call on.

"Bob," he said, trying to sound pleasant.

"Where the hell are you?" Bob yelled into his ear. "It's past ten. I have some questions to go over on your brief."

"What?" Eric said, startled. "Steve told Ryan and me to take the day off since we had been working such long hours on this case. You were standing right there, Bob."

"Oh, oh, okay, I guess. Listen, Eric, there are a few problems with the articles you cited in your brief."

"What, are you sure?" Eric questioned. The older couple suddenly stopped so abruptly that Eric almost ran into them. He sighed in frustration and inadvertently hit the older woman's arm as he walked by. He said nothing as he walked quickly away, with Bob still complaining in his ear.

Cecil followed Eric to understand what he was like and what type of person he might be. He gestured for Gail to continue down the next aisle.

Gail pushed her cart into the meat section. Gail saw the older woman who had been with the couple earlier. Gail decided to try to talk to her again, maybe get a sense of what she was like. Gail still fully planned to return this baby as soon as Alison was better. Perhaps if she could initiate a conversation with the woman, she could discover her name. The more information she had, the better. She sidled up beside the woman, who was looking at packets of hamburgers.

"Can you believe the cost of that hamburger?" the older woman said to Marge in a friendly manner. "That is way more than I can afford," she said, smiling at Marge. Marge looked at the woman. Her clothes looked old, her shoes scuffed, and her jacket threadbare. Marge's mouth turned downward in a slight sneer.

"The hamburger is always that much here. If you can't afford it, don't buy it," Marge said abruptly, plunking a large package in her cart and moving away quickly without looking back.

Brynn headed toward the dairy case. She didn't know where Marge had gone but knew she was nearby since she had heard her voice. Paul was trying with all his might to push himself out of his seat in the cart. Twice, Brynn had pushed him back down. As she selected bricks of cheese, she turned around just in time to stop Paul from taking a header straight out of the cart. Brynn pulled the cart near the dairy cases, looking back to ensure Paul was seated before grabbing the milk. There, one case over was that creamer that Eric loved. It was frequently hard to find, so she had better grab it now, she thought. She crossed to pick up the creamer. Should she get one or stock up with two? She selected two and quickly returned to the cart, placing the creamers in the bottom.

Gail and Cecil were back together. "Don't think much of that guy, the father," Cecil muttered. "He's pompous and is ignoring his family."

Gail and Cecil moved further into the store, looking around. The store, crowded and busy most of the other times they had been there, seemed quiet this morning. There seemed to be only a few children and parents present.

"Where are all the people?" Gail questioned.

"Well, now, I think God is helping us. He's narrowed our choices, so we select the right child for Alison. I think we've already found our baby. Did you see that child point at us? God was telling us that he's the one."

"I don't know, Cecil. The mother looks like she cares about him."

"Looks like she cares. You said it right there, Gail. I've told you before these people are not like us. Come on, we'll continue to watch."

The young woman was now pushing the cart and had placed the child back in the seat. Gail and Cecil followed silently. Gail was sure that the couple had no idea they were being observed. They stood facing a large row of nuts, looking back over their shoulders to observe the baby frequently.

Gail and Cecil spotted an older child around three who stuck her tongue out at them as they passed by. There was another baby in a car seat in a cart, but he was wearing a helmet on his head.

"Why is he wearing that?" Gail whispered.

"Don't know," Cecil whispered, "but something's wrong with him. That would be too much for Allie."

Gail turned the cart around and headed back down the aisle. Suddenly, Cecil stopped and gestured up the cereal aisle. The young woman was there, and now the baby happily chortled in the cart. The young woman was intent on looking at cereal boxes, but the child looked up and smiled at them as they approached.

"The puppy, the puppy!" Cecil whispered urgently.

Gail pulled the small stuffed animal from her purse as they approached the cart. Gail smiled and made the puppy wave again at the young boy. He chuckled loudly and pointed; the young woman turned around with a smile, which faded as she realized that she did not know them.

Cecil ushered Gail from the aisle.

"Gail, he said urgently, "we need to decide soon. They will remember us if we stay too long and run into these people too many times. It will be dangerous. God has given us several signs now. We can't doubt him. That baby likes us. The grandmother is rude, and the father is preoccupied. The mother took our Lord's name in vain and isn't attentive to her child. Allie could do a better job than that woman. God has clearly shown us the way."

"Oh, Cecil," Gail said, stopping abruptly in the aisle, not re-alizing anyone was behind her. The curly-haired man, still with a cell phone pressed to his ear, almost ran right into them. He sighed in frustration and clipped Gail's arm as he hurried by without looking back or attempting to apologize.

"See! They are rude, I told ya, Gail," Cecil said. "If we are doing this, it needs to happen now," Cecil said urgently. They turned back around. Gail's heart was beating so loudly that she wondered if the people around her could hear it. Cecil touched her shoulder. The young woman was right before them next to the dairy case. The young boy was intent on trying to wiggle his way out of his seat in the cart. He was pitched so far forward that Gail thought it was all too possible he might take a header right out of the cart. The young woman seemed oblivious. She turned around, said, "Oh," and pushed the child back to a seated posi-tion without saying anything more. The woman pulled her cart directly in front of a milk-filled shelf. She opened the door and started removing a carton but then glanced at an adjacent shelf and moved there quickly, leaving a distance between her cart and her baby.

"He's going to fall!" Gail whispered urgently.

"Now, Gail, we need to do it right now. Get that stuffed puppy out," Cecil commanded.

Gail did so with shaking hands. Quickly and quietly, they approached the shopping cart. The baby broke out with a toothless grin and reached for the puppy. Quicker than Gail had ever seen Cecil move, he grabbed the baby from the cart firmly yet gently. Gail was smiling and holding the small stuffed animal inches from his face. Cecil turned and walked away quickly, with Gail following, still making the puppy wave at the young boy. Cecil broke into almost a half-run. Now, they were at the doors. The automatic door slid back. They were outside. It was done.

"Hurry, Gail," Cecil said urgently.

Gail looked back at the store for just a minute. It was too late to take the child back. There was no way to explain what they had just done. They could only move on. It must be what God wanted. It had been too easy. God must have ordained the plan. Cecil was already buckling the child in the car seat.

"Alison will be so happy, Gail, you'll see. It was meant to be. It's destiny. It's destiny for all of us."

CHAPTER 15

BRYNN RETURNED TO THE CART, juggling the milk cartons in her arms.

"Ok, Paul, almost done now," she said cheerily as she bent to place the items in the cart. Paul was unusually quiet. She looked up, expecting to see him watching her from the cart's seat, but the cart was empty. His blue blanket was still there, but he was gone! Where was he?

She stiffened and looked at the seat where Paul had been only moments ago. The blanket he had been sitting on was still stuffed into the space, but Paul was gone. Brynn glanced around, stunned. How could Paul have vanished like that? She had only had her back turned for a few seconds.

Marge must have taken him. Great! Now Marge would tell Eric she hadn't been watching him closely enough. Brynn wheeled the cart away from the dairy case and started to search for Marge.

How could her mother-in-law have grabbed him out of the cart and waltzed away with him without telling Brynn? Brynn knew that Marge had done it to prove a point. Marge continually accused Brynn of needing to be more attentive to Paul. Brynn knew what was going to happen. Marge was going to act like she was helping.

"He was about to start crying, Brynn. You weren't paying attention to him at all," Brynn could hear Marge's voice so loudly in her head that it was like she was there. Her interference with and disapproval of Brynn was getting worse. Brynn was sick of it. Nothing would have happened if Eric had stayed with his family instead of wandering off to get God knows what. Brynn found she was angry at Marge, but her frustration with Eric was also growing exponentially. He never called his mother on her disapproval of Brynn, usually just rolling his eyes and telling Brynn to ignore her hurtful, hateful comments. It was getting old. She was growing tired of the lack of support. She pushed the cart hard and turned to enter an aisle to find Paul and Marge. She had wheeled down two aisles, pushing past items she knew they needed in her rush to find her baby. For some reason, she felt inexplicably nervous and wanted nothing more than to see his beautiful little face or hear his cute little giggle. Finally, she saw Marge at the end of the next aisle. Marge was turned away from Brynn, and since she couldn't see Paul in her cart, she assumed she must be holding him in her arms. Practically running, she steered her cart alongside her mother-in-law so quickly that Marge let out a surprised, "Oh! Brynn, what in the world are you doing now? You startled me!"

Brynn was also startled. The older woman was not holding Paul in her arms, nor was he ensconced in the cart.

"Where's Paul?" Brynn said, confused.

"Paul? What are you talking about? You had him with you, not me."

"I know that," Brynn snapped, "but I picked up the milk and turned around, and my cart was empty. He was gone. You came by and picked him up."

"Brynn! I most certainly did not. I've been right here doing my shopping. Do you mean to tell me that you lost your son?"

"He's not here. He's gone," Brynn said, feeling her heart jump into her throat.

"Well, for goodness' sake. Eric must have walked up and taken him out of the cart. You need to be more aware of your surroundings, Brynn. How many times have I told you that? Eric plucked him right out of the cart, and you weren't even aware of it! Careless, Brynn, so careless. Honestly!"

"Where's Eric?" Brynn said, feeling her body fill with fear.

"I don't know where Eric is. He's not with me. He's around here somewhere, though," Marge said, shrugging.

"I need to see my baby," Brynn said, tears coming to her eyes.

"Brynn, there is nothing to get so upset about. Have you finished your shopping?" Marge peered into Brynn's half-empty cart. "It certainly doesn't look like it. I don't think Eric wants to spend his entire day off in a grocery store."

Without another word, Brynn whirled her cart around and rushed through the aisles to find Eric. She could feel Marge behind her, breathing heavily, struggling to keep up with Brynn's hasty pace. Finally, Brynn saw Eric's tall frame and curly brown hair in the produce section, bending over a display of bananas.

"Eric, Eric!" Brynn called, pushing the cart so hastily that other shoppers stared at her. Eric looked up, smiling as Brynn approached.

"Hey," he said, then, seeing her face, asked, "What's wrong?"

"Where's Paul, Eric? Where's Paul?"

"Where's Paul?" he repeated dumbly. "I don't have him."

"But you came over and took him out of my cart."

"No, Brynn, I didn't. I've been right here. Maybe Mother did." Eric stopped speaking as his mother, gasping for air, reached them.

"Eric, Eric," his mother shouted, "Brynn lost the baby. My grandson is missing!" She bellowed so loudly that all the shoppers looked directly at her.

"I have to find him. We have to find him, Eric. We have to find him now!" Brynn started to race away, intent on searching each aisle, every basket for her baby.

"Brynn, stop! Stop!" Eric called. "We have to think logically," he said, but she could hear the fear in his voice beyond his measured words. "Where's the manager?" he said assertively to a young store employee.

"I'll get him?" the kid said, his voice going up on the word 'him' as if asking a question.

"Yes, get him now! We need help," Eric said adamantly.

"My grandson—my grandson has been kidnapped," Marge wailed.

"There must have been some mistake. Maybe someone picked up the wrong baby."

"How could they do that, Eric? That's stupid," Brynn snapped.

"Is there something I can assist you with?" a man in his thirties inquired. "I'm the store manager."

"Yes!" Eric responded. "Our son, nine months old, is missing from where he was sitting in my wife's grocery cart. We can't find him."

The store manager nodded and snapped his fingers at two employees. "Go to the front, Evan, don't let any customers leave right now. Tell Shelly to call the police. Sir, we've had lost children in the store before. I'm sure he'll turn up."

"But he's a baby, a baby," Brynn moaned. "He couldn't get out of the cart by himself."

"I understand, ma'am. The police are on their way."

"The police, the police, oh my God!" Marge moaned.

"Do you need to sit down, ma'am? How about a drink of water?"

"I feel faint. Eric, I think I'm going to pass out," Marge said, gasping.

Eric went to his mother to support her as she collapsed in his arms. Brynn turned on her heel and began running up and down each aisle, peering intently at each person, child, and shopping cart she passed. She made five complete circuits of the entire store before anyone could get her to stop—long after the police arrived and after Eric and Marge sat dejectedly on chairs that had appeared from somewhere.

"Your baby doesn't appear to be in the store, ma'am. Your husband gave us a very recent photo of him. That will help. Can you provide any further details about what he was wearing?" Brynn heard the police officer with the tight bun in her hair saying these words, but then everything began to shake like an earthquake. The next thing Brynn remembered was waking up on a stretcher outside the store. "She's awake, Mother," Brynn heard Eric say.

"Paul? Where is Paul?" Brynn croaked out the words from a throat that felt as arid as a desert.

Eric shook his head.

"We don't know, baby. The police are looking."

CHAPTER 16

"WE PICKED A GOOD ONE, GAIL. I can tell. God has already blessed us."

Gail shifted in her seat in the car to look at Cecil. She had been turned around in her seat the whole drive, monitoring the baby they had just stolen from the Total Foods store. The baby now looked like he was getting drowsy. He seemed stunned as Cecil quickly drove out of the parking lot, looking at them as if saying, 'Who are you? Who are you people?' But he had not cried until they had entered the highway. When he began to cry, Gail had first enticed him with the tiny stuffed puppy that interested him in the store. He had stopped crying and reached for the toy as Gail made it wave at him. She had at first kept it just out of his grasp, made the toy wave and dance. The baby chortled happily. This had gone on for several miles, but as the boy seemed about to cry again, Gail gave him the stuffed animal to hold. He smiled at her with a toothless grin and rubbed it over his face. A few more miles passed before the child threw the stuffed animal on the car's floor and wailed. Gail moved to grab the cooler and took out a bottle of milk. The boy reached for it greedily and began to suck.

"You were a hungry boy, weren't you, sweetie?" Gail said. Her affection for this child was growing with each passing mile. He seemed very sweet, good-natured, and mellow. Gail had been afraid that he would cry the whole ride back once he realized he was with strangers, but somehow, uncannily, he seemed to accept Gail and Cecil's presence. Gail rubbed her neck and looked out the window for the first time. They were almost halfway home. They were making good time. Gail looked back at the baby. He was about to drop the bottle, and she grabbed it from his hand. The movement startled the baby into a more alert state. He roused and looked at Gail.

Cecil peered at him through the rearview mirror, saying, "Hey, boy, how ya doin' back there?"

The child smiled as Cecil made a beep-beep noise as if he were a truck. It was the exact thing he used to do with Alison when she was small. Alison had always laughed at the silly noise; now, this boy also laughed. He looked at them as if trying to figure out who they were.

"Look, look, Gail. He is so happy. That proves that it is meant to be." Cecil cast his eyes into the rearview again. "You're happy, right, boy?" he said, addressing the child.

"Of course you are, Jared, my boy," Cecil said and winked.

They were ten minutes away from home now. The baby had been asleep for upward of forty minutes.

"Alison will need a lot of help at first," Gail said. She was still unsure how exactly they would explain all this to Alison, especially when you considered that the damn medication Alison was on made her so out of it. She repeatedly asked the same question and could become confused about minor things. Also, Gail was quite troubled about explaining the child's presence to their neighbors. They weren't close to many others in the trailer park. The people next door came and went so rapidly, like a revolving door, that Gail wasn't even sure who was in that trailer now. Was it the single man who never smiled or the young mother with three children? Gail didn't know. The only person they talked to was Betty, who was two trailers over, and she had been scarce since the incident where Alison had been scratching her wrist with that steak knife. She wasn't sure if Betty was avoiding them or if she didn't know what to say, but she had been around less and less. Cecil had been quiet for the last few miles. He got like that when he had something to say.

Gail wasn't sure if he had something to say or was just being quiet because the baby was sleeping, but then Cecil said, "Gail, here's what we are going to do."

So, he did have something to say, Gail thought.

"We're not staying at the trailer now. We're going to pick up Alison. You and Allie are going to pack a couple of bags. I loaded all the stuff we'll need in the trunk and that small trailer I rented last night. I'm already packed. We'll pick up other items we need for Jared on the way. We're going to Ohio."

"Ohio, Cecil! We don't know anyone in Ohio."

"I know that, Gail. You think I don't know that! I picked Ohio because we don't know anyone there. We can't be around people that know us right now. We can't just magically have a baby. People will have questions. It's not safe, Gail. We can't have any suspicion around us. We can't afford to have anyone sniffing around and asking questions. I rented a house for us there for the short term. We have it for three months."

"Three months! How can we afford that? And besides, what about your job, Cecil? You can't just not go to work for three months!"

"Relax, Gail. I have this all figured out. Ohio had some of the cheapest rentals. The house is small, but we'll have privacy. And my job? Well, no worries there. I quit last week."

"Cecil, what? What are you saying? How will we live? Is that why you didn't go to work on Friday?"

Cecil nodded. "Relax, Gail, just relax. I've been thinking on this plan for a while now. I've been saving money from each paycheck for over six months. We won't have much but will have enough to get by. Maybe while you and Alison care for Jared, I'll find a job in Ohio to help with expenses. We'll lay low there with the baby. We'll get Alison off that damn medication. It doesn't do anything for her except make her goofy. No one will have any questions about where that baby came from that far from home. We can get there in less than five hours, so the drive won't be that bad. When we come back, we tell a little white lie. The baby is your niece's kid, and she has developed a drug problem, that Oxy shit. Alison is watching her baby for a little while until she gets better."

Cecil looked at Gail as if he expected her to protest, but Gail nodded. It did seem that he had it all planned out. Cecil didn't know yet, but this would fit her narrative of borrowing the baby and giving him back once Alison was better. Cecil peered at Gail intently.

"Ok, Cecil, I think that might just work."

Cecil let out an audible breath and reached over to grab her hand.

"God has blessed us. This will all work out. Don't worry about one thing, Gail, not one thing."

CHAPTER 17

IT WAS THEIR FIRST NIGHT in the small rental house in Ohio. Alison and Jared had both been so tired from the drive. Alison had seemed especially confused in the car on the way there. Gail had a sneaking suspicion that Alison was taking more medication than she was supposed to. However, she was undoubtedly prescribed enough, even if she only took it as the doctor directed! Gail wasn't sure if Alison was taking more of the medication on accident or on purpose, but it didn't matter now. She and Cecil had convinced Alison in the car that it would be a good idea for her to get off all the medication.

"We'll help you," Cecil implored as he drove. You have a baby to take care of. He needs you."

Alison had agreed to give Gail all her bottles of pills. Gail would dole them out to her, cutting down the quantity slowly.

"That's how you're supposed to do it. I read about it online," Cecil said authoritatively, if not smugly. Jared had cried more when they had put him in the small crib than he had since they had taken him. They had gotten through it, though. Gail had encouraged Alison to rock him in the small rocker Cecil had the good sense to bring in the trailer. When they finally got Jared down, Gail could tell how tired Alison was, but she also seemed wired at the same time. Gail patted her shoulder.

"I think you need a pill to help you sleep tonight, honey."

"Mom, I want to stop, just like we talked about."

"Oh, we will, but slowly, just like your dad said. I think one is truly warranted tonight, honey."

Alison nodded. Gail sat in the rocker, ensuring that Jared stayed asleep in the crib and that Alison slept in the small single bed in the same room as Jared. Finally, feeling assured that they were both out, Gail rose and crept out of the room, silently closing the door.

"Well, they're both asleep now," Gail said, rubbing her neck as she entered the small living room where Cecil sat. She sniffed the air once again. This room smelled like a dirty, wet dog. She would have to give the carpet a good clean and remind Alison not to put Jared down on it until it was cleaned. Cecil smiled at his wife.

"Good," he said, patting the seat next to him on the couch so she could come sit. Gail sat down. Cecil seemed so sure that everything was fine, but Gail was unsure. She frowned.

"Cecil, we must come up with a perfect story about where Jared came from if anyone asks when we return home."

"Don't you worry," Cecil said, patting her knee and still seeming to be in an excellent mood even though she was questioning him.

"I've been praying on that exact question for days now, Gail, and I have come up with—well, God has given me the perfect story. I told you before. Jared is Alison's cousin's baby. The cousin lives here in Ohio. That's why we came here for a few months. The cousin gave Allie custody of her baby because she's addicted to those pills that Oxy, they talk about all the time on the news."

Cecil stopped and smiled broadly at Gail as if his story solved everything.

Gail sighed.

"Cecil, you mentioned that story to me in the car when we first took Jared. Alison doesn't even have cousins. Both you and I are only children."

Cecil's face darkened with anger—the anger she and Alison had come to know so well and so assiduously avoided.

"Gail, I know that," he snapped. "You think I don't know that! People sometimes have very good friends that they call cousins. This is my best friend's daughter. She and Alison were close when they were younger. This will work, Gail. Also, never say again, 'when we took Jared,' put that whole story out of your mind. The true story is we picked Jared up here in Ohio and Alison will raise him from now on. People shouldn't be digging into our business that closely anyway. Betty is the only person you are close to in the trailer park."

"Was close to, Cecil, was."

Gail and Betty's friendship had undoubtedly faded.

"Well, see, that works out, too, then. God is setting it all up for us, Gail. I know he is leading us. If anyone asks us too many questions, we tell them to mind their business. Alison can say she doesn't want to talk about it. At church, they know she had a troubled past; they'll leave her alone."

Gail nodded.

"Okay, but we have a deeper problem than what we say. Cecil, we need Alison to remember this story and be able to tell others about her fictional cousin if they ask."

"Well, I prayed on that part, too, Gail. Don't think I didn't. First, while we are here, we get Alison off all those useless pills the doctors gave her. She agreed to that in the car, right?"

Gail nodded.

"I guarantee that her memory will improve once she is off them. As for her remembering the story, do you recall when Alison was in high school and she almost flunked biology?

"Yeah?" Gail said with a question mark in her voice, not understanding the connection.

"I quizzed her on the body's bones every night, remember?"

Gail nodded.

"We went over and over and over the names of all those bones, and then what happened?"

"Alison got an A on that test," Gail replied.

"Exactly! I plan to do the same thing now, only with the story about Jared. I'll quiz her every single night. This will work, Gail. God is going to make this work. It is what God wants!"

CHAPTER 18

ALISON, CECIL, AND GAIL had only been in the small rental house in Ohio for two days. The house was in a shabby neighborhood. The people around them didn't seem very friendly. Gail had waved at a neighbor yesterday, but the woman had looked down and not waved back. When Gail mentioned this to Cecil, he said, "Good, that is exactly what we want. We need to keep to ourselves, Gail. Now, don't go out there trying to make friends. God has taken us this far with the baby, so don't mess it up now. The less people know about us, the less they see us, the better it will be for all of us, including Jared. You and Alison have enough to do with taking care of the baby. Plus, you won't even have me around to help during the day. The foreman said I should know whether I got the job today or tomorrow, and he even told me it looked favorable."

Cecil had already interviewed for two jobs, and the one in the ball-bearing factory might work out.

"She still needs a lot of help," Cecil said, nodding toward Alison, holding Jared on her lap while seated at the scarred kitchen table.

"You focus on her and that baby and forget everyone and everything else. You hear me?"

Gail nodded. Cecil was right. They had come this far. She couldn't do anything to mess it up right now. There was no going back. The only way out was to move forward, and for now, that meant going along with Cecil's plans. Cecil poured himself another cup of coffee and gestured toward Gail to ask if she wanted one. She nodded and returned to the sink to finish their breakfast dishes. Cecil sat down at the table across from Alison and Jared. He smiled at them. Alison looked happy, happier than she had in months. She gently bounced Jared on her knee and bent down, planting kisses on his head. He chuckled and reached out to grab her blonde hair. He was a happy baby overall. Cecil reached out to Jared, wiggling his fingers, and Jared grabbed his hand. Suddenly, Alison sighed, and a troubled look appeared on her face.

"Daddy," she said, furrowing her brow. "This is not my baby. My baby died." She hesitated. "Didn't he?"

Cecil dropped Jared's small hand and slammed his hand down on the table. His face immediately contorted into an ugly shape.

"Alison Marie," he said in a loud, authoritative voice as he pointed at her. "Never say that again! You hear me! I told you that is your baby. Your baby is right there."

He pointed at Jared.

"But Daddy, my baby died. I remember. I mean, I think I remember."

"He did not!" Cecil screamed, half rising from his seat at the table.

"That is your baby, right there! God gifted you with that baby. God gave Jared to us, to all of us."

Cecil slammed his fist on the table several more times. Jared, who had been watching him the entire time, looked stunned and began to wail.

Alison murmured, "Shh, shh," trying to comfort him while looking at her mother as if imploring her for assistance. Gail rushed over, drying her hands on the dish towel, then holding her arms out to take Jared. She rubbed his back as she paced around the kitchen. Alison remained at the table, looking down and beginning to trace the scars on the table with a slightly shaky finger. "Look at me," Cecil said in a somewhat lower voice.

Alison slowly raised her head until she met her father's eyes. Cecil stared at his daughter piercingly.

"He is your baby," he repeated in an almost menacing tone. His tone and entire demeanor were so frightening that Gail stopped walking, clutching Jared tighter and slightly shivering.

"Never question the Lord, Alison. You know that verse, 'Do not put the Lord your God to the test'? You know better! Am I clear?"Cecil questioned, moving his eyes to take in his wife and daughter.

"We never speak of such foolishness again," Cecil continued to stare at them.

Gail nodded first, and then Alison followed suit. Alison reached out her hands for Jared, who was still whimpering.

"Alison, you do understand me?" Cecil repeated in a slightly less aggressive tone.

"Yes, Daddy," Alison whispered, afraid to say more. His response to what she meant to be only a simple question had been so aggressive, so frightening. She nuzzled Jared as he put his head on the nape of her neck. She just wanted to put this entire conversation out of her mind. Her mother stood numbly in the middle of the kitchen floor as if rooted there. The phone began to ring.

"Well, now," Cecil jumped up from the table, smiling. "Who could that be? It must be about the job! Ladies, I am about to become gainfully employed once again."

CHAPTER 19

ALISON SIGHED. They had been at the rental house in Ohio for over two months. Alison felt jittery without any pills. She hadn't had one in almost a week now. She couldn't go back on.

"So proud of you, baby," her father frequently said. "And you know who else is proud of you? Your baby boy, Jared, is proud of you, too."

She couldn't disappoint her father now. Plus, she didn't even know where the pills were anymore. Her mother had them if there were even any left. She heard the door slam. Her father was home from work. She looked up from the magazine she had been looking at and looked over at Jared, sleeping with his arms sprawled over his head. She smiled. She loved him so much. Cecil opened the door quietly to their room and entered.

"Hey, Allie, girl, ready for our practice session before I take my shower?"

Alison nodded. She looked at her father. He smiled at her. He didn't seem as tired today as he did sometimes when he came home from work. He seemed to be in a good mood. She knew she was thinking clearer off the drugs. She had to ask him one more time. She just had to. Hopefully, he wouldn't fly into a rage, but maybe this time, he would answer, and perhaps this time, he would tell her the truth.

"Ok," Alison said, and she watched her father waiting for her to recite the story they practiced every night.

"But, Daddy," she said softly, "I love my Jared, I love this baby, but my real baby died, didn't he?"

He glared at her and stood taller, reaching his full height and towering over Alison's diminutive frame.

"No, Alison," Cecil said, avoiding her question.

"Your baby is right there sleeping in that crib. God blessed you with a baby. You lost your husband, but you have your baby right there. Now, tell me again where he came from."

Alison sighed. How many times was he going to ask her this question? She was so tired. Yet she knew he wouldn't stop until she replied and replied correctly. She repeated the rehearsed lines once again.

"My cousin has a drug problem. She gave me custody of her baby because she couldn't take care of him. It upsets me, and I don't like to talk about it."

"Good girl!" Cecil crowed. "We'll practice again tomorrow." Cecil started to walk away.

"But, Daddy," Alison's brow furrowed. She knew she was pushing him. If her mother were here, she would tell her to stop before he got even angrier. Alison opened her mouth to question her father one last time. It was as if Cecil knew what Alison was going to ask. He stood up tall, once again towering over Alison.

He said in a firm, loud voice, "Alison, do not question the Lord."

His voice was getting even louder. Alison looked over at the sleeping Jared. Her father was going to wake him if he didn't stop.

"God gave you that child. God gave all of us that boy. If you question God's grace and goodness, he will take it all away."

Alison's heart seized as she looked at Jared. She felt so very, very tired. She couldn't lose him! She couldn't lose anyone else. She would never be able to survive.

"Cecil," the door to Alison and Jared's room opened, and Gail stood there. "What in the world are you yelling about in the baby's room with him sleeping right there? You'll wake him! Dinner is almost ready now, and you haven't even taken your shower yet, have you, Cecil?"

"Nope, I'm going now," Cecil mumbled, exiting the room.

"I need to finish dinner," Gail murmured, leaving Alison alone. Alison peered into Jared's crib. Amazingly, he was still sleeping. She looked down at him.

"Oh, Jared, I love you so much," she said in a voice barely above a whisper.

CHAPTER 20

"SIT DOWN, BRYNN," Marge said in a commanding voice. "Goodness, you are so scattered. Sit here and try to relax. Drink the coffee I brought for you."

Brynn sighed. The last thing she wanted to do was talk to Marge. She always had to make a subtly cutting remark and then deny that she had said anything hurtful. There was no way to win against her! There never had been, but she had gotten infinitely worse since Paul had been missing. Brynn had already updated her on what the police had said concerning the investigation: absolutely nothing new. Brynn felt that the police were losing interest. She shared that with Eric, and he solemnly agreed. She would not share that with Marge. Brynn reluctantly sat down. She had nothing more to say to Marge and only wished fervently that she would leave. She fantasized about going to the door, opening it, and breezily saying, "Bye, now," but she knew she would not do so. Marge would immediately tattle to Eric and accuse her of being rude.

"So, how are you feeling, dear? Still not getting out much, I see."

Marge's eyes scanned over Brynn and the ratty sweatshirt and sweatpants she had slept in last night and had not bothered changing out of.

"Not much," Brynn acknowledged. "I like to stay near the phone in case the police call about Paul."

"Isn't that what cell phones are for?" Marge sniffed.

"Service is spotty here, you know that. I don't want to drop a call."

"Ok," Marge said and sighed. "Is it easier for you with Paul gone, dear?"

"Easier? Why would you say such a thing?" Brynn was startled at the casual cruelty of the statement. "Of course, it's not easier. I miss him with every fiber of my being. I worry all the time about him."

"Ok, dear, ok, don't get upset. It's just that I've always wondered if you wanted to be a mother, Brynn. You were always so neglectful with him when he was here. You didn't watch him closely. I wondered if you might feel some relief now that he is gone."

"That, Marge, is a terrible, horrible thing to say. If I tell Eric you said that, he will be mad."

"Brynn, once again, you are misinterpreting what I am saying. Paul changed your life very quickly. You didn't finish your degree and only had two semesters left. You and I both know that Paul was an accident, that you didn't mean to conceive a child. Eric even told me so; don't you dare lie to me. You were just careless."

"What about you, Marge?" Brynn sneered. "Are you happy? Find it easier now that Paul is gone."

"What a thing to say to me, Brynn. Of course not!"

"Paul may not have been planned, Marge, but he was always wanted. He was wanted from the very second I realized I was pregnant. Also, you do understand how conception works, right?" Brynn said snidely. "I didn't do it all by myself. Eric was right there, too. Will you ask him if he is relieved that Paul is gone?"

Marge sniffed and frowned at Brynn as she rose from her seat at the table and grabbed her purse. "There is no having a civil conversation with you, is there, Brynn? You are just so ready to argue all the time. I do have one more question for you, Brynn."

Brynn nodded and braced herself for more disapproval, knowing it was coming.

"Who was responsible for the birth control, Brynn? I do wonder about that."

"That is none of your business. If you want the answer to that question, ask your son."

Marge shook her head as Brynn opened the door. Brynn could feel a pounding headache pooling right behind her eyes. Why not? She was growing so, so tired of all the disapproval. Something had to give. Something had to change—and change soon.

CHAPTER 21

BRYNN FLINCHED as she heard her mother-in-law's car pull into the driveway. Was she going to come over every single week now? She was starting to feel better. It was only 9 a.m.—early for Brynn—and she was already up and showered. She planned to pour a cup of coffee and clean the house a little. She was determined not to fight with Eric tonight. No matter how pleasant their conversations might be, they always ended up arguing and hurting each other's feelings. Brynn had read that to have a good day, you express thankfulness before getting out of bed. Brynn had done so for the last two days, studiously avoiding the thought that seemed to be knocking on the door of her conscious mind: *Thankful, Brynn, really? What do you have to be thankful for? Your baby is gone!* Brynn had ignored the thought this morning, repeating sentences of gratitude: *It's a bright sunny day, I have a beautiful home, and my husband loves me.* She stumbled on that one. "Maybe my husband loves me," she finally said. She was determined to have a good day; the last person she wanted to deal with was Marge. Oh, well, she was here. She would have to power through somehow. Marge knocked loudly on the door and exclaimed, "Oh!" when Brynn immediately opened it.

She looked Brynn up and down.

"Well, I thought you might still be in bed."

"No, Marge, I'm up. Come on in."

Marge nodded and looked around the kitchen. Her eyes immediately held on to the dishes piled in the sink. Brynn hadn't had the energy to put them in the dishwasher last night, and Eric had rushed off to his office, mumbling about having a brief to finish.

"I'm planning on cleaning the house today," Brynn remarked as Marge stared at the dirty dishes.

"Ok," Marge murmured.

"Would you like some coffee?" Brynn asked politely.

"Do you have a clean mug?" Marge replied.

Brynn imagined herself replying snarkily, "No, Marge, I don't, but here's a dirty one. Eric and I always drink from dirty mugs." The thought of the reply caused Brynn to smile slightly, and Marge knit her brows together.

"Yes, of course, I have a clean mug," Brynn forced herself to say the sentence politely.

"Alright, then," Marge assented.

Brynn crossed the kitchen, turning the coffeemaker on.

"How are you doing, dear?" Marge inquired.

"I'm better. I'm trying to be positive." Brynn hesitated. "I made a gratitude list this morning before I even got out of bed. I thanked God for all the positive things that I have in my life."

Marge sniffed as Brynn handed her the coffee.

"Really, Brynn? I came here to check on you. Eric worries about you, but here you are, just fine and talking about how happy and grateful you are. My son is in so much pain, and you are happy and grateful even after all that has occurred? Do I need to remind you, Brynn, that you lost a baby? Or have you just entirely moved on from that, too? And maybe you should clean the house since you no longer have a job. No wonder Eric looks so tired all the time. He works all day and then has to come home and clean. It is patently obvious that you're not going to clean. Eric says you're depressed, but we are all upset about Paul. You need to snap out of it. Depressed? I don't think so! You're using that as a crutch to avoid doing things you don't want to do."

Brynn closed her eyes. She could not let Marge ruin this day. She was trying so hard.

"Brynn, are you even listening to me?"

"Yes, Marge, I have heard every word you said."

"Well, Brynn, did you know that Eric stopped at my house last night after work?"

"No, I didn't know that," Brynn said, shaking her head. However, it explained why Eric arrived home forty-five minutes later than usual.

"The poor boy is so distraught. He is worried about Paul and if the police are doing all they can to find him. He worries about you. He mentioned that you weren't exactly stable and said that you stay in bed for most days. That is why I decided to check on you. I was trying to see if I could help, but I get here, and you're not in bed. You're up and around and trilling on and on about how happy and grateful you are. It doesn't make any sense, Brynn, now does it?"

Brynn sipped her coffee and again had an inappropriate vision of throwing the hot coffee right in Marge's smug face.

"Marge, I read about the gratitude stuff, and I am sure I never said I was happy. Making a gratitude list is supposed to make you feel better. I feel awful about Paul, and I miss him so much!"

"Sometimes I wonder about that, Brynn, I do!

"What are you saying?"

"Do you truly miss Paul?"

"Miss Paul? Of course, I do! It feels like part of my body is missing. My whole body aches for him every single day."

"But you are the one that told Eric you weren't ready to have a baby, isn't that, right?"

"Eric told you that! That conversation was between us."

"Well, he did tell me. When I see you up and dressed and looking so good, I can't help but wonder if you might be happy because now you don't have the baby that you never wanted in the first place."

"Marge, I said that to Eric right after discovering I was pregnant. I wasn't even showing yet! I was young, and I was scared. I wasn't even sure Eric was ready to have a baby. I thought he might break up with me. We decided to keep the baby, and I have loved him ever since. I loved him when I was pregnant and fell in love with him even more after he was born. What you are saying is just not true! When was Eric talking about me not wanting the baby—yesterday?"

"Oh, no, no, a long time ago, Brynn, not now," Marge said with irritation.

Then why bring it up now? Brynn thought.

"Eric was talking last night about how you are not getting along. I feel so sad for him, Brynn. How much can one man take?

And now I hear that you aren't even sleeping in the same bed? Men have sexual needs, dear; you must know that!"

Ok, Brynn thought, *Eric has a huge mouth, which he should keep shut!*

"Our relationship is none of your business, Marge."

"But it's true, isn't it? You aren't sleeping with him, having sex with him?"

"Marge, this is the last thing I want to discuss with you."

"So, it is true, then. I knew it! Brynn, you were a terrible mother, and now it seems you are working on being a terrible wife." Marge's comments, playing into all of Brynn's fears, cut so close to home that her words sliced into Brynn like a razor blade. She staggered and pulled out a kitchen chair to sit down, collapsing into it with her head in her hands. She finally looked up at Marge, coolly sipping her coffee.

"You've mischaracterized everything I've said."

"Oh, but, Brynn, they are your words, not mine, right?" Marge stood and picked up her purse. "I told Eric I would check on you, and now I have. Here's a tip, Brynn: see if you can put the dishes away before Eric comes home. You have all day. Maybe then Eric will have something to be grateful for!"

CHAPTER 22

BRYNN STIRRED ON THE COUCH. She heard a key in the lock at the front door. It had to be Eric! He was home already! She looked at the clock. She had slept for hours. She shouldn't have taken the extra anxiety pill. She had paced back and forth, beginning to cry as soon as Marge slammed out of the door that morning. She had felt nonfunctional, and she had planned to get things done that day. She had decided to clean the kitchen, but she couldn't think or concentrate while she was this upset. She had gone to the bedroom and gulped an extra pill—just one. She needed something to steady herself, that was all. She remembered returning to the kitchen and opening the dishwasher to stack the dishes, but then she felt so sleepy, so very tired. A twenty-minute power nap on the sofa, surely that couldn't hurt! She briefly remembered waking up and seeing the clock hands pointing at 1:30. She had rolled over on the couch and gone back to sleep, thinking she still had hours before Eric would arrive home.

"Hey, baby," Eric said, smiling at her and setting his briefcase on the floor. "Taking a little nap?"

"Oh, Eric, I meant to get more done today! I, I—" she stopped.

If only Marge hadn't come over. Should she even mention her? Even bringing up her mother-in-law's name seemed to lead to a big quarrel these days.

"Well, I see someone started to clean the kitchen. Was my mother helping you? I asked her to come over and help you."

"You did? You asked her to come 'help' me?" Brynn made air quotes as she said the word help.

"Brynn, please don't start. Let's try to have a good night."

"I want to have a good night, too, Eric! Why wouldn't I? Believe it or not, I felt better before your mother arrived."

"Why wouldn't I believe you, Brynn?"

"Oh, I don't know, Eric! Because you tell your mother very private things about us that are none of her business."

"Brynn, I don't know what you are talking about. I stopped by Mother's last night. She asked how you were doing. I mentioned you could use a little help, maybe even a little motivation to get up and around. She offered to come over and help you."

"Oh, she was so helpful, Eric! You told her I wasn't ready to have a baby. I thought that was a private conversation between us."

"What! We didn't talk about that last night. That's old news, anyway. Why would you even bring it up?"

"Your mother brought it up, not me. Oh, and thanks for telling her we're not getting along so she could throw that in my face. And the sex part—the fact that we don't have sex—is not something I want to discuss with your mother, of all people."

"Oh my God, Brynn! I did not tell my mother that we weren't having sex. I don't talk about my sex life with my mother! That is just creepy!"

"Well, she somehow knew we weren't getting along, and she said that you had sexual needs."

"Brynn, ick! I may have mentioned that we were fighting some, but I didn't put all the blame on you. We're both stressed, Brynn. It's not all you. As far as the sex stuff, I didn't mention anything. She might have been fishing for information—you know how she is. I think she is worried we might break up. She had a hard life, you know. She spent years in a bad marriage with my father. I know she doesn't want the same for me."

"She's bitchy to me every time she comes over here. I want it to stop."

"That's a little harsh, Brynn. You need to cut her some slack."

"Why? She never cuts me any slack. She would be more likely to cut my wrists if she could get away with it."

"Brynn, don't even talk like that. I think you both misunderstand each other. She only wants the best for you, and I know that is true."

Brynn shook her head and rose from the couch unsteadily.

"I have dishes to finish, Eric. The dishes your mother did not help me with, okay?"

CHAPTER 23

IT WAS TURNING OUT to be another awful, bleak day. Brynn couldn't stand it anymore! Sometimes, she would wake up and, just for a few moments, feel happy seeing the sun blinking through the curtains. But then, like a ton of bricks falling on her head, she would remember. She would remember it all. Paul was gone. And now, six months later, the police checked in very infrequently, and in the last month, if she was honest, not at all. Her relationship with Eric was in tatters. They were so distant, so polite with each other. She had no idea what his true thoughts were or what his true feelings were anymore. The house she loved so much no longer gave her any pleasure. Cleaning was a burden, and housework was often left undone for days or weeks. Dishes would pile in the sink until they spilled over onto all open counter spaces. Eric would eventually get sick of the mess and load and unload the dishwasher. He never asked Brynn what she did all day or how she occupied her time. She did not know if he avoided asking to avert confrontation or did not care. They were so far apart mentally and physically. She was not at all interested in sex. It had only gotten worse as the months progressed. She couldn't imagine touching Eric, and she certainly couldn't imagine being touched herself. How could she be allowed to experience pleasure with Paul gone? It wouldn't be right. Brynn once again thought about what the use of living was when she felt this much sadness. She felt lead in her stomach, and a boulder of pain was sitting squarely on her shoulders yet again. She heard a noise outside that sounded all too much like a car door slamming shut. She peeked out through a barely lifted curtain and groaned. There was her mother-in-law striding briskly up the driveway. Marge was the last person she wanted to see and the only person who seemed to visit these days. However, if she stopped to consider, she could not think of one person she would be interested in seeing anyway. Brynn's relationship with Marge had continued to deteriorate substantially if that was even possible. Her negative comments used to be veiled but were now increasingly overt. Every time Brynn said something to Eric, it seemed that he was much more supportive of his mother than he was of her. A day already starting bad was about to be made substantially worse. Of this, Brynn was sure. Brynn advanced to the front door, flinging it open and stepping back without saying hello. Marge, carrying a bag that looked like it contained groceries, nodded at Brynn but continued walking right past her and entered the kitchen. She put the bag down and began pulling out food and putting it in the refrigerator and the freezer. Yes, Eric's favorite ice cream bars and a large piece of steak. What had Eric done? Had he asked his mother to come over with a care package? Brynn stared at the food with a sullen look on her face.

Marge finally spoke.

"How are you doing, Brynn?"

"I'm okay," Brynn choked out. The last thing she would do was tell her mother-in-law how she felt and how desperate she was becoming. Marge stopped and looked at Brynn. Her eyes scanned her up and down. Brynn was sure she was taking in her lank, unwashed hair and the ratty T-shirt and sweatpants she wore.

"Okay, that's good," Marge said, clearly forcing herself to smile at Brynn. "You're finally feeling better, then?"

Brynn merely nodded.

"Well, I must say I'm glad to hear it. I brought each of us a cup of coffee," Marge said, handing Brynn a cup of take-out coffee. The food was now all put away. Marge pulled out a kitchen chair and indicated that Brynn should also sit at the table. Brynn wished more than anything that she would get ready to leave, but that didn't appear to be happening. Brynn sat down reluctantly. Marge sipped her coffee. Brynn took a sip as well. It couldn't be possible that her mother-in-law had come to check on her to see if she was okay, could it? Could she possibly confide how awful she felt to this woman? Might she listen and try to help?

But just as Brynn had these thoughts, her mother-in-law cleared her throat.

"Well, Brynn, you say you're doing better. I must say I'm glad to hear it. Brynn, if you're doing better, I think it's time for you to think about finding a job. I mean you have nothing to stay home for now. You don't have a baby to take care of. I think it's time for you to get out there. Help Eric. It will take some of the pressure off him. I worry about him so much! Eric works so hard, and here you are, just sitting around the house daily," she sniffed.

Brynn's heart plummeted. Marge was not here to help her. She would never help her. No one would ever help her.

"Did Eric ask you to talk to me again?" Brynn questioned.

"No, no, of course not, but I can't help but see how hard he is working. You could help him if you just would."

"But what if Paul is found? What if he comes back? I should be availab—"

Marge held up a hand to stop Brynn's barrage of words.

"Oh, Brynn, we both know that's not going to happen, right?"

"Why would you say such a thing? What does that even mean?" Brynn questioned.

Brynn stared at her mother-in-law and fantasized that it was her mother sitting there instead of Marge. Days like this, she thought with a sigh, made her miss her mother more than ever. It had been Brynn and her mother alone, just the two of them, since Brynn was six months old. Her father had walked out when she was a baby.

"He chose the booze over us, baby," her mother would say.

It was not entirely appropriate to tell a child, but Brynn had heard that sentiment for as long as she could remember. Her mother had died of a sudden, massive heart attack when Brynn was a freshman in college; how Brynn wished that her mother could have met her son. That she could be there now, to help her, to support her during this staggering loss of her baby, her Paul. But she wasn't there, was she? Brynn thought morosely, and it did her no good to wish for something that would not occur. The clouds were increasing in the sky, and Brynn noticed them as she gazed out the large window in the living room. The sky was growing ever darker, like her own mood. Why couldn't Marge come over when Eric was home? She knew Eric wouldn't be home on a weekday. At least when Eric was there, he would deflect some of the worst barbed comments that Marge was sure to make, but now she was alone with her.

Marge took a sip of coffee.

"Brynn, you don't have anything to do, do you? You're not going out? Eric tells me that you never go out, that is."

"No, no, I'm not going out."

"Brynn, I need to speak to you about something without Eric present. I don't plan on staying long. I wouldn't want to bother you."

She put undue emphasis on the word bother.

"It's fine," Brynn said. Should she offer Marge some pastry to go with the coffee? Of course, she had none. She hadn't been to the store herself in weeks. She moved to the cupboards, looking for something she could serve that wouldn't look lame. She found nothing except a half-empty box of Oreos that was probably stale. Putting those out would look worse than offering nothing.

"What are you looking for, dear? Did you lose something?"

Brynn smoothed down her hair and tried to affix a smile on her face.

"I thought we could have something to eat. Are you hungry?"

Brynn asked, then realized it was stupid. She thought, *you just looked and have nothing to offer her. What will you do if she says yes?* Brynn held her breath.

"No, no, I'm fine. Sit back down, dear."

Brynn nodded and pulled out the stool from the kitchen island.

"So, Brynn," Marge began. "I wanted to come over when I knew Eric would be working. It can be hard to talk to you when he is around."

"Okay," Brynn assented.

"You must know that there are some disturbing things in the papers about Paul's disappearance."

"I've heard," Brynn said, "but I mostly stay away from the newspapers. Eric told me that some people are writing untrue things. There are theories about how Paul disappeared. Eric calls them armchair quarterbacks. He said I would be disturbed by what they said, so I haven't even bothered. I—I'm upset as it is."

Brynn swallowed hard. She did not want to show emotion around Marge. She was sure she would not be supported but would more likely be seen as hysterical and unhinged.

"Well, Eric told me not to tell you what I have been seeing, so I would appreciate it if you could be mature enough to keep this conversation confidential. Can you do that, Brynn?"

"Okay," Brynn agreed hesitantly.

"So, do you know the theory that is being bandied around about Paul now?"

"No, Marge, I don't think I do."

"Well, some people, and not just a few, it seems quite a few to me, think it would be impossible for someone to be so quiet that they could steal a baby from your grocery cart right under your nose. I mean, there would have been movement and rustling around, and why would Paul not cry out when being picked up by a stranger?"

"I know," Brynn agreed. "I have thought those exact things. I don't know how it was possible, how it happened, but it did!"

Brynn cradled her head in her hands. She was developing a huge headache.

"Anyway, Brynn, I don't know if you even know this, but I have already asked Eric. I told him not to tell you. I don't know whether he did or not?" Marge questioned.

Brynn shook her head. "I don't know. I don't know what you're talking about."

"Well, Brynn, I'm not going to mince words. I am going to be forthright and ask you. Did you have anything, anything at all, to do with Paul's disappearance?"

"What!" Brynn gasped. "What are you saying? What are you saying to me?"

"Now, don't get all hysterical," Marge said, raising a hand to indicate that Brynn should calm down. "We are just having a frank, adult conversation. Some of the theories I have read are quite plausible."

"What theories! I don't know what you are even talking about. Marge, I love Paul. I want my baby back each minute of every day. I miss him more than you know. Sometimes, I don't even want to live in the world without him."

Marge sighed.

"Eric said if I talked to you, you would get upset and be unreasonable. Please calm down. We are just talking."

"Why would I do that? How would I do that? You think I kidnapped my own baby?"

"Here is what they are saying. You should be reading some of this stuff on your own. It's good to be informed, you know. Anyway, some of the theories are crazy, really out there, but the ones that make sense say that you set the whole thing up. You knew it was going to happen."

"Why in hell would I do that, Marge? Give me one good reason."

"Well, Brynn, you're young. Maybe you wanted your freedom back. We all know that Paul wasn't planned, don't we? He was an accident. You didn't even get to finish school because of him. Maybe you are missing the life you could have had without him. Eric works a lot. I know that. Here you are left alone with an infant."

"Marge, this is so preposterous I don't even know what to say."

"Brynn, we both know that you weren't the most attentive mother. How many times did I tell you to watch him more closely? Many people think you didn't want to be a mother."

"So, what did I do? I asked someone to kidnap my child?"

"Did you?" Marge said, looking at Brynn with probing eyes.

"My God, I can't answer that! I think I'm going to be sick."

"Look, Brynn, I just want a direct answer, and then I'll go. You might have been paid a lot of money for him. They say babies on the black market demand a high price."

"We don't need money, Marge. You know that."

"Brynn, Eric has money. We know that, but what if you wanted to leave Eric? What if you wanted to be done with it all and start over? How would you? We also know that you do not have your own money. You and your mother never had any money, isn't that true? Look, Brynn, if you have made some huge mistake, I'm here to tell you there might be a way out. Eric's father and I had a lot of investments. I have more money than I will ever need. I'm more than prepared to pay to buy Paul back. Money isn't an issue. I can meet whatever figure they demand."

Brynn sat stunned, shaking her head back and forth.

"So, Brynn, what do you have to say? I can even give you a stipend to leave and start over with a whole new life. What do you say?"

"You think I'm involved? You think I know who stole my baby? That I wanted him stolen, taken away?

"Well, Brynn, you never answered my question, did you? You didn't say it wasn't true; you said you couldn't answer my question."

Marge sat back in her chair, looking pleased as if she had discovered a clue. Brynn got up so quickly that the tall stool she had been seated on almost fell over. She crossed to the door, opened it, and gestured with her hand that Marge should leave. "Here's your answer, Marge. I don't know who stole my son. I don't know how they got him out of the cart so quickly and quietly, but apparently, they did. I love my baby whether he was planned or not. I want him back. I will always want him back. Now leave my house and don't return unless Eric is here."

Marge sniffed and picked up her purse.

"We were only talking, Brynn. I was only telling you what I had seen in the newspapers."

"Get out!" Brynn hadn't meant to scream the words, but she realized too late that she had.

Marge walked past her and out the door.

"Oh, and I will tell Eric. I'll tell him everything."

Marge didn't turn around; she kept walking to the car as Brynn slammed the door. Brynn realized she was shaking and unsure what to do to stop it.

CHAPTER 24

BRYNN HAD FELT SO BAD, so morose after Marge left that she didn't know what to do. Thoughts of hurting herself and exactly how to do it pinged through her mind. She walked aimlessly and restlessly through the house. She was so, so tired of feeling bad. Something had to give. Finally, in her endless pacing, she found herself outside Paul's door. She hesitated and opened the door. Neither she nor Eric regularly entered the room, choosing for that door to remain firmly closed day after day. But now, Brynn twisted the handle and opened the door. Everything was the same. It looked like Paul had never left. Brynn peered into the empty crib. She pretended that Paul was lying there. She gently rubbed his little back. Well, she ran her hand over the empty space where he should have, could have been lying. She knew he wasn't there. She wasn't delusional. But she felt a sense of relief pretending that he was there. She quickly snuck out of the room and tiptoed across the floor, pretending he was sleeping. She grabbed the baby monitor, flicking it on. She entered the adjacent bathroom and looked at her reflection in the mirror. She was a mess! Her hair badly needed a wash, and she also needed a shower. If I hurry, maybe I can get cleaned up while Paul sleeps.

She grabbed a towel and hurriedly turned on the shower. She stripped her clothes off and jumped in while listening for cries on the baby monitor. It felt so good to be clean. She toweled off rapidly. She ran into the bedroom to get some clean clothes and quickly dressed before returning to Paul's room. She felt so much better pretending he was there. Her mood was lifting. She peered into the empty crib.

"Still sleeping," she whispered. "You're a tired baby! You rest."

Maybe she could clean the kitchen since Paulie was taking an extra-long nap. Before she realized it, hours had passed. Brynn had cleaned the entire kitchen and had started to organize the refrigerator. She looked up at the clock. It was almost time for Eric to come home. Hours had flown by instead of the usual dragging of time. She turned back to the refrigerator, but she heard a car door just then. Eric was home. She ran to the door to greet him, smiling as she opened it.

Eric smiled back and said, "Baby, you look better. Feeling better today?"

Brynn nodded and hugged him.

"We have to be quiet. Paul is sleeping."

"What—what did you say?" Eric said, startled.

"Paul is sleeping," she repeated. Then, a thought jolted through her like a lightning strike. *Oh, no,* she thought, *I said that out loud. I was pretending, but saying it makes it real.*

"Brynn, what—what are you saying?" Eric repeated.

"Are you saying that Paul is here? Paul is back?" Eric dropped his briefcase in the entryway and ran to Paul's room. Once there, he was confronted with an empty crib. Brynn watched from the doorway. When he turned back toward her, she noticed he had tears in his eyes.

"Brynn," he said in a quiet voice rife with emotion, "what are you doing? What is happening?"

"I was only pretending that Paul was sleeping. It made me feel so much better."

Eric ran his hands through his thick, curly hair.

"But, Brynn, you know he's not here, right? Right, Brynn?"

Brynn nodded and looked away.

"Your mother upset me earlier today. You won't even believe what she said to me." Brynn opened her mouth to say more, but Eric interrupted.

"So that is why you are playing pretend? Pretending that our missing child is here. God, Brynn, I don't understand you. You've upset me terribly. I thought somehow, some way, that Paul had come back!"

"Thanks so much for your support, Eric," Brynn said, her voice dripping with sarcasm.

"What?" Eric questioned somewhat cluelessly.

"You think it's my fault that our son is missing, too."

"Brynn, don't be ridiculous. Of course, I don't think that. Look, this is hard, so hard for all of us."

Brynn continued to glare at her husband, saying nothing more.

Eric swallowed and ran a hand through his dark, curly hair.

"It's just," he sighed, "my mother is needy." "You know that. She needs attention. She needs support. She's gotten worse since my dad died; you know that. She's very fragile."

Brynn put her hands on her hips and glared at him fiercely.

"She needs support, and I don't? Is that it?"

"No, Brynn, you don't get it. You are strong. She's not. If I don't assuage her, cosset her along, indulge her even, she'll make everything so much worse. I can't deal with that right now. I have to be on my game at work, dealing with the police, making phone calls, all of it."

"Eric, just because I'm strong, if I am, doesn't mean I don't need support, either."

"Brynn, I do support you. I support you all the time, by the way."

"Wow, now you sound like your mother! Is that a veiled way to mention that I don't work, so you support us monetarily, too? How dare you make this about money now!"

"Brynn, are you looking for a fight? Is that it?"

"Of course not," Brynn spat back. "This is the worst thing that has ever happened to me, to us."

She amended her words 'to us' at the last second. She saw hurt flash across Eric's eyes ever so briefly.

"Brynn," Eric said but stopped, hesitating and rubbing his beard.

Brynn stared at him.

"What, Eric? If you have something to say, say it."

"The person who took Paul must have snuck up so quietly and quickly that you did not notice anything."

Brynn quickly took a breath. "You do agree with your mother," she said in a hushed tone. "You think I am responsible for Paul's being taken. You think I'm negligent! My God, Eric!"

Eric held up a hand in protest.

"You don't know how much I wish I had been there. You don't know how often I replay the scene in my head. You don't know how much I wish I hadn't wandered off."

"Why? Why do you wish that? Because if you had been there, it wouldn't have happened. It wouldn't have happened if you had been there because only your wife cannot care for her child alone."

"I didn't say that, Brynn. You did."

"I can't believe you. You think your mother is right. You are saying the same things your mother said last week. You think I did something wrong, that I caused Paul to be stolen."

Eric looked down and did not reply, not even with a nod or a shrug. Brynn spun on her heel, walking away from Eric and out the door. She let the door slam behind her with a loud bang. Once outside, she stood in the yard, looking around aimlessly. She had nowhere to go. She wasn't exactly angry, not sad, but much closer to devastated. Instead of feeling too much, she was feeling too little. She felt dead—so dead inside.

CHAPTER 25

ANOTHER SATURDAY MORNING, the day began with an argument yet again. Brynn slammed the bedroom door so hard that the windows shook. The slam drowned out Eric's voice, calling out to her. She hurriedly locked the door before Eric reached it. She heard his heavy footsteps walking quickly down the hallway. He jiggled the doorknob.

"Brynn, open the door so we can talk."

Brynn stood just on the other side of the door, holding her head in her hands and using her arms to obscure everything around her.

"Brynn," Eric called again, this time more urgently. "Brynn, open the door!"

Brynn lowered her arms from her face. "No!"

She was going to add, *I need a few moments alone*, but before she could get the rest of the words out, she heard Eric say in an angry voice,

"Don't be a child!"

His disapproval, combined with the crazy theories about Paul, was too much. Brynn felt rage surge through her body.

"Go away, Eric! Go away, now."

"Brynn, I am trying to help you. How much more of this am I supposed to take?"

"Get away from me," Brynn screamed as loud as she could, her voice turning shrill as she reached the final word of her sentence.

"Whatever!" she heard him say in a low voice.

She heard his footsteps recede, and she breathed a sigh of relief. Brynn moved to the bed and sat down heavily on the edge. It was only then that she realized how much her hands were shaking. Saturday—only two days since Marge's last disastrous visit. Eric and Brynn had not talked about Paul since Brynn pretended that he was back home and safe in his crib.

But now, another visit with Marge had gone so wrong, so fast, and descended into an argument between Brynn and Eric as soon as she left. The last time Marge was at the house, Brynn told her not to return unless Eric was there. She had threatened Marge that she would tell Eric everything she had said to her, but she had not. Accusing Brynn of kidnapping her own baby and offering to pay her off. The accusations were ludicrous, and Eric looked so tired for the next few days when he came home from work, mumbling something about the big case all the associates were working on. She had said nothing more to him about his mother. But now, this Saturday morning, there she had been. Her car had slowly pulled into their driveway. It was early, just after eight a.m. She made sure Eric was home, Brynn thought grimly. It was unlikely that he would have gotten out of the house that early on a Saturday morning. Eric moved to the door, opened it, and hugged his mother, remarking, "You're out and about early this morning, Mother."

Marge sighed and gave a sideways glance at Brynn without saying hi.

"Well, I needed to ensure you were here, didn't I?"

"Is there something you need to talk to me about, Mother?"

"Not really. I just wanted to check on you and see how you were doing. Have you heard anything new about the case, about our Paul?"

He's not yours; he's mine, Brynn thought sullenly, realizing that her face was coalescing into a disagreeable sneer. Eric ran his hands through his hair.

"Ok," he said, giving Brynn a quizzical look.

"We haven't heard any new information."

He looked first at his mother and then at Brynn.

"Is something going on between the two of you? Something's not right."

"Well, Eric, I have no idea what Brynn has said to you. I am sure she told you that I am no longer welcome in your home."

"What, what are you talking about?"

"I didn't say that," Brynn said in a voice that she realized was too loud and harsh. "I told you not to come by if Eric wasn't home. I never said you weren't welcome here."

"Brynn, why can my mother only come by when I am here? She's come to check on you a lot these last few months, and I appreciate it. I thought you did, too."

"Eric," Brynn started to say, but before she could say more, Marge interrupted.

"Look, Eric, I have no idea what she has said to you about the incident, but Brynn, well, poor Brynn, I think she might be getting somewhat delusional."

"I am not delusional, Marge, and you know it."

Eric held up a hand.

"You better start at the beginning right now because I have no idea what either of you is talking about."

"Well, son, I was over here two days ago to check on Brynn and see if you needed anything. I asked Brynn if she had heard anything about Paul, and she just went off and went crazy. I guess I inadvertently upset her by asking about Paul. I understand, I do, but all the yelling and hatred were unnecessary, Brynn. She ended the conversation by yelling at me and telling me never to return to this house again."

"What! That's not right," Eric said, looking at Brynn with an accusing expression.

"You're leaving some key points out of the story, aren't you, Marge? Like how you accused me of being somehow involved in my son's kidnapping. What about the part where you offered to pay me off if I told you where Paul was and how you could get him back?"

"Mother! You said that to Brynn! That is beyond crazy."

Brynn continued.

"And I never said she wasn't welcome here. I told her not to return unless you were home, Eric."

"Oh, Brynn," Marge shook her head and reached out a hand as if she was going to touch Brynn's shoulder, but Brynn deftly moved out of her reach. "Poor dear, you are so upset you misunderstood much of what I was trying to say."

"I heard what you said that day. I heard it all very clearly, loud and clear, in fact."

"Eric, I never accused her of being involved in the kidnapping. I asked her if she thought an additional reward for information might be in order. I did ask if there was anything else that Brynn remembered about that day—if she saw something or heard something that she had failed to tell the police."

"If I knew something, why wouldn't I tell the police?" Brynn snarled.

"See, Eric, poor dear, she gets so quickly upset. Only after I left and thought about it did I realize how much I had upset Brynn."

"Why didn't you tell me about this, Brynn?"

"I tried to talk to you. You snapped at me, remember? And then you were so tired when you got home from work, Eric. I didn't want to bother you."

"Bother me! I deserve to know if there is a big misunderstanding like this."

Brynn watched as her mother-in-law nodded in agreement with him.

"Didn't go quite the way you just told him, did it, Marge?"

"Brynn, watch your tone. Mother is here to apologize to you. Aren't you, Mother?"

"Of course, dear. Brynn, I know you take medication and see a therapist, but maybe you need more help than you are getting. I am just so pleased to be welcome in your home again."

"Who said you were!" Brynn snorted.

"Brynn, stop," Eric said in a harsh voice.

Brynn looked first at Eric and then at Marge. Her head was beginning to spin, and she felt physically ill. "I can't, I can't do it." She turned and fled the room.

"She's gone, by the way," she heard Eric mumble on the other side of the door, so apparently, he hadn't walked away.

"Brynn, open the door so I can talk to you."

Brynn said nothing, staring at her bare feet. She heard him try the locked door one more time.

"OK, have it your way, then. I can't reason with someone who is being completely unreasonable."

Brynn continued staring downward at her feet, then the wood lines on the floor. She was losing Eric. Paul was gone and Eric was drifting further and further from her. Was she imagining it, or was he more and more supportive of Marge and less and less supportive of her? A year ago, they would have laughed at Marge's penchant for drama, but now Brynn was alone, and no one understood her point of view. Eric was now much more ready to side with his mother and leave Brynn alone. The pain Brynn was feeling was becoming intolerable; her whole body hurt, anxiety churned through her belly, and her heart was beating too loud, too fast. She crossed to the en-suite bathroom to take an aspirin, but as she reached for the bottle, she saw the Percocet sitting there that had been prescribed to Eric after he had injured his knee playing soccer. She picked up the bottle and shook it. A significant number of pills were still present. She looked at her reflection in the mirror as she closed the medicine cabinet, the bottle still clutched in her hand. As she peered closer at her reflection, she glared at herself. Her face took on an angry, distorted appearance. *Take them. Take them all,* a mean, surly voice urged. Brynn shrugged and popped two pills into her mouth. She hastily grabbed a paper cup of water and swigged the pills down before she could think further of it. She returned to the bedroom and crossed to her dresser drawer. This is where she kept the anti-anxiety pills, the benzos, that her psychiatrist had prescribed. The first prescription hadn't seemed to work—a paradoxical reaction, her therapist had told her, meaning they had worsened her anxiety rather than improved it. She removed that bottle now, along with the bottle of the pills that she was currently taking. There were a lot of pills in both bottles. *Take them! Take them all!* she heard the voice say again. *Leave me alone, all of you, leave me alone!* Brynn said fiercely in her own mind. Still, she opened both bottles and poured out a small handful. She stared at them for several minutes before opening her mouth and palming them all in. She grabbed the cup of water still present on the dresser and swallowed them all. She stood, waiting, feeling nothing, absolutely nothing, and maybe that was the point. Had she taken enough to overdose? She had taken a relatively small dose in the scheme of things, but her body wasn't used to pills. Was it possible she had taken enough to die? *Who cares?* She heard the mean voice sneer at first, but her next thought was, *what if we find Paul? What if, by some miracle, we find him, and he comes home? I can't be dead! No, no, I don't want to die! I don't want to die! I can't! I can't die!* Brynn was hot then cold. She was starting to feel dizzy. *My God.* She had made the most colossal mistake of her entire life. She crossed to the phone on the nightstand beside Eric's side of the bed, picked it up, and keyed in 911 with no more thought than she had given to gulping the pills in the first place.

"What is your emergency?" a detached voice said. "Fire, medical, police."

"Medical," Brynn said in a voice now shaking with fear. "I took a bunch of pills, I did, just now. I don't want to die. Help me!"

"Stay on the line, ma'am," the voice said firmly.

"I need your address; I'm sending an ambulance."

Brynn gave her the address but then hung up. She ran to the bedroom door, unlocked it, and yelled frantically for Eric.

"Eric, Eric, the ambulance is coming! I took a bunch of pills. I took too many pills."

Eric thundered down the hallway.

"What the hell, Brynn! What are you saying? What did you..." But she saw his gaze go to the pill bottles on the bed. Brynn felt her mouth become cottony—her body too warm. Eric moved to the phone.

"I called them. I called them already," Brynn slurred.

"Oh, I feel so funny," Brynn said, moving to sit on the bed. In the distance, she unmistakably heard an ambulance's wail.

CHAPTER 26

BRYNN HEARD THE DOOR OPEN as she lay on the couch covered with her favorite warm, furry blanket. She fluttered her eyelids, but as she heard Marge's voice, she snapped them back closed. *Marge is the last, the very last person I want to see or talk to,* Brynn thought miserably. They had only been home from the hospital for a matter of hours. Brynn's stomach was still hurting from the medication they had given her. She rolled onto her side, facing the brown fabric of the couch. She had no choice but to pretend she was deeply asleep. Another confrontation with Marge. And on the same day! No way she could handle that. She heard approaching footsteps and then heard Eric whisper, "Shh, I think she fell asleep."

"Are you sure, Eric?" Marge said loudly, clearly not caring whether she woke Brynn or not. "I wanted to speak with her," Marge continued in the same loud voice.

"Mother, lower your voice," Eric remonstrated. "Come on, let's go to the kitchen. Leave Brynn alone. You can talk to me."

Brynn waited for the kitchen door to close, but instead, she heard the kitchen chairs being pulled out as if they were sitting down at the table. Eric had forgotten to close the kitchen door. Brynn would be able to hear every word they said.

"Coffee, Mother?" she heard Eric inquire. Marge must have nodded affirmatively because she heard Eric flick the coffee-maker on.

"Well, what did they say at the hospital?"

Eric sighed. Brynn knew he would run his hands through his mop of curly hair.

"They gave her medication. It made her throw up. They said she hadn't taken enough pills to kill herself. They did a psych consult. We discussed the possibility of her staying in the psych ward. Brynn was very against that. She said she had her own therapist, that she hadn't wanted to die and that she just wanted to go home. They asked her a lot of questions. The doctor left and even had a phone consultation with Brynn's therapist. Everyone agreed that she could leave. Brynn is to see Toni, her therapist, twice this week. The appointments are already scheduled."

"Why, Eric, why would Brynn do such a stupid, foolish thing? I cannot believe how much that girl puts you through!"

"The doctor called it a cry for help. Brynn repeated over and over that she didn't want to die. She was frustrated and upset. The doctor also said he thought a stronger medication change was probably in order for Brynn. Between you and me, I don't think Brynn even takes her medication all the time. That might be part of the problem. I will talk to her about that later, but not today."

"Of course, she doesn't take her medication correctly," Marge said and sniffed.

"What do you mean by that, Mother?"

"She's careless, Eric, thoughtless. She always has been. It's part of the reason you are in your situation."

"What are you talking about?"

"Paul might not be missing if Brynn had been paying attention to her surroundings."

"Why, I am sure..."

"Don't go there, Mother. Just don't. Not today of all days. Brynn is in significant pain, and she had to feel desperate to do what she did this morning."

"But what did she do, Eric? You said the doctor said that she didn't try to kill herself."

"He said it was a cry for help. And thank God she wasn't close to being successful."

"A cry for help, Eric, or a desperate, pathetic bid for attention?"

"Mother!" Brynn heard him use the name almost as an epithet.

"Eric, you are upset, too, and you don't do anything as stupid as Brynn did this morning. She seems to be trying to garner as much attention from you as possible. She is trying to make you feel sorry for her. You should be comforting each other on your loss. But no, with Brynn, it's all one way. It's all about her. Maybe she could work harder to find Paul if she could stop thinking of herself for just one minute. You can't talk to her about anything, Eric. I assure you that was all I was trying to do when I was here the other day. Talk to her about Paul, strategize what we could do and where we would go from here. Instead, she became entirely unreasonable and accused me of the foolish, awful things she said this morning. I don't believe for one minute that those pills were a cry for help. I think she knew all too well what she was doing. She is trying to get you to pity her. She is putting all the responsibility on your shoulders while she does what? Sleeps on the couch day after day?"

"Mother, we have all been through an extreme trauma. That is what the doctor at the hospital said. Brynn is not manipulating the situation or me. She is upset. Is she mishandling it? Yes, she is, very badly."

Brynn heard Marge sniff.

"I don't know how you put up with it all, son. You're a saint."

Brynn felt a single tear run down her cheek. She raised her hand out from under the blanket to wipe it away.

CHAPTER 27

BRYNN'S MOUTH FELT THICK AND COTTONY. She felt anesthetized without feeling drowsy. She had to admit that she had liked the feeling of the new medication at first. She certainly was able to feel it kick in, and the crippling anxiety, the pit in her stomach, was gone, but she was beginning to dislike this feeling of nothingness, this intense brain fog. It was as if a curtain had been pulled over her feelings, both good and bad. Yet she was taking each pill on schedule, never missing a dose, just as Eric had requested. He had called her out for not taking her last medication and had asked that she at least try—take them, give them time to work, he had urged. She had reluctantly agreed, but now, though she felt medicated during the day, she was wide awake at night, tossing and turning endlessly, waking Eric up repeatedly. They both agreed that she would discuss the medication at her next appointment with Toni. Brynn had just laid down on the couch, Eric reading in the easy chair beside her. She pulled the blanket up and nestled into the pillow that now stayed on the couch.

"Baby, take a little nap if you can," Eric said soothingly.

"You barely slept at all last night."

"Maybe, maybe I will." Brynn realized her words were slurred. Damn medication! Brynn felt like she had not fallen asleep at all, but she must have because she heard Eric talking to somebody quietly, and he was no longer in the adjacent chair. Was he on the phone? She started to sit up but then heard Marge's voice and lay back down. Did she have to deal with her yet again?

"She's sleeping, Mother," she heard Eric say. "I see no need to wake her. She barely slept at all last night. She needs the rest."

"She's sleeping again, Eric? Does the girl do nothing but lie on the couch!"

"Mother, I told you she couldn't sleep last night."

"Well, maybe if she didn't lie around so much during the day, she could sleep at night."

"That's not it, Mother. You don't get it. She's struggling with the medication."

"She's taking it this time?"

"Yes, she is, but I'm not sure it's helping her. Anyway, thanks for the groceries. I appreciate the help; that was a great deal on those steaks. I see why you didn't want to pass them up."

So that was her excuse for coming over this time, Brynn thought. She had brought groceries once again.

Brynn nestled back into the pillow. Maybe she could fall asleep, but just as she thought she might drift away, she heard Marge's voice ask Eric, "How is that dear girl at work? Katherine, isn't that her name?"

"Shh," Eric whispered fiercely.

"It's Katrina. Her name is Katrina, and she's fine. I mean, I guess she's fine. Mother, lower your voice," Eric whispered urgently. His tone caused Brynn to perk up.

Who? What were they talking about?

"Katrina, that's a pretty name, isn't it? She's also very easy on the eyes, isn't she, son?"

"I don't know. I haven't noticed," Eric replied.

"Well, I'm glad you have a good friend at work to talk to. God knows you need the support. She seems like she cares about you."

Brynn felt her heart beat faster. Who were they talking about? Eric had mentioned no new colleagues at work.

"Does she have a boyfriend, Eric?"

"I don't know, Mother. Why would I know that? Look, this isn't appropriate to talk about, especially not here with Brynn right in the other room."

"I understand, dear. I'm just glad you've met someone."

Met someone, met someone? Brynn repeated in her mind. What the hell was going on? Eric and Marge continued talking about the steaks and then about her lawn. The woman, Katrina, was no longer mentioned. Brynn lay there, repeating those few sentences in her mind. Finally, she heard the door open and heard Marge exit. She lay there with her eyes open, waiting for Eric to enter the room. She latched onto his eyes as soon as he entered the room.

"Hey, you're awake," he said warmly.

Brynn felt her stomach curdling. If she had been able to think, she might have thought of a different way to get her questions answered, but thanks to the medication, she couldn't think straight. She stared at Eric with a frown and abruptly said, "Dating someone new, Eric?"

Eric sighed loudly, ran his hands through his hair, and sat down heavily.

"I'm married to you, Brynn. You weren't supposed to hear any of that."

"Oh, but I did, Eric. So, who is Katrina? I'm glad your mother likes her so much."

"Brynn, it's nothing, ok? Katrina is just one of the legal assistants. She's been there about three months."

"If you two are so close, why didn't you ever mention her to me?"

"I don't know, it never came up."

"How does your mother know so much about her? You talk about her to your mother, just not me."

"Brynn, if you must know, Katrina has been trying to help me. Two weeks ago, after you left the hospital, she came into my office to drop off some files. She found me crying at my desk. It had all gotten to be too much —the stress of Paul, the worry about you, dealing with my mother. I was sitting there crying, and luckily, she was the one who walked in, not one of the partners. That would be a way to get promoted and become a senior partner, wouldn't it? Crying like a baby! Anyway, she took me downstairs for coffee. It was the best thing. I needed to get out of there. And before you ask, I haven't gone anywhere with her, only downstairs for coffee and only that one time. She listened to me. She let me talk about all that has been going on. She's had her own trauma. She seemed to get it. She showed me some breathing techniques that can help with stress. I can show you sometime if you would like. She also showed me this thing called tapping. You tap on meridian points in the body. It is very calming."

"That doesn't explain how your mother knows so much about her," Brynn said tersely.

"Well, it was the first day, that Monday after you left the hospital, that Mother stopped by the office to check on me. My assistant told her I was downstairs with Katrina. She met her that day. Katrina is a warm, outgoing person. She was kind to Mother, and I guess she remembered it. That's all, Brynn. It's nothing."

"Why keep it such a big secret if it's nothing? Why keep it so hush-hush from me?"

"I'm not, not really. It just never came up. You have a lot on your mind. I don't tell you all the minutiae that occurs daily at work."

Brynn flipped over on the couch, facing the back of the sofa and away from Eric. She felt him stand up and touch her shoulder gently. "Brynn, it's nothing. I promise you it's nothing, okay?"

Brynn did not turn to face him and flinched away from his touch. She felt relieved as she heard him move away. She let out a breath as she heard his footsteps recede and eventually fade into nothingness. Brynn felt sure Katrina was a much more significant part of Eric's life than he was willing to admit.

CHAPTER 28

BRYNN SIGHED. She wasn't sure she agreed with Eric's assessment that she needed to get out of the house more. It had been a year since Paul had been taken, but she still found it physically painful to be around other people. Why did it seem that everyone was so loud? Their voices and laughter cut right through her with knife-like intensity.

She longed to be home and wrapped up on the couch with the multicolored afghan around her. She was not home, though, but in this crowded clothing store. She did not want to buy anything. She picked up a sweater desultorily and then put it right back down. Eric had wandered off, claiming he needed to get some jeans.

"You'll be fine here, baby?" he had asked.

She knew her answer was supposed to be yes, so she nodded, even though she wanted to scream, no, Eric, I am not all right. Get me the hell out of here now! She looked around. He must be coming back for her soon. He wouldn't leave her here too long, would he? Brynn heard the giggle of a young child, and she flinched. She looked down the aisle just in time to see a lady pushing a stroller with a dark, curly-haired tot in it. The child looked sturdy, about the same body build as Paul, Brynn thought idly. Her heart ached as she remembered her missing son. She found herself following the mother and child without seeming to have made an actual decision to do so. She rounded the corner, putting her in the same aisle as they were. The child released a chortle, and Brynn felt her body stop breathing. That laugh sounded so much like Paul. The visuals and sounds of Paul played in an almost constant loop in Brynn's mind. No, it couldn't be. It was impossible. Brynn edged closer to get a better view of the child. She gasped. The boy had the same type of hair as Paulie. This child was about the same age that Paul would be now.

"Nothing here for us, Brandon," the lady said, speaking to the child. "Let's go."

Brynn jockeyed around an older lady who was partially blocking the aisle. Now, she was right beside the child. She bent down, and she saw it! No, no, no. It couldn't be. The boy had a bright red nose: the tip was red, like Paul's birthmark. Brynn stood back up, but the mother was already on the move, pushing the stroller quickly down the aisle. Had she noticed Brynn observing and was now trying to get away? Brynn followed quickly. Her head swiveled as she looked around futilely for Eric. Why was the woman hurrying so much? Was she aware Brynn was following? What did she have to hide? What was the rush? Now, the woman was exiting the store. Brynn was right behind her. She couldn't let her get away. She could jump in a car and vanish if she got to the parking lot.

"Whee, Brandon!" the woman exclaimed as she pushed the stroller over a speed bump. The child let out a giant guffaw. That voice, his voice, sounded exactly like Paul. Brynn ran up so she was right beside the woman. She looked at the child again, noting his nose's red tip.

The woman looked at her, concerned. Brynn had to do something before it was too late.

"That's my baby! You have my baby!" she screamed hysterically. She attempted to grab the stroller, but the woman wrenched the handle away from Brynn. The woman screamed herself.

"Help! Help me!" she yelled.

Brynn grabbed for the stroller again. The child began to cry loudly.

"It's okay, Paul, it's okay," Brynn soothed.

"Call 911!" the woman screamed. "This woman is trying to take my baby!"

It seemed only moments, and maybe it was, before the police arrived and before Eric came running out of the store with a bag of jeans clutched securely in his arms.

"What is going on?" the officer asked the sobbing woman.

"This crazy lady first followed me in the store, watching my son. I tried to leave quickly, and she kept following me. She tried to kidnap my son!"

"I did not!" Brynn screamed back. "You stole this child from me a year ago! That is my son! It looks like him. It sounds like him! Tell them, Eric! Tell them that is our baby."

"Brynn," Eric said, closing his eyes. Brynn was becoming irate. She was not crazy, and she knew she was right!

"I know this child is my son," she said, appealing directly to the police officer.

"I know it is him because his nose is red. My baby has a bright red birthmark on the tip of his nose. See? Look at the baby's nose! It's bright red!"

"Seriously?" the other woman snarled sarcastically. She looked down at the child in the stroller, looking up at all the adults surrounding him.

"Officer," the woman said respectfully, "may I get something out of my purse."

The officer nodded, but Brynn realized he was watching the woman closely. The woman pulled out a wet wipe towelette, leaned over, and vigorously wiped the young child's nose. All the red immediately disappeared.

"He ate a cherry popsicle right before we went into the store," the woman said, glaring at Brynn.

"Oh," Brynn said, looking down. She watched the woman and child walk away. She heard Eric talking to the officer. She heard him apologize and saw the officer look at her sadly and nod.

"Let's go, Brynn," she heard Eric say. "Let's get you back home."

CHAPTER 29

BRYNN WAS LYING ON THE COUCH. Eric had walked by twice. She quickly closed her eyes, faking sleep. They had spoken little since yesterday's incident in the store.

"Why, Brynn?" Eric had said when they were in the car headed home. Brynn had shaken her head.

"I don't know, Eric. I was so anxious. I thought it was Paul."

Eric sighed. "But clearly it wasn't him. Why didn't you come and find me?"

"I didn't know where you were. Eric, what if it was him? I couldn't let him get away, could I? I had to follow. I had to find out!"

"Oh, Brynn," Eric said, and the conversation concluded with nothing more said. Brynn heard Eric walk by the couch once again. What was he doing? Was he going to keep pacing by her until she woke up? She opened her eyes, looking directly at him.

"Hey, have a nice rest?" he inquired.

"Mm-hmm," she assented, even though it wasn't so.

"Do you feel like talking about what happened yesterday? I think we need to."

"It's over, Eric. I made a mistake. That's all. Maybe it's even the medication. It makes me feel awful, Eric. I feel spinny and weird. I have strange thoughts."

"Well, if that is the case, maybe you should stop taking it."

Brynn shook her head no.

"No, I feel even worse when I don't take it. It's like I'm going to jump out of my skin."

Eric rubbed his hands through his hair.

"Okay, you feel bad when you take it and when you don't."

He was frustrated with her.

"What do you want me to say?"

"I don't know," Brynn said morosely.

"Brynn, we need to do something. You're not getting better. It's almost where I'm afraid to leave you alone. I'm not sure what you might do. I thought going out might help you, but I'm afraid of that, too. If you're going to accost strangers, think every child you see is Paul. Well, that's not working. Brynn, it's been long enough now."

"What, Eric? I should get over it! Forget all about Paul. Just put him out of my mind. Maybe I can pretend he never existed like you do."

"Brynn, I don't pretend he never existed. My heart is broken too, you know. It's just going on this way isn't good for any of us."

"Been talking to your mother again, Eric?"

That last sentence, 'going on this way,' sounded like something Marge had said to her only last week.

"Brynn, I'm not trying to fight with you. I want to help you but can't because you won't let me. I think you need more. I know you don't want to hear it, but maybe it is time to consider some inpatient treatment."

Brynn shook her head no vigorously.

"I have a therapist, Eric."

"Oh, I know, Brynn. I also know that you keep canceling appointments. Saying you have a therapist that you never see isn't helping. I think you need more, or maybe you should try attending a few appointments."

He was frustrated with her, making Brynn feel the whole world was against her. She threw the blanket off her legs and jumped off the couch.

"Thanks for the support, Eric. And, by the way, I never wanted to go to the store anyway. I went to humor you."

"I don't know what you want, Brynn. I don't know how to help you."

"What do I want, Eric? I'll tell you what I want. I want to be left alone. In fact, I might want to be left alone for the rest of my life!"

Brynn pushed past him and exited the room.

CHAPTER 30

BRYNN HAD NOT MISSED HER WEEKLY THERAPY appointment in over two months. She hated to admit it, but Eric had most likely been right. His mention of her going to an inpatient treatment facility had certainly scared her enough that she had begun attending her therapy appointments faithfully. Brynn considered what she and Toni had talked about at this session.

Gaslighting! So that was what it was called. Marge had been doing it to Brynn for years —ever since Brynn had met her, even before she married Eric. And Eric always made excuses for his mother. He always supported and took her side, no matter how cruel her words were to Brynn. Therapy helped Brynn understand so much.

"Make no mistake, Brynn," Toni, her therapist, stated, "there are reasons for everything, but because Marge is hurt now or in the past, it does not give her a reason to hurt you. Of course, her son should be supportive of her, but you are his wife and deserve his support. You are not required to take her abuse."

"If I walk away from her, I am afraid it will mean I have to walk away from Eric, too. He always says he knows what his mother is like. He talks a good game, but, in the end, he always asks me to be the one to compromise. He says she is upset because her husband died, or she is upset about Paul, or she is getting older. It's always something, and she manipulates him constantly!"

"Brynn, I can't speak to their relationship dynamic, but I can encourage you to talk to Eric. Your feelings are valid, and you are not selfish or unreasonable. Talk to Eric, and Brynn, tell him how you feel.

"But then after that?" Brynn inquired.

"What are the next steps? We don't know that yet, but you must do what is best for you. It's your life, and you deserve to live it."

CHAPTER 31

"BRYNN, THERE'S SOMETHING I would like to talk about during this session," her therapist said, flipping her ever-present notebook open. Brynn nodded.

"I even have a book that I think might help you."

"Ok," Brynn said, "you know I love to read."

"In the last session, you talked about Eric and how he said he thinks Paul is dead."

Brynn nodded, remembering her painful conversation with Eric not so long ago. "Eric believes Paul is dead. I think that helps him cope with the loss, but when I have that thought, Toni, I don't even like to say those words aloud or even in my head. The thought that Paul might be dead destroys me. I do want to move on, though. You know that. I don't know how."

"That's why I think this book might help. We, as a culture, are generally quite uncomfortable with the unknown. The book is *Ambiguous Loss* by Pauline Boss. I have a copy for you right here," Toni said, reaching behind her to the bookcase, which sat directly behind her chair.

"Have you ever heard of the book, Brynn?"

Brynn took the book the therapist handed her and studied the title.

"No, I haven't heard of this author or ambiguous loss. I know loss all too well, though," Brynn sighed ruefully.

"Ambiguous—I know what the word means. It means not clear, undefined."

"Think, Brynn, how might that apply to you."

"We don't know if Paul is dead or alive. It's hard to grieve him because a tiny spark, especially a tiny spark inside of me, tells me that he may—that he could come back. There's no closure."

The therapist nodded.

"Makes it hard to move on, doesn't it? Not knowing gets in the way. The author has suffered her own ambiguous losses. Her husband suffered from Alzheimer's, and he left her long before he was gone physically."

Brynn ran her hand over the cover of the book.

"I can't wait to read this."

"I think it might help you, Brynn. Read it, and we can start discussing it during the next session. The uncertainty you and Eric have concerning Paul is a lot to deal with. The lack of information about his whereabouts and his status—alive and well or dead—is uniquely troubling. I think Ms. Boss articulately explains a great deal of the pain that you are going through. And, Brynn, just because it appears that Eric has it all settled in his mind doesn't mean he does. Don't sell yourself short. You are coping right here, right now. I see in front of me a young woman who is doing the very best she can in an impossible situation. You are coping far better than you give yourself credit for."

Brynn nodded, unable to speak. Tears came to her eyes, and the lump in her throat seemed to expand. Brynn stood, leaning down to grab her coat.

"See you next week?" she inquired quietly.

"Of course," Toni smiled at her warmly.

CHAPTER 32

"MAMA, MAMA," Brynn heard a young boy call out in the mall parking lot.

Brynn hesitated very briefly, then continued walking to her car in the parking lot without looking back.

Brynn smiled as she exited the mall. After her therapy appointment, she had picked up a new sweater and some underwear, which she badly needed. Another year had passed, and now she knew that she could go into a store and not be distracted by the young children there or think that every young boy she saw was Paul, which was a significant improvement.

"Mama, mama," she heard the child call again.

Yes, the brief glimpse she had of the child in the stroller clearly showed a child who would be about Paul's age now. The young boy she glanced at had curly dark hair like Paul's and appeared to have a body build just like Paul's.

"Mama, mama," the child called again, louder this time. His mother was right there with him. Why was he calling for her so loudly?

All these occurrences would have in the past been clues to Brynn and would have caused her to rush over or follow the woman and the child immediately. But no, the child was not her baby. Those days of running after strange women and young boys were done. Over now. Brynn had continued her search for over six months, but now, she was medicated and seeing a competent therapist she liked. She was trying with all her might to move on from her trauma, from the horrible thing that could not be undone. No, that boy was not her baby. Her baby was gone and was not returning, never returning. Brynn had not thought losing hope was the way to move on, but it was. Waking up each day and thinking, hoping that Paul might return, had been driving her insane. She would not return to inpatient hospitalization again, ever. Her stay had been awful. It had been apparent over that interminable period of three weeks that Brynn had to move on. She had to move on or give up and go insane. She had thought at the time that killing herself was a viable option, but even that had not worked out for her. She knew deep down that she wanted to live. But all that was in the past now. She continued to move away from the mother and child with deliberate speed. The boy was still calling out, "Mama, Mama!" he said with greater intensity.

She allowed herself to look back. The mother, a slight blonde woman, was bending down to the stroller, attempting to console her son. Brynn shook her head and moved onward toward her car.

"Mama," the boy still trilled even as his mother bent before him.

"Shh, Jared," she soothed. "It's okay."

The boy tried to twist in the stroller to see behind him, calling out "Mama" loudly and more insistently one last time. He turned back as the woman offered him a soft blanket festooned with cavorting dogs. The child grabbed the blanket, rubbing it over his face and nose. The child's nose had a bright red dot barely visible on the tip.

"Let's get you home for your nap, Jared," the woman said. "We've driven a long way. You must be tired."

The child had stopped calling out now. Brynn felt her shoulders relax as she heard the shrill voice no more. She was almost in her car. She clicked the key fob to unlock the doors. She thought to herself, *Eric would be proud*. She had continued past the child like a normal human being. *I'll have to tell Eric*, she thought as she slid into the car. Then she remembered Eric was no longer in the home she would return to. Eric was not there and would not be returning. She wasn't even sure where Eric had gone when he had moved out after her hospitalization. Was he staying at his mother's? Was he staying somewhere else? Was he staying with someone else? Brynn had no idea. She felt momentarily sad, but there had been no connection between them for some time now. Brynn wasn't even sure that she truly missed him—or did she miss the life they used to have? The house was big, much too big for one person. If she were indeed going to move on, she would need to move out to leave the house and the life they once had. She remembered how she and Eric had driven to the beach and looked at the small cottages that were so prevalent along the shore. Maybe she would drive there now and look at some of the cottages. She might feel better in a much smaller house. They could sell it if neither she nor Eric wanted to live in their home. The price they would get would probably more than cover the cost of a small beach cottage. She would go this afternoon and see if she liked anything down there. If she saw something, she would talk to Eric. If they were moving on, why not go all the way with it? It was probably time to say the word "divorce" as well. Eric probably thought she wasn't stable enough for heavy conversations, and they could prolong this stasis, this holding pattern for years, but why? Why not rip the band-aid off and be done with it? It was time. It was finally time.

CHAPTER 33

ERIC WAVED AT HIS MOTHER as he pulled out of her driveway. She was so hard to live with. She was always in his business, always hovering over him.

"You look tired, son. Do you want something to eat? What can I do for you, Eric?"

You can leave me alone; that would be a start. He had thought that many times but never said it. It would only hurt her feelings. Thank God Katrina had again invited him over for dinner at her apartment. He loved spending time with her. She was calm, gentle, and a great listener. When he told her how difficult living with his mother was, she suggested that he move in with her. She had made it very clear that she had an extra bedroom and offered it to him as a friend, nothing more. He had declined, even though his heart soared at the suggestion. He was beginning to have feelings for Katrina, even though he had not acted on them at all. They didn't even hug or chastely kiss when saying hello or goodbye. Sometimes, he saw Katrina looking at him and wondered if she might feel something for him, too. It was too early, though, way too early. Brynn was still living in their house. They were separated, but divorce was never mentioned. He didn't want to push Brynn. If she brought up divorce, it would be one thing. She still seemed fragile. He was sure she didn't want to get back together, but he didn't want to push. Why was life working out so differently from what he had envisioned only a few short years ago? His life wasn't supposed to be like this! He pulled into Katrina's driveway. She opened the door of her condo and waved at him. He smiled at her, parked the car, and waved back.

CHAPTER 34

"OK, THAT'S THE LAST OF THE STUFF from the attic."

Eric had just returned from putting the two boxes in Brynn's car.

"I don't know how your mom's boxes got mixed up with my stuff, but you have them now. I'm just glad that Katrina…" He hesitated as he said his girlfriend's name. "I know you wouldn't want to lose keepsakes from your mom."

Brynn nodded. The closing on their house had finally gone through. All the paperwork was signed. They were finally free and clear of the house. Brynn intended to pay off the mortgage she had taken out on the beach cottage tomorrow with her share of the proceeds. Eric ran his hands through his curly hair awkwardly as if he didn't know what else to say. Brynn looked up at him.

"Eric," she said quietly, "I'm not mad anymore. I'm not mad at you about anything. I don't have anything against Katrina. It was over between us a long time ago. Even when we were still living in the same house, you know we weren't together as well as I do."

Eric nodded and gave Brynn a serious look.

"I will always care about you, Brynn. You must know that. I want you to be ok. I only wish the best for you."

"Eric, I'll be ok. I am seeing someone now. It just started, but" Brynn trailed off.

"Katrina is a good person, Brynn. I'm sorry about the way you found out. I should have told you myself, not wait for ever-helpful Mother to blurt it out."

They both laughed. Then Eric looked very serious.

"Brynn, I never cheated on you. Katrina and I didn't get together until after I moved out, and even then, not immediately."

"It's ok, Eric, really."

Suddenly, Brynn got a faraway look in her eyes.

"I think he's alive, you know," she said, her eyes glistening.

"Paul, you know, I think he's alive. He would be three years old now. He lived in my body for nine months, Eric, and I've always thought that my body would tell me if he was gone, left this world, deceased. And I don't feel that at all. I feel that he's out there somewhere."

"Brynn, please, don't torture yourself."

"I'm not, I'm really not. I have come to terms with never seeing him again, but unless something happens and this feeling changes, I don't; I can't believe that he is dead."

"Oh, Brynn," Eric said sadly. He started to reach out an arm to touch her but then pulled back, letting his arm drop leadenly to his side. Brynn realized there was nothing more to say. They stared at each other for one more minute before Brynn softly said, "Have a good life, Eric."

"You too, you too," Eric repeated as he coughed and cleared his throat before walking away.

CHAPTER 35

BRYNN STARED AROUND THE BEACH COTTAGE. Every corner was loaded with boxes. She had more things than she had room for. She was going to end up putting quite a few items in storage. She stood silently in the middle of the living room. She could smell the ocean through the open windows. She thought she could hear the gentle waves whooshing in and out if she listened hard enough. It was quiet here, and she felt calm. She knew she slept better here than in the vast house she and Eric had shared. After Eric moved out, she had been alone in that house for months. How many times had she heard things creaking and strange noises, especially at night? The house was so large that it was difficult to get up and find the noise source. She had kept the bedroom door locked at night and even installed a deadbolt on the door, but still, she had often jarred awake at night. In this small cottage, getting up and looking around was easy, ensuring no intruder was there. She felt safe. At first, she had thought that she might feel lonely. But she didn't. She had been lonely in their old house. A big house meant to provide shelter for many more people than just her. Also, walking by Paul's room daily was like negotiating a minefield. Even with the door resolutely closed, it was hard to pass by, knowing that all the baby items were still inside. It was too easy to imagine what might have been, what life would be now if Paul were still present, still living in that room. Brynn remembered all too well that time she had pretended that Paul was there. Eric had looked at her as if she was crazy, and she guessed she had been a little crazy. She had been crazy then with grief. But now she had a new start. It wasn't what she wanted. She thought she and Eric would grow old with their children. Why was life working out so differently from what she had envisioned only a few short years ago? It wasn't supposed to be like this!

CHAPTER 36

EIGHT MONTHS EARLIER

DAMN! ALISON HAD DRIVEN over an hour out of her way to that new large toy store located in the high-end mall. She hadn't wanted to tell her parents where she was going or be accused of using too much gas. So, she had snuck out quietly with Jared. She was taking her son with her to buy his birthday presents, but he was so young he wouldn't realize what they were doing. However, Jared began to cry and become whiny before they entered the store, repeatedly yelling "Mama" even though she was right beside him! Once inside, every single item, no matter how small, was too expensive and out of her price range. They had left with nothing, and Alison had cried silently as they drove home.

CHAPTER 37

GAIL SIGHED. Jared was turning two tomorrow, and she and Alison had been working hard to make him a cake, buy balloons, and get ready for their small party. They had just returned from the Dollar Store. Alison had wanted Jared to have a lot of presents to open.

"Like you used to do for me, Mom," Alison had said urgently.

None of the items they had bought for Jared's birthday were expensive, and watching Jared open them would be fun. Alison had found more at the inexpensive Dollar Store than at the larger toy store. Still, she was frustrated, wanting to buy more even after they had run out of money.

"Maybe I'll have a job by next year," she said in frustration.

Gail nodded. Alison tried to take care of Jared and help around the house, but more days than not, she couldn't even get out of her own way. She couldn't even get out of bed several days out of the month. They had cycled now through so many different medications, and none of them seemed to help Alison with her depression or her anxiety. Alison had cried in the car all the way home from the store. Gail had been glad they had left Jared at the trailer with Cecil. He was much too exposed to Alison's cycling moods. Gail wasn't at all sure that Jared was turning two. He was a sturdy, stocky boy.

"Big for his age," Cecil would crow, "and a smart one, too!"

But was he just two? Gail thought he might be closer to three years old. They had no way of knowing, so they used the date they had taken Jared for his birthday.

"He's taking a nap," Cecil said, stretching as they entered the trailer with all the shopping bags.

Alison put all the bags she was carrying in the kitchen and hurried to the bathroom. She always tried not to cry in front of her father. He would always make an insensitive comment like, "What's wrong with you now? You have nothing to be depressed about."

Alison was learning to hide her true feelings more and more when near her father.

"She's upset again?" Cecil questioned brusquely.

Gail sighed. "I wish Alison was getting better. I do, but sometimes I think she's not, Cecil."

Cecil stood, yawning and rubbing his belly.

"It's a slow process. We have to give her time. Jared helps her. He is helping her. Look, she was out and about with you because of him."

"I know," Gail said, sighing, "you are right. She wanted to buy him more things, and when we ran out of money, she even mentioned that maybe she could have a job by his next birthday."

"Well, there you go, then that's an improvement," Cecil said.

"I just, I wish; I was hoping we could give him back by now."

"What?" Cecil said in a too-loud voice, his eyes narrowing.

Gail was so tired and worried about Alison that she had said it out loud — the thought she had every few days and the scenario she played out in her head almost every night. She had never mentioned her plan to Cecil all these years, but she might as well go ahead and tell him now.

"Cecil," she said quietly and starting very tentatively.

"I have always hoped that we could give Jared back someday. He belongs to someone else. He was loved. The stories I read in the paper said that his parents loved him. His real mother was young, just like Alison. She must miss him terribly."

Cecil crossed to where Gail was standing with a harsh, mean look in his eyes. He reached out and grabbed her arms so hard that she let out a yelp.

"Cecil," she yelled, "you're hurting me." She looked toward the bathroom and the bedroom where Jared was sleeping. She didn't want Alison or Jared to see or hear what was happening. Gail tried to pull her arms away, but Cecil tightened his grip and pushed her back until she was right against the refrigerator, the handle cutting uncomfortably into her back. Gail flashed back to years ago. She was a young girl, and her mother told her not to marry Cecil.

"He has a mean streak, Gail. Mark my words — and the drinking! He drinks way too much. He is not a good man."

Her mother had repeated these words for months. But she had married Cecil, and he had never hurt her. He had never hit her or Alison. He had not had a drink since Alison was a baby. But now he was hurting her, and Gail flinched as aggression and anger shot out of his eyes.

"Give him back!" Cecil yelled, but then he looked toward the bathroom as if he feared Alison might hear. He lowered his voice and repeated, "Give him back!" in a voice just above a whisper. The quieter tone somehow seemed even more frightening than the raised voice.

"We can never give him back. He's ours now, Gail. Don't you understand that? If the truth were ever to come out, we would all go to jail, even Alison. Do you think that a court, some high-falutin judge, will believe that Alison knew nothing about the baby being stolen? You will ruin all our lives, and I mean Jared, too. I never want to hear you say anything again about giving that boy back. It's not happening. It will never happen. Are we clear?"

Gail was frightened by the look, a murderous look, which was present in Cecil's eyes.

"Are we clear?" Cecil repeated, tightening the grip on her arms. Gail nodded as Cecil slowly released his iron grip on her arms.

CHAPTER 38

GAIL LOOKED AROUND THE TRAILER, perplexed. She and Cecil had only been at the store for forty minutes, maybe less. But now, returning home, both Jared and Alison were gone. Alison had not mentioned that she would be going out. She didn't have a car. She couldn't have gone far. She guessed it was possible she could have walked to the nearby playground with Jared. It was improbable because she and Cecil should have passed her on the drive back to the trailer. Plus, you could see the playground from the road, and Gail was quite sure, well, almost sure, that the playground had been empty as they drove by. Gail began to unpack the groceries with a frown on her face. Cecil slammed the door as he entered with the last two bags.

"Where's Allie girl? Where's the boy? I thought they'd come running as soon as we pulled up. Wait till I tell Jared I found that cereal that he likes." Cecil chuckled.

Gail tried to keep her voice light but could tell she was not entirely pulling it off.

"Not here," she said, trying to sound cheerful and unconcerned. "They must have gone out."

"Gone out! Where could they have gone on foot? The only place would be the playground, and that place was empty when we drove past."

So, Gail had been right.

"Did Allie tell you she was going out?"

"No," Gail said, shaking her head and staring at the package of chicken as she placed it in the refrigerator.

"Huh," Cecil muttered. "She should have left a note, so we don't worry. Maybe I should drive around and see if I can spot them."

"Cecil, that will waste gas. Alison is an adult. She knows what she is doing."

"I hope so, Gail. I hope so."

Gail heard worry in her husband's voice. Alison wasn't exactly stable. She had only recently started going out. Gail had been happy about it at first. She knew she was going to Speedy's and was sure she had a few drinks while there, but where else was she supposed to go in this town? She could go to Bible study with Gail, but almost all older women were there, and Gail could understand why that did not interest Alison. She needed to be around people her age. The younger people did hang out at Speedy's, so why shouldn't Alison? She knew all too well that some unsavory characters hung there, but Alison knew enough to avoid people like that. But where was she now? In the middle of the afternoon? She hadn't taken Jared to Speedy's! Where could they possibly be?

"I don't like it, Gail. The girl worries me."

"Cecil, we can't be with her 24/7."

"I know that. I just want..."

But then the blare of loud music interrupted Cecil's sentence. A car's tires crunched on the gravel outside their trailer. A noisy engine revved, and then the music abruptly stopped. Both Cecil and Gail hurried to the trailer door to look out. A bright red car with a white stripe on the hood sat in their driveway. A tall young man with blonde shaggy hair jumped out.

He's so skinny, Gail thought. *Who is this guy?* And just like that, the passenger door opened, and Alison jumped out. She was giggling about something and had a giant smile on her face. *She looks happier than I have seen her look in years*, Gail could not help but think.

"Who the heck is that guy?" Cecil thundered.

The young man reached back toward the car, pulling the seat forward. Jared jumped out of the back seat. Gail noted that he also had a big smile on his face. Jared held his arms out, and the man picked him up, lifting him off his feet and spinning him in a wide circle. *They look so happy. They all look happy*, Gail thought as she looked at her husband, who had a deep frown on his face. Alison gestured toward their car as if saying, "My parents are home." The young man shrugged and looked toward the trailer. Jared was already running ahead toward the door. Gail and Cecil took a step back as Jared burst through the door.

"Grandpa, Gammy, you have to meet Johnny. He's so cool!"

Cecil made a sound that sounded like a growl. Gail forced a smile as the door opened again, and Alison walked in, followed by the young man.

"Where were you, Alison Marie?" Cecil said immediately.

"Your mother and I were worried. You didn't leave a note or anything!"

Alison looked back at the young man, who gave her a half-smirk.

"I'm fine, Daddy. We're all fine. I want you to meet my friend, Johnny. He dropped by and took us for a ride in his car."

"It was fun, Grandpa," Jared said excitedly. "We went so fast!"

"So fast! That doesn't sound safe," Cecil grumbled, looking at the man disapprovingly.

"Daddy, stop, just stop," Alison said, shaking her head. "It wasn't that fast. It just seemed fast to Jared. Aren't you even going to say hi to Johnny?"

The young man stuck his hand out. A beat passed before Cecil extended his hand and shook.

"Nice to meet you, Johnny," he said in a voice that sounded as if he thought it was anything but nice.

"And this is my mother, Gail," Alison said.

"Hey," the young man said, flipping his head to get the hair out of his eyes.

"You live around here, son?" Cecil inquired. "What's your last name? I might know your people. We've been living here for years."

"It's Morrison," the young man replied, "but I'm not from around here. Needed a new start, so I thought I'd try this place. So far, it's working out great." He smiled at Alison and patted her on the butt.

Gail looked down, feeling her cheeks redden.

"How did you two meet?" Cecil asked.

Gail realized his questions sounded more like an interrogation than a casual conversation.

"We met at Speedy's, Daddy."

"Oh," Cecil snorted.

"Yeah, I seen Alison there a couple weeks ago, but last night I finally got the nerve up to talk to her and man, I am glad I did."

He snaked his arm around Alison's waist. Cecil opened his mouth as if he was going to ask another question, but before he could, Johnny said, "Hey, Babe, I gotta get moving. See you there tonight?"

"You sure will," Alison said, beaming.

"Hey, kid," Johnny called out. "Be good. Later, scrub!"

"Johnny, can we go for a ride with you again?"

"Sure, anytime," Johnny said, smiling at Jared.

"Yes!" Jared said.

"Bye, baby," Johnny said, wrapping his arms around Alison and giving her a long, passionate kiss.

Oh, my! Gail thought and looked down once again.

"Later, babe," he said as they disengaged.

"Nice to meet you, Johnny," Gail said, her mouth dry. It felt like her tongue was sticking to the roof of her mouth.

"Yeah, you too," Johnny shrugged. He opened the door, and Alison followed him out. Gail and Cecil exchanged a look. Gail watched the young couple standing next to the car, and she looked away again. He began to kiss Alison with the same passion and familiarity he had used in the trailer.

"Where did you go with that guy, Jared?" Cecil inquired.

"You found my cereal!" Jared said. "Thanks, Grandpa! Can I have some now?"

"Jared, no," Gail said. "It's too close to dinner. You know that."

"Where did you go with that guy, boy? I asked you a question."

"We just rode around. Doesn't Johnny have a cool car?"

"I guess," Cecil muttered. They all heard a loud engine start and then skidding tires as Johnny pulled out of the driveway. Alison reentered the trailer.

"What?" she said as she looked at her mom and dad.

"I'm not sure about your new friend there," Cecil said solemnly. "I'm not too sure he's the best role model for Jared."

"Oh, Daddy, what are you talking about? You don't even know him! Don't judge him already."

"Well, Jared said he drove very fast. Doesn't sound safe to me."

"He didn't drive fast. It just seemed like it to Jared. We had fun, didn't we, Jared?"

"Yeah, Johnny's cool, so cool," Jared repeated.

"What is wrong?" Alison said, the smile fading from her face. "You two can't stand to see me happy? Is that it? Would you rather have me moping around this trailer for the rest of my life? No one is doing anything wrong. I'm an adult, not some stupid kid. You should be happy for me. I haven't been happy in so long."

"Oh, honey, we want you to be happy," Gail said. "It's just that we don't know your young man yet, and we want Jared to be safe. Jared is almost five years old now. He needs a good role model."

"Jared is safe! I'm his mother, you know. I know how to take care of him," Alison snarled.

"Now, Alison, don't get mad," Gail implored.

"Jared," Alison called out, "want to walk to the playground before dinner?"

"Oh, yeah!" Jared said, putting down the cereal box he had been reading.

"You don't need help with dinner, do you, Mama?"

"No, Allie, I'm fine."

"Is it okay with you if I take Jared to the playground, warden?" Alison said, giving Cecil a scathing look.

Cecil shrugged.

"We'll be back," Alison said. "Come on, Jared."

She slammed the door harder than she needed to on the way out. Cecil and Gail looked at each other. Gail sighed.

"Did you see how happy she looked when he was here? Maybe it could be a good thing, Cecil. At least she is out with people again.

"She needs to meet a nice man, a good man, a churchgoing man and Gail, you know as well as I that is not what that man is."

"Cecil, we don't know him yet. He deserves a chance. Jared seemed to like him. Alison deserves to be happy."

"We'll see, Gail, we'll see. I'm keeping a close watch on that one, though!"

CHAPTER 39

JOHNNY'S CAR ROARED INTO THE DRIVEWAY. Jared immediately picked up his jacket. "Ma, Johnny's here! Let's go!"

"Ok, Jared, I'm coming," Alison said, smiling.

"Where are you all going now?" Cecil said in a disapproving voice.

"We don't know," Jared answered. "Johnny has a big surprise for us. Come on, Ma, I can't wait!"

Alison followed Jared out the door, stopping to kiss Gail goodbye but breezing past Cecil.

"Still don't like him," Cecil muttered as the car squealed away.

"Oh, Cecil, maybe you should give him a chance."

"Why? He isn't showing me anything I want to see. They stay out late every Saturday night now. Alison isn't getting up for Sunday service. I've invited that man to church with us three times, and he has never come. He's a bad influence on her. I know it."

Gail nodded. She wasn't sure about Johnny herself, but what could she do? If they said too much, it would only drive Alison away.

"Okay," Johnny said, turning the loud music blaring through the car down. "You two close your eyes and keep them closed until I say so. Absolutely no peeking, scrub! Hear me?"

Jared nodded, closing his eyes and throwing his hands over his face.

"Where are we going, Johnny?" Alison inquired.

"You'll see, baby, we're almost there."

Alison felt the car slow. They hadn't driven far—they were only about fifteen minutes from her parents' trailer.

"Not yet, not yet, keep 'em closed. Both of you!"

Alison felt the car come to a stop.

"Ta-da!" Johnny yelled out. "Open up!"

Alison looked around, confused, as Jared yelled out, "Wow!"

"Well, get out, scrub. Let's look around."

"Johnny, what is this?" Alison questioned.

"It's our new home, baby," Johnny said, pleased.

"What?" Alison said.

"Look at the yard, Johnny! I love it. We have room to play ball here. Is that a badminton net? No way!" Jared said excitedly.

Johnny reached up above the car's visor.

"I have the key. Let's go inside and look around."

"Johnny!" Alison exclaimed.

She knew where they were. They were at Trail Heights, the upscale trailer park near her parents' more rundown complex. This trailer looked nice. It had a front porch attached, with room for a couple of chairs. As Alison touched the railing, it shimmied. Alison looked down.

"You'll see. The place needs a little work, but nothing I can't handle." Johnny put the key in the lock. It stuck. Johnny twisted it, trying to make it open. He finally slammed into the door with his shoulder, and the door swung open.

"Oh," Alison said. This trailer was much larger than her parents. The kitchen counters looked almost new. There was a slider that led to the backyard. Alison could see Jared racing around the yard.

"Keep looking, baby," Johnny said with a giant smile. Alison walked toward the back.

"The bedroom's big," Alison remarked as she stared at a set of built-in shelves.

"This way, baby, look at this."

Alison followed Johnny down the hall. He opened another door with a flourish. "Oh, my!" Alison said. "Jared can have his own room! He won't have to share with me anymore."

"That's right, baby! And the bedrooms are not right next to each other. We'll have the privacy to do what we want in our room, if you know what I mean!"

Alison continued walking through the trailer, a massive smile on her face.

"Johnny, look at the bathroom. It doesn't have just a shower stall! It has a tub and a shower."

"That's right! The toilet needs some work, but I know a little about plumbing, so that won't be a problem."

"Ma, Ma! "Come here," Alison heard Jared calling.

"Johnny, did you buy this place? Did you buy this place for all of us?"

Johnny nodded as Alison threw her arms around him.

"Well, not exactly. I told Mr. Barnes, the owner, that you would buy it, though.

"What!" Alison said, confused.

"Ma!" Jared yelled with more urgency.

Alison crossed to the slider and opened it.

"What, Jared, what exactly do you want?"

"Look at this yard, Ma. I can play a lot of games out here! Can we get some rackets? We can all play badminton! I'm going to count my steps to see how big the yard is!"

"Ok, Jared, you do that," Alison said, closing the door.

"See, he loves the place, baby. I knew he would."

"What do you mean, Johnny? I'm buying the trailer?"

"Well, I've talked to Mr. Barnes several times now. We give him the first and last month's rent plus a small stipend, and it will be a rent-to-own situation. You can use the money you got from the military. What better way to use the money than this?"

"Johnny, there isn't that much money left."

"That's why we'll rent to own and not purchase it outright. We'll both chip in for the monthly rent. Jared is only going to get bigger. He needs his own room and a place to play. And the best part is we can be together every night. No more checking in to motels for sex and no more doing it in the car. I'm getting way too old for that, Alison."

Alison nodded.

"And you'll be away from your dad. No more Mr. Grumpy, 'Let's worship the Lord,'" Johnny intoned, mimicking Cecil. "All we have to do is go to the office, and you'll sign some papers. We can do it right now, Mr. Barnes said, but if you want to wait till

Monday, he said that would be fine, too. Just don't let your parents talk you out of it."

Alison nodded. The money she had gotten from the military after Jared's death was going so fast. It hadn't been as much as she had thought it would be. She needed to be careful. She had given her parents some of it. Cecil had been so grateful to get that back tax bill paid off. Also, Alison's work situation, or rather lack of work, quickly ate up the money.

"What do you say?" Johnny said expectantly.

"I love the place, Johnny, but I want to make sure I have enough money. Will it just be my name on the lease? Why isn't it both of our names?"

Johnny sighed. "Alison, I have something to tell you."

CHAPTER 40

SO, JOHNNY HAD LIED to her about being incarcerated. Well, Alison had known that without knowing. She sensed that Johnny had been in trouble, and there were too many time gaps between the jobs he had mentioned. He hadn't wanted to tell her he had admitted because he feared she wouldn't want anything to do with him.

"And then I met your father," he had said. "Mr. Holier Than Thou, he would have never let you go out with me. Plus, the kid, I bet even now, if he knew, he wouldn't want Jared near me."

Alison had nodded her head reluctantly. Cecil was, if nothing else, very judgmental. Johnny was right; her father always thought he knew best and had all the answers.

"Baby, you have to get away from your dad. He's too much. He treats you like you're twelve. And Jared? He's going to start rebelling against all that Bible shit being rammed down his throat."

There were just so many reasons for them to move out. So what if it were her name alone on the new trailer? It meant she would be financially responsible for all of it. Johnny said he would help with the bills, and Alison believed that he meant it, but still, it would be great to have an equal partner. *It will be better once we're married*, Alison thought to calm her rising anxiety. Johnny had never mentioned marriage, but she knew he must be thinking about it just as she was. The money from the military, Jared's death benefit, was going so fast. Alison was sure that her parents thought there was more money left than there was. This trailer would eat up another hefty chunk of the money, and then they would have to keep up with the monthly payments. But it would be fine with Johnny there to help. She would have to work more, that was all. They liked her at the store. She could get more hours. She couldn't loan Johnny any more money to buy weed. That was an expense she could cut out. She sighed. Now that she knew about his past, they would need to talk. The last two times she had given him the money for the weed, she had questioned why it cost so much. He said he got a better deal by buying in bulk like he was buying toilet paper at a big-box store! She hoped he wasn't selling. With his record, he would be in big-time trouble if he got caught. Once, when she had questioned him about needing more so soon, he had called her out.

"Alison, of course, it goes fast. You partake as much as I do."

They should both cut back. She would mention this to him. Plus, she didn't want drugs around Jared. She would be less stressed without her father breathing down her neck every moment. If she were more relaxed, she wouldn't need to get high. *So that was one more win*, she thought. She gazed down at the bank statement that she had just received. The money was undoubtedly going quickly. If she weren't careful, it would all be gone. Thank God she had Johnny. Alison felt that she was at a turning point. Her life was finally turning around for the better. It would only be up from here.

CHAPTER 41

ALISON SIGHED AS SHE LOOKED at her father sitting across the small kitchen table from her. She could tell he was going to bring up her moving out of their trailer and into her own yet again. He wanted her to stay with them, she knew. Why didn't he realize that all his negativity was only doing more to drive her away? She had told Jared at least five times not to mention Johnny and that he was planning on living in the new trailer with them. Jared had readily agreed. He wanted to move so badly. He loved the yard and the badminton net at the new trailer. Plus, it was closer to his friend Jackson's house. Cecil rode Jared as hard as he did Alison —always with disapproval, always wanting him to practice prayers and memorize Bible passages. He was a five-year-old boy! He wasn't interested in all that. Why didn't Cecil realize how hard he was to be around sometimes?

"More potatoes, Jared, Alison?" Gail inquired.

Alison looked down. Poor Mama always tried to gloss over everything and ensure no controversy. *It won't work, Mama,* Alison thought. *He will talk about us moving, no matter how often you ask about potatoes!* Cecil cleared his throat. *Here we go,* Alison thought, looking down and stabbing at the roasted chicken with more force than needed.

"What's wrong with this trailer, Alison Marie? You've lived here all your life. Your mama is always here to make good food for all of us. When you need to go out, there's always someone here to care for Jared. Nights you go out with that man, you know Jared is safe and well cared for. It's not so easy to be alone, you know."

"Nothing is wrong with this trailer, Daddy, but you are missing the whole point."

"Did you hear Pastor Mike's sermon this morning? It was all about the importance of family. And family—that is what you have right here."

"I know what he said, Daddy. I was there. Look, the new trailer has a huge yard with grass."

"And a badminton net, Ma, don't forget that!" Jared interjected.

"Jared is only going to get bigger. He needs room to run and play. He'll have his own room at the new trailer. Jared and I can't share a room forever. Daddy, you must realize that."

"Well, I've been thinking on that, even praying about it. We might be able to make Jared a room right here. If we got one of those partition things, we could block off part of the living area and make the boy his own space."

Gail looked up and grimaced slightly.

"What?" Cecil said belligerently, frowning at his wife.

"Cecil," Gail said, sighing, "the living room is small as it is. How could Jared have any privacy if he's crammed into a corner of the living room?"

"I have a vision, Gail."

"You have to give it a chance."

"What do you think, boy?"

Jared looked at Alison. *Poor baby*, Alison thought. She could tell he was trying hard not to say the wrong thing.

"Tell him, baby, it's okay," Alison encouraged. "You have a right to have an opinion, Jared."

"Grandpa, I like the new trailer. It's so much bigger. I have more room to play. Johnny will teach me to throw a football, and I need room to run for passes."

Cecil made a sound like a growl. "All I hear lately from both of you is that man's name! 'Johnny this, Johnny that!' Your young man missed Sunday service again, didn't he, Alison?"

"He might have had to work, Daddy."

"On the Lord's Day? That's not right. Alison, are you moving out so you can live with that man?"

"That man has a name, Daddy, and no, I'm not moving for Johnny. I'm moving because it's best for Jared."

"I don't like it, Alison."

"I'm an adult, Daddy. You can't stop me."

"If you two plan on living like man and wife, you need to be married in the eyes of the Lord!"

"Daddy, Johnny may visit us, but he's not moving in; I've told you that before," Alison fibbed again.

"How are you paying for this trailer anyway?"

"Daddy, I've told you three times now. Mr. Barnes is letting me do a rent-to-own situation. I give him a small down payment, then pay the rest month to month. You know where the money is coming from. I'll use some of the money I got from the military—Jared's death benefit."

"You need to save that money for the boy."

"Daddy," Alison said, slamming her fork down. "This is for 'the boy,'" she gestured, making air quotes. "What better use of the money than to give Jared a better place to live? Jared wants to move. Don't you, baby?"

Jared nodded vigorously.

"Why don't you both come with me to see the trailer after we eat? You'll see how nice it is."

Cecil snorted. "How are you going to make these monthly payments?"

"They like me at the store. I'm going to ask for more hours. And if I run short some months, Jared's money is there. Johnny said he would help me if I needed a loan."

"Why would he do that if he's not living there?"

"Because he cares about us, Daddy. Look, we plan to get married eventually, just not immediately."

Cecil sighed. He looked at Gail, who nodded.

"I guess I could help you a little until you get on your feet."

"Okay," Alison said, smiling slightly.

"It's for the boy, Alison Marie, not for you. And if I find out that man is sleeping there, I'll stop the money just like that," Cecil said, snapping his fingers.

"Thanks, Daddy," Alison said, smiling and looking down to hide her exuberance. Mama must have talked him into this idea. Maybe, for once in her life, something finally might be working out.

"Grandpa, can we go see the trailer after we eat? You're going to love it! I'll show you my room!"

"I guess, boy, I guess. We should all pray and ask God for guidance right now."

Alison nodded. Cecil could say as many prayers as he wanted as long as he was being this agreeable. Alison couldn't wait to tell Johnny.

CHAPTER 42

GAIL WAS SURPRISED when she heard the light rap on the trailer door. She was even more surprised when she opened it to see Betty standing there. Although the two women used to be very close, they'd drifted away after Jared's arrival. It was even earlier than that. Betty had kept her distance ever since that awful day when Alison had been caught by Betty running that steak knife over her wrist. Gail had felt sad about the widening gulf between her and Betty, but when she complained to Cecil, he had said it was better to keep some distance from others.

"We can't risk anyone finding out where Jared came from," he had said solemnly.

He had been an infant then. How quickly the years had passed. Jared would soon turn six. Gail had seen Betty and her husband only briefly ever since, often waving from a distance but never conversing. Now, Betty was right at her door as if she had come over for a friendly visit as she had done all those years ago.

"Betty, how great to see you!" Gail exclaimed, smiling warmly. "Please come in. Do you all have time for a coffee?"

Betty smiled back and nodded but seemed nervous and uncomfortable to be there.

"Is Jared here? Alison?" Betty questioned, looking around the trailer as Gail moved into the kitchen to make the coffee.

"No, just me," Gail said.

"Cecil is working, and Alison and Jared are at their trailer."

"Oh, ok, good," Betty said.

Gail looked at her quizzically. They spent the next several minutes engaged in innocuous conversation about the weather and the new list of rules the association had issued regarding the upkeep of the trailers.

"It is so good to see you, Betty. I am so glad you stopped by," Gail said as she placed the steaming cup of coffee before Betty.

Betty grimaced and said, "I hope you still think that after you hear what I have come to say."

Gail shook her head. "What are you talking about, Betty? What is going on?"

Betty sighed and quickly sipped the coffee before saying, "I am not trying to be nosy and interfere, but we were such good friends once, and I think you should know."

Good friends once, Gail winced at the phrase. "Please say what you have to say, Betty. I'm all ears."

"Okay, okay," Betty said, rubbing her hands together. "Harold says it is none of my business, and I shouldn't get involved, but it seems to me that it must be said, especially since a child is involved."

Gail frowned. She was feeling increasing frustration with Betty's alluding to something without saying anything. Clearly, it concerned Alison and Jared.

"Please say what you came to say, Betty."

"Well, Harold and I went out for a burger last night at Speedy's. Alison and that young man she's been seeing were there. Johnny, that's his name, isn't it?"

"Yes, Johnny," Gail acknowledged.

"Well, they were drinking a lot, I must say, round after round. I don't think Alison was even aware I was there. She certainly didn't say hi to me."

Gail held up a hand to stop Betty. "Betty, they are young. I am not surprised that they drink a little bit. If you were worried about Jared, you must know he was with us. So, the two of them were enjoying a night out. Jared was safe. Alison is a good mother," Gail said stridently. No one would ever know that Gail sometimes wondered if Jared was well cared for. She wanted Alison to be a good mother, and maybe wishing it—saying it— might make it true.

"Betty, I also know that Johnny lives with Alison and Jared. Cecil hates it. He says they need to get married to live like a married couple. You know, Cecil, he has even told Johnny that it is sinful to have sex without being married. But, young people, Betty! You know as well as I that they all live together without being married these days. It may not be right, but Alison seems happy. Jared likes Johnny. He hangs all over him every time I see them together. I would rather Alison be out with friends than hang around our trailer with us and never go out. You know what she used to be like, Betty. Can you tell me that seeing her out and about is worse than how she used to be? She was sad and depressed all the time! She is finally off all that awful medication. Betty, so what if she was having a few drinks!"

Betty looked down, shaking her head. "Gail, no," she said quietly. "All that is not what I have come over here to say. I don't care if Alison lives with a man. That is her business. And having a few drinks. Harold had a few drinks while we were there, so who am I to judge?" She hesitated once again. "While we were eating, that Stevie Saunders came right up to their table and sat down."

"Oh!" Gail involuntarily shuddered. Stevie Saunders was a notorious drug dealer. He had been in and out of prison several times even though he was no older than Alison, maybe even a few years younger. "Well, they probably know each other from school, Betty."

Betty nodded. "I know, I know. Neither Harold nor I wanted to jump to conclusions, and if that was all I saw, well, I probably wouldn't even be here telling you."

"Go on," Gail said, feeling increasingly frustrated.

"Well, anyway, Harold had to get up and go to the bathroom. He had to pass right by their table. When he walked by on his way back, Harold clearly saw Stevie pass something to Johnny, and Johnny gave him some money. Harold saw it clear as can be."

"You can't be sure it was drugs," Gail said, not wanting to believe in the possibility.

"I know, I know," Betty acknowledged, "it's just… I wanted you to know, what with Jared and all. You know what happened with Suzy; it took her years to get clean."

Betty's daughter, older than Alison, had spent the better part of ten years addicted to heroin.

"Betty, Alison is not Suzy!"

"I know that Gail, I do, but I know how this all goes. It starts so slowly. You convince yourself it's just a little drinking. They're young, blah blah blah. I don't want to see Alison go down that road."

"Cecil will have a fit if he hears any of this!"

"That is also why I am telling you."

"Cecil will tell Johnny to leave. Alison and Jared will be devastated!" Gail ruminated, rubbing her forehead.

"I told Harold not to say anything to anyone, and I won't be saying any more. I just thought you should know."

"Ok, so I know," Gail said shortly.

Betty stood. "I think it's time for me to go."

"Maybe you should," Gail said. She looked down as Betty made her way out the door. She blinked her eyes, trying not to cry. She would talk to Alison, question Jared, watch closely, and make it all okay. The most important thing was that Cecil did not find out. His assured overreaction would only make everything worse.

CHAPTER 43

"WHAT DID YOU HAVE FOR DINNER TONIGHT, JARED?" Gail asked, trying to keep her voice casual. She moved her body slightly to look out the window. Alison was still talking to her father in the driveway.

"Gammy, it was so good! Mom made turkey, mashed potatoes, and green beans with onion thingies on top, just like you make. Johnny was there, and we all prayed before eating."

"Oh, my, how nice!" Gail remarked, trying to hide her surprise. Alison had never been much of a cook. Gail was surprised she had made such a big dinner, especially on a weeknight. She was sure Alison had worked at least half a day today. She had been so worried when Alison and Jared moved out that they would live on fast food and frozen pizza, but apparently not. So maybe Johnny was a good influence on Alison instead of a bad influence, as Cecil frequently complained. Johnny must have helped Alison buy all that food. For all she knew, maybe Johnny had cooking skills. He might have helped make this big dinner. Alison must have picked up some cooking skills from Gail. Gail had been making them hearty dinners for years.

"Did Johnny help your mom make all that food?"

"No, he played outside with me."

"Well, that's nice, Jared."

Alison must have made all that food to please Johnny. She would have to tell Cecil this. The trailer door opened, and Alison and Cecil came inside.

"Grandpa, you said you'd show me how to throw a baseball when I came over."

Cecil chuckled, moving close to Jared and ruffling his hair.

"I did, boy, I did. I remember. Get the ball and my old glove from the closet. Let's get outside before it starts to get dark."

Jared ran to the closet.

"Slow down, Jared," Alison yelled. "Don't run in the house."

"I have to hurry Ma, before it gets dark!"

Cecil smiled. "Won't get dark that fast, boy!"

"Come on," he said, opening the door as Jared returned carrying the softball and the glove.

Gail turned to Alison.

"Well, Alison, Jared told me what you all had for dinner tonight."

Alison sighed.

She must be tired from working today, Gail thought.

"I know, Mom, ok, I know! I'll do better tomorrow. It's just that I worked half a day today, and then they asked me to stay an extra hour. With Johnny gone this week, I have more to do. It's hard to keep Jared occupied sometimes. He has so much energy. I know he needs to eat better."

Gail furrowed her brow. Nothing made sense.

"With Johnny gone? What are you talking about?"

"Oh, it's just a temp job at that new production center in Osage. He'll be back next week, but it was too far for him to drive back and forth."

"Oh, I thought Jared said you all ate together tonight."

Alison shook her head. "No, not tonight."

"But still, you made a good meal for Jared. Good for you, Alison."

Alison frowned at her mother. "Mama, don't be sarcastic. I don't like it. It's not like you. Look, I said I would do better tomorrow."

"What?" Gail said. She was growing ever more confused. "But Jared told me you had turkey, mashed potatoes, and green beans for dinner tonight."

"Tonight?" Alison said in a questioning tone. "He said that? We stopped at McDonald's on the way over here. Like I said, I know he needs to eat better."

"Why would Jared say you had turkey if you didn't? And he said Johnny was there with the two of you."

"I don't know," Alison shrugged.

Gail stared at her daughter. A shiver jolted through her body. If Jared was lying about dinner and Johnny, what else was he lying about? What was going on over there?

"Are you ok, Alison?" Gail questioned.

"I'm fine, Mama. Why wouldn't I be?"

CHAPTER 44

ALISON OPENED THE DRAWER that had held Johnny's T-shirts. She looked again as if rechecking the drawer might make the items appear. Nope, all gone. This time, unlike six months ago when he had taken that temporary job in Osage, all his clothes were gone. His shotgun and his motorcycle magazines, too. He had left for good this time, no doubt. The fact that he had taken all the pills plus the bag of weed probably upset Alison the worst. He had left her with nothing; she had paid Stevie for that bag, not Johnny. Now, what was she supposed to do? Call Stevie herself? She didn't feel safe around him, the way he always leered at her. Maybe Johnny would come back? *No*, Alison thought, shaking her head. She knew deep inside that this time; Johnny was gone for good. Sure, he had disappeared for a few days a week before but had never taken all his things. Jared was going to ask for Johnny endlessly. What would she even tell him? She hated seeing Jared upset, and he loved running and playing with Johnny. For all of Johnny's faults, he had never failed to treat Jared kindly. How could he get up and leave like that? Not saying goodbye to her was one thing. She understood they hadn't been getting along for months, but why do that to Jared? *Hurting me is one thing; hurting my kid is unforgivable, loser*! she thought. Alison breathed shallowly as fear and panic began to course through her body. How would she survive without Johnny? She would be alone with Jared, with no one to help her. She couldn't and wouldn't move back to her mom and dad's trailer. Being around her father was unbearable with his judgment, his Bible quotes, and his belief that he was always right. She had needed Johnny's money for rent and groceries. She had just started working at the new Dollar Store. They seemed to like her. Maybe she could ask for extra hours. But then she would have to find someone to take care of Jared. She would have to drop him off with her mom and dad. It was the only choice. No way she could afford a babysitter. She would talk to them about watching Jared before asking for more hours. First, she had to tell Jared that Johnny was gone. It was better to do that than to wait for him to ask endless questions. She would go to her parents' trailer tomorrow right after they returned from church. Maybe, for once, her father would be proud of her for taking the initiative to ask for more hours instead of judging her as he usually did. If she called Tanya, Jared's friend Jackson's mother, she could probably get her to watch Jared for a few hours tonight. She would need a drink or two after talking to Jared and in anticipation of talking to her mom and dad tomorrow. She would go to Speedy's for a quick drink or two tonight. Maybe Stevie would even be there. It would be preferable to see him in a public space. He must have at least some weed left.

"Jared," she called. "Come in my room and talk to me. I have something to tell you."

CHAPTER 45

ALISON SHOULDN'T HAVE HAD THE FOUR DRINKS last night. She had a thundering headache as she knocked on her parents' screen door. Her father opened the door, still dressed in his church clothes, and gave her a disapproving look. Jared pushed through the door.

"Hi, Grandpa, hey, Gammy," he said happily.

"Hey, boy," Cecil said, his eyes softening as he looked at Jared.

"Missed Sunday service again, didn't you, Alison Marie?" her father questioned as he closed the door.

"You haven't been to church for months," he grumbled. "The Lord sees, you know. He knows what you do," he thundered.

Alison shrugged. *I'm more worried about you seeing than God,* she thought.

"Alison, if you won't go to church, then at least let me drive by and pick up Jared. He can go to church with us. He needs to be at Sunday School. He needs to learn about the Bible and Jesus, his savior. 'Raise a child up in the way he should go, and he will not depart from it.'"

Okay, here we go, Alison thought. *He's quoting scripture already.*

"Alison, you must get to services. It's the most important thing you can do for that boy."

Alison sighed. "I will, Dad, next week we'll go for sure. It's out of your way to stop by to pick up Jared. I'll get him there myself. I promise."

The last thing I need is you sniffing around my trailer and judging me, Alison thought.

Cecil shook his head. "I hope you mean that promise, Alison Marie. I really do."

Gail walked into the living room carrying three cups of coffee on a tray.

"So where is your young man, Johnny, this morning? I hope he is not working on the Lord's Day. Jared, I have poured a big glass of milk for you on the kitchen counter. It's chocolate," Gail trilled.

"Yes!" Jared said with a fist pump and ran into the kitchen.

Alison picked up the coffee, looking down. Johnny's gone. Was she going to have to lead with this news first? Her parents looked at her expectantly as if waiting for a reply. Jared returned to the living room, carrying his large glass of milk. He looked at the three adults.

"Gammy," Jared said, taking a large sip of milk, "Johnny left us. He had to go live somewhere else, but it's okay because Chad came over and stayed with us last night. He—"

"Jared!" Alison shouted, and she shook her head slightly. Jared immediately stopped speaking.

"Oh, no, Allie," Gail said sympathetically.

Cecil glowered.

Well, I might as well go ahead now, Alison thought. *Get it all out there.*

"I did have something to ask you. I am going to ask for more hours at the store, and I was wondering if you could watch Jared sometimes so I can work longer. I need the money now."

Gail started to nod immediately. She opened her mouth to say something, but Cecil held up a hand to stop her. His words were clipped.

"Alison, I will not be helping you pay rent if men live there. I have told you that before!"

"Fine, Dad," Alison replied. Why had she come over here in the first place?

"I am not asking you for money. I just told you I want to work more hours. And no men live there, so you don't have that to worry about."

"Well, then, who the heck is Chad?" Cecil questioned.

"He's just a friend that needed a place to stay last night."

"Where did he sleep?" Cecil snarled and looked at Jared as if he might provide more information. Jared looked down.

CHAPTER 46

"JARED," ALISON SAID SERIOUSLY, bending down to his level to look him right in the eyes. "You can't ever tell Gammy and Grandpa about anything happening here. You can't tell her who is sleeping over. You can't tell her about the parties we have or about the medicine that I need to take."

"Is Johnny coming back here to stay and have a sleepover?" Jared said, hopefully. He liked Johnny best. He would play ball with him and chase him in the yard.

"No, baby, Johnny is not coming back."

"How about Ray? Is he coming back to stay?"

"No, Ray is gone, too. Listen, Jared, Mommy is very serious. If you ever talk to Gammy and Grandpa about what is happening here, they'll take you from me. You won't be able to live with me anymore. You'll have to move back in with them."

Jared nodded and frowned. "I won't be able to read my comic books at Grandpa's. He hates them. He says they are not godly. The only superhero I should be reading about is Jesus."

"See, Jared, that is exactly what I mean. You won't be able to have your comic books at Grandpa's. You won't be able to do anything fun. What happens here is a secret, Jared. Our little secret. When Gammy asks how everything is going and when she asks how I am doing or who is staying here, you have to say that it is just the two of us and everything is fine. And that's it. Do not tell them anything else. Do you get it, baby?"

Jared nodded.

"Ok, let's practice," Alison said. "Gammy has just asked how I am doing. What do you say?"

"I say 'fine'?" Jared said with a question in his voice.

Alison nodded. "That's right. Try that again but say it with more confidence."

"How is your mom?" Alison repeated.

"She's fine, everything is fine."

"Good boy," Alison said and ruffled his hair. "Who stays with you in the trailer?" Alison asked.

"Just Mom and me," Jared said, smiling at his mother. He enjoyed her undivided attention while they played this word game.

"Way to go, Jared," Alison said and held out her hand so he could give her a high-five. "Now, that is what you say every time they ask. Just say that every single time and don't provide any more information. Got it, baby?"

Jared nodded.

"I'm going to see if I can find some money for you so you can buy a couple of new comic books tomorrow, okay?"

Jared nodded and threw his arms around his mother's waist.

CHAPTER 47

BRYNN RUBBED HER HEAD. The headache would not disappear, and the sour stomach was even worse. She knew all too well why she felt this bad. It was, once again, too much wine last night. Brynn was much happier in the beach cottage where she had been for over two years. Her Paul would be eight years old; she had thought last night. A third grader, she imagined him bursting through the door and shouting, "Mom!" anxious to show her some pictures that he had drawn. Those images, of course, were nothing but fantasy, and she was resigned to never seeing her baby again. She still did not believe he was deceased, though. She probably never would. Thinking of Paul last night and then checking Eric's wife's Facebook page and seeing that she was pregnant had made Brynn feel sad enough that she had opened yet another bottle of wine. *Only one glass can't hurt*, she remembered thinking. *Isn't wine good for you? Resveratrol or something in it that's healthy.* She had meant to have only one glass, but one had easily led to two, then three, and after that, who knew how many? She had lost count. Brynn had reduced her depression medication and tapered off as her psychiatrist had recommended. Was she self-medicating with the wine? *Probably,* she admitted. She moved out of the bedroom and into the kitchen, where the wine bottle was still on the counter. *Oh, no, less than a quarter of the liquid left.* She had drunk almost the entire bottle last night! No wonder she felt so bad! Damn, now she would have to go out and buy more again. A voice whispered to her, *Have a glass now. Finish it off early. It might even help your hangover.* Brynn reached into the cupboard to grab a glass but suddenly paused with her hand on the door handle. *What are you doing? Just who do you want to be?* she heard another voice whisper. *Is this how you want to live? I know you're sad and lonely, but drinking more and more—is it helping?* Brynn shook her head. She felt that she was at a crossroads. She could almost see two paths lying in front of her. Continuing down the one littered with wine bottles would lead to certain consequences. And none of those consequences were good if you considered how she felt right now. Or there was the other path: she could stop drinking or, at the very least, drastically reduce her consumption. She could face life, her feelings, her pain without crutches—no more pills, no more alcohol. She stared off into the distance and saw the fork in the road ahead. She projected into the future. She saw an older woman, overweight, alcoholic. This person was bitter and angry. She rubbed her eyes and projected herself down the other path. She still saw an older woman with gray hair, but this woman was physically fit. This woman was also standing alone in the beach cottage, but she was smiling and felt better in her body. Brynn picked up the bottle of wine. She stared at it for several minutes, then poured the remains down the sink. She looked out the window. It was bright and sunny today. Maybe she would go for a run on the beach. Tomorrow would be Sunday. There was a small church two blocks over. There was a sign out front that said, "All are welcome." Maybe she would go!

CHAPTER 48

BRYNN SMILED as she exited the psychiatrist's office and headed through the parking lot to her car. She only checked in with him now once a month. He had just suggested that they could extend the check-ins to every three months. Brynn had nodded her agreement.

"Know, Brynn, I am here if you need anything. I still believe that continuing weekly counseling is crucial for you."

Brynn had agreed to this as well. She enjoyed talking to her counselor. Toni always suggested useful strategies, such as meditation and breathwork. She was a great sounding board—someone to talk to regularly. Brynn was continuing to lead a lonely, almost solitary life. Toni encouraged her frequently to get out more and socialize. Brynn tried, but it was often easier for her to keep her own company. It was hard to make new friends and even harder to answer simple questions that new acquaintances would ask, such as, "Do you have children?" or "Have you ever been married?" It was so hard to meet new people without the awful story of Paul rolling out of her mouth. Paul would now be eight years old. She hated seeing the sympathy cross others' faces when she told even a part of her story. Some looked stricken, not knowing how to respond, and some people would act like they couldn't get away from her fast enough. *Don't worry. It's not contagious. You won't lose your child just because I did,* she would think as she watched these people walk away. No, it was easier to keep her own counsel, to stay apart and separate. Brynn found herself thinking more and more about getting a job. She had been volunteering at the food bank for the last two years but was beginning to want to do more. Money wasn't a problem for Brynn. She had the rest of the proceeds from the house with Eric and the alimony she had received in the divorce settlement. It was a nice-sized check that came in monthly. Brynn had not requested alimony from Eric, yet Eric had insisted.

"This never happens," her lawyer had affirmed.

Brynn reluctantly agreed to accept, and the money came in handy. She hadn't had to think about work for several years. She had time to heal and to keep all her counseling and psychiatric appointments. She could afford a good health plan that covered all her needed treatments. It felt good being off all that medication, and Brynn rarely drank now —maybe a glass of wine now and then, but one bottle could easily last her a month, maybe more. Eric no longer called her to check in as he did for the first two years after the divorce. She secretly followed his wife, Katrina, on Facebook. So, she was pregnant again. Their first son was cute, with dark, curly hair like Paul's. It seemed that Eric was thriving in his life.

Suddenly, an idea snapped into Brynn's head just like that. She shouldn't get a job. She should go back to school. She had only one more year to finish. She could get her degree and then find a good job—maybe some work-from-home accounting thing. She knew solitary would serve her best. The state college was only two towns over. She should go there and see if she could sign up for classes. Some might even be online. How easy would that be? Once she graduated and had a decent job, she could contact Eric and tell him she no longer needed the alimony. She knew he had plenty of money but could use more with his growing family. It would be the right thing to do. Brynn smiled to herself. She couldn't wait to start her initial research about the college. She would tell Toni her plan at the next appointment. She knew Toni would think it was a great idea.

CHAPTER 49

ALISON WAS SITTING in the school hallway in the too-small chair, waiting for her appointment with Jared's second-grade teacher. Parent-teacher conferences—she hated them. She hadn't come last year, although she had lied to her mother and told her she had been there. Her head was hurting so badly. How much longer was she going to have to wait? If she had only taken a pill before coming here or if she hadn't drunk so much the night before. But she drank almost every night. She hadn't taken a pill because she wanted to be entirely straight to talk to Jared's teacher. She hadn't chosen an appointment time when the notice had come home. She was hoping to ignore the whole thing just like last year. Instead, the notice was sent home again with Jared, and that time, "your presence is strongly requested" was high-lighted, and the word "strongly" was underlined. *Oh, shit,* what did that mean! Alison couldn't believe that Jared was in trouble at school. He consistently got all fours, the highest possible mark.

"What the heck is a four?" Cecil groused when Jared trium-phantly handed him the report card with a huge smile on his face.

"It's like an A, Dad. He got all As," Alison said.

"Well, why don't they just say that then? Have to change everything with their high-class ideas," Cecil complained. Then, he looked at Jared and smiled.

"You're a smart one, huh, boy? Smartest one in this family!" he said, giving Jared a big high-five before he began to complain about Jared and Alison missing Sunday service the previous week.

"We were sick, Dad, I told you that."

Cecil made a harrumphing sound and shook his head.

Alison looked up and down the school hallway. The door to Jared's classroom was still firmly closed, which meant the prior parent was still inside. Alison wished Gail was here with her for support or to chat to pass the time. Gail would have been thrilled to be invited to attend with Alison, but Alison was afraid that her mother would find out how many days of school Jared actually missed if she had accompanied her. Attendance had to be the reason she had been strongly requested to come to this meeting. Alison knew there were too many days when she was too tired or too hungover to help Jared get ready for school. And if he missed the bus and she felt too sick to drive him or if she had already taken a couple of pills and felt too high to drive, he didn't go. She wasn't going to risk driving high. And speaking of high, she needed a pill right now. One wouldn't even make her high. It would just take the edge off. She should have taken one, but the problem was that her stockpile was dwindling without Brandon around. She was going to have to call that piece of shit Stevie Saunders soon to get more. She couldn't chance running out. Stevie overcharged her terribly and leered at her whenever she was alone.

"Mrs. Jensen? I'm so sorry for the wait. I'm Miss Cavendish," the young teacher chirped. Come on in," she smiled warmly.

They entered the room, and there were more impossibly small chairs to sit on. Alison pulled out a tiny chair and sat down.

"I'm so glad you made it, Mrs. Jensen. Jared tells me that you work a lot."

Alison nodded. She hadn't had a job in over a year, but that was her baby boy, always covering for her.

"I hope Jared is not in any trouble. He's a good boy," Alison said, trying to smile.

"Oh, no, Mrs. Jensen, not at all. Jared is a pleasure to have in class. He's very bright and picks up new concepts right away. He's ahead in all the subjects. I do wish we had more resources here. My last school had a talented and gifted program, and I know that if we had one here, Jared would qualify, but there are not enough resources here, unfortunately. I try to give Jared supplemental work and special projects as much as possible."

Alison smiled, relaxing slightly for the first time. So, it was all good news.

"Thank you for helping him," Alison said.

Miss Cavendish suddenly frowned.

"There is only one problem I wanted to talk to you about."

"Oh?" Alison questioned.

"Jared is out a lot. He misses a lot of days. I can catch him up when he comes back, but still," she trailed off. "I asked Jared if he was sick every day he was out, and he didn't want to tell me at first, but then he admitted that you were working, and he hadn't made the bus in time. Please don't think I'm judging you. A single mother raised me, so I get it. But Jared needs to be in school. He wants to be in school. If you can't get him ready in time or must leave for work before the bus, is there anyone else who could bring him?"

Alison thought, *Yeah, my mom and dad, but then they'll be all up in my business.* Alison sighed in response, "I'm sorry, we'll do better. I don't leave for work until after the bus."

"*Yeah, right,* she thought, *because I don't leave for work at all, lady!* I could ask my dad to help. He lives nearby."

Even as Alison said these words, she thought, *Nope, not happening.*

"That's great, then," Miss Cavendish said. "Jared's attendance is my only concern."

Alison smiled. "We'll work it out. We'll do better."

Alison had to think of a way to get Jared moving. Maybe if he had his own alarm clock, he could get up all by himself.

The teacher continued to talk.

"Let me show you his latest artwork. He drew a picture of you."

Alison smiled and nodded yet again. How many pills did she have left? She was taking a handful when she got home. She had earned them after this.

CHAPTER 50

"I CAN'T—I WON'T KEEP GIVING YOU THESE PILLS, Alison. They are quite addictive, and I'll be frank with you: I'm not a psychiatrist, and I'm not sure what is best. Prescribing these benzodiazepines for short-term use is not a problem, but Alison, it's been over a year now. You need to get into counseling."

Alison sighed. Damn, damn, the only reason she had driven here was to get more pills. When she got home, the gas would be almost on E, and her welfare check wouldn't come in for two more weeks. She could not ask Cole for more money; she had already done so twice. He would think she was only using him for money. He had only been living with her and Jared for six weeks. She knew her parents didn't have extra money, and the last thing she needed was to listen to her dad harangue her about her lifestyle and then rant about her absence at church yet again.

"You need to see a counselor, a psychiatrist," the doctor repeated.

Alison sighed. "Money is an issue. I have Jared to support."

"I know, I know," the doctor nodded, seeming sympathetic, but Alison caught him surreptitiously glancing at his watch. "Rita can give you the names of some local counselors."

"How am I supposed to afford them?" Alison couldn't help snapping.

The doctor nodded. "I understand. I wish this state had passed the additional Medicaid plan. Believe me, it would help many of my patients. Maybe you can work out some payment plan with one of the counselors, though."

Alison nodded. Great, she was leaving here with nothing, absolutely nothing.

"You take care now," the doctor remarked jovially and whooshed out of the room.

Alison did call the list of counselors Rita, the doctor's secretary, had given her. What else did she have to do? By the time she got home, there wasn't enough gas in the car to make it to the grocery store and back. There were four names on the list. Two were not currently accepting new patients, and the third had recently closed their local office. "But we can see you at our office in the city," the receptionist had chirped.

"No thanks," Alison said as she hung up. Yeah, right, she could not drive into the city once a week or even once a month. It would be an over two-hour round trip. It was impossible! Finally, she was to the last name on the list. Yes, they were accepting new patients. They even had an opening the next week.

"Just give me your insurance, hon, and we'll get you all set up," the receptionist said warmly.

"Well, I don't have insurance right now," Alison explained.

"Oh," the receptionist said, and Alison so clearly heard the warmth fade from her voice.

"So, you'll be a self-pay patient, then?"

"Yeah, yes, I guess," Alison said, clearing her throat.

"Payment is due at the time of service, and you won't be allowed to carry a balance. Do you understand?"

I understand you think I'm scum, some loser, Alison wanted to scream, but with difficulty, she kept her composure.

"Yes, I understand. What is the cost per session, please?"

"It's one fifty per session, which is with the doctor's discount for self-pay patients. Dr. Rosen recommends coming in once a week to start so we can assess and see exactly what you need."

"Oh," Alison said, drawing in a breath. She couldn't afford this!

Dr. Rosen recommends once a week, but if you can't swing that, he will allow you to come biweekly. Does that work for you?"

Three hundred dollars a month! She could never afford that. She needed to eat. Jared needed to eat.

"Ma'am, hello, does that work for you?" The receptionist sniffed.

Alison sighed loudly. "Oh, never mind," she said, throwing the phone down on the kitchen table. Alison still had her head in her hands five minutes later when Cole opened the door to the trailer and walked in. He crossed to her immediately. He smelled strongly of alcohol.

"What's wrong, baby?" he said, kneeling in front of her.

"The stupid doctor wouldn't give me any more pills. He said I needed counseling, and I called the counselors, Cole, but they either won't take new patients, or they cost an arm and a leg. I don't know what I'm supposed to do. I feel awful, and no one will help me."

Cole shook his head.

"Baby, you don't need the stupid doctor or counseling. You need a little something to make you feel better. I have something right here that will fix you up."

He patted his pocket.

"I thought you said Stevie was all out of the Oxys?"

"He is, baby, but what I have is better than the Oxys all day and cheaper, too."

"Cole, is it what I think? I don't do that shit! I also don't want needles here around Jared."

"Baby, baby, we're not injecting drugs—no way—just a little snort here and there. Maybe a little chasing the dragon when the kid's not around. It will make you feel better, Allie, I guarantee that. No more doctors and counselors with their high-priced la-de-da. What do you say? I can tell you need a boost. I do, too. It's something we can do together."

Alison hesitated. Her heart beat hard, and her hands and feet started sweating. She was on the way to a full-blown panic attack. She looked up at Cole. He raised his eyebrows at her. She felt she was making a decision that could not be undone, but she needed something—she needed help now.

"Okay, sure, why not," she said. "Let's do it."

CHAPTER 51

ALISON SMILED TO HERSELF as she finished wrapping Jared's birthday present. She had spent more than she should have on the video game console, but it was all Jared had talked about for months. He played games on it at his friend Jackson's house. He would be so excited when he saw it. Even with Cole paying half of the cost, Alison knew she would struggle to afford other things they needed for a couple of months. *Even food,* she thought ruefully. But it would all be worth it to see Jared's smile when he opened the gift after they returned from their trip. She glanced at the clock in the kitchen and yelled out Jared and Cole's names.

"It's almost time to go. We don't want to be late!"

She heard Jared yell back, "Coming, Ma!"

She thought she heard a grunt from the bedroom, which meant Cole was finally getting up. Hopefully, he wouldn't be too hung over. Jared was going to love this part of his birthday surprise. The tickets to the aquarium had also been expensive, and she hadn't dared to ask Cole to contribute more, so she had paid for them all herself. There was a special shark exhibit there this month, and when not playing video games, Jared and his friend Jackson always talked about sharks. Jared always told Cole his newest shark fact, which made Cole and Alison smile. Ever since Jared had been a baby, it had been important to Alison to make a big deal out of Jared's birthday. He deserved much more than a stupid cake and some chintzy presents. She remembered the year her dad had gotten her a new Bible. He had been all smiles, but he hadn't even gotten a children's Bible, so the large tome was impossible for Alison even to try to read. She had been so disappointed. Birthdays like that were never going to happen to Jared. No matter what it took, Alison would make sure of that!

Suddenly, both Cole and Jared burst into the room. Jared ran right to the large, wrapped present.

"Can I open it now, Ma? Can I?"

"No," Alison said, smiling and mussing his hair with her hands.

"We are leaving for your special adventure in five minutes. You can open it when we get back."

"Ma!" Jared said, with only mock disgust and a huge grin. Cole crossed to the refrigerator and popped open a beer.

Alison frowned. "Cole, really, a beer? It's only 9 a.m."

"Happy birthday, kidlet," Cole said, punching Jared in the arm.

"Yeah, Alison, but I'm pretty sure they don't serve drinks at the aquar —"

"Shh," Alison yelled out loudly. "Don't say it, it's a surprise.

"Jared, run and get your jacket so we can get going."

Jared nodded and ran for his room.

"Alison, Cole whispered, It's a long ride. Just wait while I take a little boost. Hey, don't think I forgot about you. I stopped by Stevie's on the way home last night, and guess what he had?" Cole said, smiling.

"I thought he said he was all out."

"Guess he got some in. Anyway, here's some Oxys for me and you."

Jared walked into the room with his jacket on and zipped just then.

"What's that?" Jared said as he noticed Cole handing two pills to Alison at the same time that he popped some in his mouth.

"Nothing, kid, it's nothing, Cole said, just a little medicine for me and your mom."

Alison palmed the two pills quickly. "I just have a little headache, baby, that's all. You ready to go, birthday boy?" Alison said brightly. "We have a long ride."

Jared frowned at both of them but then nodded slowly. "Where are we going?"

"It's a surprise, baby. You'll see when we get there!"

CHAPTER 52

A MILE FROM THE AQUARIUM, Alison turned to Jared in the back seat and said, "Close your eyes. Keep them closed until I tell you to open them."

Jared nodded. Alison waited until Cole had pulled into the parking lot before she said enthusiastically, "Jared, open your eyes!"

Jared immediately popped them open.

"The aquarium, Mom! I've been wanting to come here for months."

"There's more," Alison said, smiling at Cole, who smiled back.

As they made their way to the entrance, Cole suddenly pointed, "Look at that. I think there's someone you know waiting outside."

Jared looked and saw his friend Jackson excitedly waving back at him.

"What, wow!" Jared said, jumping up and down. "You got Jackson and his mom to come! You guys are the best."

Cole pointed at a poster on the door as they made their way to the entrance line. "Imagine that—there's a special shark exhibit. You boys aren't into sharks, are you?"

"Are you kidding!" Jared yelled. "We love sharks!"

"Yeah, this will be great," Jackson exclaimed.

As they waited in the entrance line, there was a loud commotion on the other side where people were exiting. A young child, probably under a year old, was screaming at the top of her lungs. She was so loud that people were turning to look.

"Shh, Carrie, shh," the mother encouraged to no avail, bouncing the child in her arms.

"Katrina, let me take her," a large man with dark curly hair said. *He must be the father*, Alison thought. The man held out his arms to the screaming child. The woman grabbed the hands of two other young children, walking with the man. A slightly older boy was walking ahead of all of them. This boy was sturdily built, just like Jared, and appeared only a few years younger. He, too, had curly black hair. *He resembles Jared a little*, Alison thought. The screaming baby began to quiet once in the man's arms.

"She's better with you, Eric," the woman said, smiling.

Jared continued to stare at the family, his eyes taking in the man's large build and hair so much like his own. The family was walking away now, and Jared was still following them with his eyes.

"Jared," Alison whispered, leaning down to his level, "don't stare; it's rude."

"Move, boys, we're next in line," Cole said.

"I can't wait, huh, Jared?" Jackson said, nudging his friend.

Jared nodded. "Yeah, me too," he agreed, but he looked back again, watching the family retreat, unsure why the strangers had captured so much of his interest.

CHAPTER 53

"JARED," ALISON SIGHED, EXASPERATED. "Why didn't you say something earlier?"

"Because, Ma, Cole said he would take me to the store, but he hasn't been here in three days now."

Alison crossed the room to pick up her purse, knowing she would find no money inside.

"Jared, I can't, I can't. I have no money for the posterboard and markers. When is the assignment due anyway?"

"I told you," Jared whined out his words. "Tomorrow, it's due tomorrow! I wrote the report already. I need to draw a graph."

"Well, what am I supposed to do? There's no money here."

"Ma, let's call Gammy and Grandpa. I left some posterboard and markers there a month ago. They might still have them."

"Jared!" Alison rolled her eyes. She was in no mood to see her mother or her father. They would ask her how Cole was. She couldn't tell them she hadn't heard from him in over a week. Alison had a sneaking suspicion—well, not so sneaking—that he was gone, had left them, and moved on. Moved on without so much as a goodbye. They hadn't been getting along for months, but she had expected more from him than this.

"Ma, please, will you call Gammy to see if they still have the posterboard and the markers?"

"Okay, Jared, okay," Alison said, picking up her phone. As she waited for her mother to pick up, Jared said, "What are we having for dinner? I'm hungry!"

Alison shook her head. There was only a little milk and a case of beer, courtesy of Cole, in the refrigerator.

Where were they? The phone was ringing, and neither of her parents was answering.

"I don't know, Jared. Mac and cheese?"

"Mac and cheese again! We've had that twice this week already."

"I guess we could pick up a burger if we go out. I think I have a coupon."

"Yuk, Mom, again!"

Just then, her mother answered the phone breathlessly.

"Hey, Ma, what's wrong? You okay?"

"Oh, I'm fine. Your father, though, is still not feeling well."

"Oh, that's too bad. Listen, Jared said he left some posterboard and markers at your trailer. Do you still have them? He needs them for school."

"We sure do. Cecil stored them in the kitchen cabinet because he thought Jared might need them later."

"Ok, great, we'll drive over and pick them up."

"It will be good to see you two! Is Cole coming too?"

"No, Mama, Cole's not coming. He's busy."

"Well, why don't the two of you stay for dinner? I made a nice stew for your dad."

"Stay for dinner?" Alison questioned, trying to calculate if she could be around her father for that long without getting supremely aggravated. Hovering just over Alison's shoulder, Jared heard her and yelled, "Yes!" with great exuberance.

Gail chuckled and said, "Well, I hear Jared wants to come for dinner. Please say yes, Alison."

Jared was nodding at her stridently.

"Alright," Alison sighed. "We'll be over in a few minutes."

CHAPTER 54

ALISON STAGGERED and had to grab onto the railing on her parents' porch as her mother opened the door for them. Damn, she had only taken a little—a small boost in the bathroom before they left. Better to handle her father if she was a little high. Stone cold sober, and he was much too hard to take. Had she taken more than she meant to? Was the smack Cole left behind stronger than what they had been taking?

"Are you okay, Allie?" her mother questioned, concerned.

"I'm fine, just fine," Alison realized her words were slightly slurring, and she saw her mother give her a look. She would have to tread very fucking cautiously.

Jared burst into the trailer ahead of her and ran right for the kitchen cabinet. "There they are," he said gleefully, pulling out the posterboard and a pack of markers.

"Your grandpa said we should save them for you, that you would need them again."

"Thanks, Gammy," Jared said, smiling.

Alison sat down heavily on the couch. Great, now she was feeling incredibly sleepy.

"That smells good, Gammy."

"I'm glad, Jared. Are you hungry, boy? It will be ready in a few minutes. I just put the biscuits in the oven. They'll be done soon."

"Where is Dad?" Alison asked.

"He's lying down. I'll wake him up for dinner."

He's napping? My dad?" Alison said, surprised. Cecil had always yelled at Alison when she napped in the middle of the day.

"Sleeping is what you do at night," he would say. "Idle hands, Alison, lead to the devil's work."

Gail slowly nodded. "He doesn't want anyone to know, Allie, but he has been feeling poorly for months. I finally convinced him to see the doctor, and we have an appointment later this week."

"Wow," Alison said.

Cecil avoided doctors at all costs. He must feel bad, she mused. Jared was sitting on the floor, taking each marker out and testing it to see if it still worked. Alison had been about to say something but instead found her head nodding forward. She jerked. She had almost fallen asleep. Gail frowned at her.

"Allie, are you okay? Why are you so tired? You're not sick, are you?"

"No, Mama. I'm just tired. I picked up some extra hours at the store, and I've been working a lot."

"Oh, okay. Not at night, I hope. Who is staying with Jared while you work? Is Cole helping out?"

"No, Mama, Cole…" Alison cleared her throat as she realized her words were still slurred.

Jared jumped in, looking up from the floor where he sat.

"Cole has a new job. He isn't home anymore during the week."

He does? Alison almost said, then realized with a start that Jared was covering for Cole's absence by making up a lie. Alison nodded mutely.

Gail frowned. "You're not leaving Jared alone while you work, are you, Alison? He's a little too young to be left alone, especially at night. Maybe Cecil can come over if he starts to feel better."

Jared nodded his head no.

"No, Gammy, it's okay. I'm not alone. Gary is watching me."

"Who in the world is Gary?" Gail questioned.

Jared hesitated for only a second.

"He's in high school, and when Mom works, he watches me. He gets to the trailer before I'm out of school because high school gets out earlier than we do. Gary's cool," Jared replied enthusiastically.

"You must be paying him, though. Alison, how can you afford that?"

"No, no, Gammy, he does it for free."

"Does it for free! Why would the young man do that?" Gail questioned.

"He's, he's…" Jared looked piercingly at his mother, and she realized that he was making up another lie on the spot.

"He's a Boy Scout, and…" Jared trailed off, but Alison was somehow able to think quickly enough.

"That's right, Mama, he's a Boy Scout and working on his Caregiver badge or something like that. He needs to earn so many hours working with children."

"Oh, okay," Gail said skeptically. Just then, the oven timer dinged. "The biscuits are ready," Gail said brightly. She removed them from the oven.

"I'll wake your father, and then we'll eat."

As Gail left the room, Alison and Jared exchanged a look.

"You've got it all figured out, haven't you, baby?"

Jared shrugged.

"Want a glass of water, Ma? Don't fall asleep when Grandpa comes out. He won't like it."

"I know, baby, I know."

"Jared," Alison whispered, "we don't really know a Gary, do we?"

"No, Ma, we don't," Jared whispered.

CHAPTER 55

"GRANDPA, WHY DO YOU BELIEVE IN GOD? How do you know he is real?"

Jared was questioning Cecil. Alison rolled her eyes. This conversation would not go well. Alison knew her father hated to be questioned. She had told Jared to go easy. Her father, after a year of delays due to his reluctance to see a doctor and then an even longer wait for his referral to a specialist, had been recently diagnosed with cancer. She was sure her father wouldn't want to talk much at all. Jared, on the other hand, liked to discuss anything and everything. He was becoming very interested in current events. She couldn't recall caring about what was happening in the world when she had just turned thirteen. Jared always asked her, "Do you know what they are doing in China right now? You know, the coral reefs are really in trouble, Ma!"

A smart boy. He was such an intelligent boy! Must have inherited all that inquisitiveness from Jared! He certainly wasn't like her.

Her father cleared his throat. "I was lucky that my parents brought me up right. We attended church every Sunday and never missed a week."

Alison looked away. That was definitely a veiled—not really so veiled—dig at her difficulty getting up for church on Sundays.

"I know God is real because I was taught about the Lord from a young age and because the Bible, the Holy Word of God, says so.

"But Grandpa, there are a lot of other religions, you know. There's Buddhism, Judaism, Islam."

"I know that, boy," Cecil thundered, "but there is only one true religion, and we are fortunate enough to be a part of it."

"But how do we know that our religion is the one true religion? I bet the kids who are brought up Muslim and Jewish are taught that their religion is the best."

"Jared, we have the Bible that tells us what to think."

"But, Grandpa, the other religions have their holy books, too. The Koran, the Talmud."

Alison watched as her father interrupted Jared again.

"Who is telling you all this, Jared? Are you learning this stuff in that school you go to? I knew you should have left there and enrolled at Holy Trinity Academy years ago!"

"Dad, we can't afford that school, and you know it," Alison interjected.

"Still, if that is what they are teaching him there, to question the one true God, it's high time he left that place."

"No, Grandpa," Jared said. "I'm not learning about those other religions at school. I found a book about the Great Religions of the World, and I've been reading it."

"Don't believe everything you read in books, boy. A lot of books are written by those overeducated idiots who don't have a clue what they are talking about. The only book you should be spending time with is the Bible. I've been telling you that for years, Jared!"

"But I want to learn about different things. It's fun!"

"Fun! If these books teach you to question the Lord, they should be thrown out. No, more than that, they should be burned. Leading a young person down the wrong path!"

"Grandpa, you haven't even read the book. You don't even know what it says!"

"Well, Jared, maybe you should start spending some time doing something more productive than reading nonsense. You know Mark, Bob's son, has been going to work with his dad when he's not in school. His father is teaching him all about plumbing. I wonder if they might let you tag along sometimes. Now, plumbing could be useful for you to learn, Jared."

"I don't want to be a plumber!" Jared shouted.

"Jared," Alison admonished.

Jared had not yet learned that it was always better to agree with Cecil, whether it was what you believed or not.

"What is wrong with plumbing, boy? It's an honorable trade, and they make great money."

"I want to go to college, Grandpa. I already know that!"

"And who do you think is going to pay for that?"

"They have scholarships and loans."

"And what do you need a college education for? I sure don't know many people around here who have a degree. Sounds like a waste of time and money, Jared."

"But I know what I want to be. I want to be a lawyer. I like to discuss issues, and Mom says I'm great at arguing, right Ma?"

Alison smiled.

Cecil snorted, "A lawyer! That's even more school—longer than four years! That's impossible for someone like you. What a foolish idea, Jared. I don't know many lawyers, but from what I've seen on TV, they're all fools. Overeducated idiots who don't know a thing. I doubt they can even repair things in their house when they break. Alison, are you encouraging him in this foolishness?"

"Dad, I think Jared can be whatever he wants to be. He is smart enough to do anything he wants."

"Well, it's not so smart to doubt the Lord. It's not so smart to forget to honor his special day every single week, Alison Marie. It's not so smart to ask a lot of stupid questions that no one can answer."

"Daddy, you can insult me all you want, but do not call Jared's questions stupid! Just because you can't answer doesn't mean he shouldn't ask them."

"A plumber, a mechanic, a job like that is the way to go, Jared."

Jared shrugged his shoulders.

"Working with your hands, doing something meaningful is what God wants for all of us."

"Lawyers do something meaningful," Jared replied. "They help people with problems."

"Don't talk back, boy. I know what I'm talking about. I've been out there. I know how the world works. Alison, you are letting him get away with way too much. My daddy would have slapped me down for saying far less."

"Daddy, he's just talking. He's not disrespecting you because he doesn't agree with you."

Cecil shook his head.

"Boy, you need to start reading less and getting outside more. Get your hands dirty. It would be good for you. The only book I want to discuss with you is the only one worth reading: the Bible, the holy word of our Lord."

"Okay," Jared said, "I'll talk about the Bible with you. Did you know Karl Marx said that religion is the opiate of the masses?"

"What the hell does that even mean? And who is this Karl person? Does he live around here? What church does he go to? Is he your age?"

"No, Grandpa," Jared said, smiling. "He lived in Germany a long time ago."

"Well, then, why the hell do I care what he thinks? You know, Jared—" Cecil gulped in a large amount of air and began to cough uncontrollably. He gasped for air and held up a finger to say "wait." Gail immediately came out of the bedroom and got a glass of water for Cecil from the tap. He continued to hack but eventually stopped long enough to take a couple of sips. He gasped and leaned on the counter for support.

"That coughing is getting worse, Daddy."

"It's fine. It's not the cancer. It's allergies, I think," Cecil said.

Gail shook her head. "We need to make another appointment with the doctor."

"I told you, Gail, no. I don't need that doctor or some damn treatment that he mentioned. There's another group of overeducated idiots that think they know everything!"

Gail shook her head. Cecil walked slowly to the living room.

"I'll just sit down for a minute, and then I'll be fine."

Alison looked at her father with a worried expression.

Cecil looked at Jared.

"Promise me, boy, you'll get out there and not just sit and read all the time. You know, I heard Mr. Anderson needs some help on the horse farm; that might be a good use of your time, Jared. And Alison, get that boy and yourself to Sunday services next week; I beg you!"

CHAPTER 56

BY THE TIME JARED WAS FIFTEEN, Cecil had become very ill. They had waited months, almost a year, before he had agreed to start treatment. By the time they had started the chemo, the cancer was quite advanced and had metastasized.

"Whatever the hell that means," Cecil would grouse between coughing fits.

"Spread, Dad, it means it has spread through your body," Alison would say firmly.

It had only been six months later that Cecil had passed—or gone home, as they all repeated. Gammy, who had been so attentive to Jared when he was younger, had gotten very distracted caring for Cecil. She stopped following up on how Alison was caring for Jared. There were weeks when they didn't even see her at all. After Cecil's death, Gail had been exhausted for many months. By the time she was feeling better and was up to questioning both Alison and Jared about their lifestyle, Jared, with little coaching from his mother, had become quite the accomplished liar. Gail never mentioned having Jared move in again.

Jared sighed loudly and looked right at his mother with a harsh expression on his face.

"You can stop calling it medicine; I'm old enough now; I know what the shit that you and Bobby take is."

Alison stood up, trying to make herself as tall as she could. With a start, she realized that her fifteen-year-old son was as tall as she was. He would soon outgrow her, and in another couple of years, he would quite possibly tower over her.

"Jared, don't swear," she tried to say firmly. Jared snorted.

"You need to respect me. I'm your mama. If you don't, I'll send you to live with Gammy, and I don't think you want that."

Jared rolled his eyes. "Yeah, Ma, that threat doesn't work anymore. Gammy is getting old. There is no way she would ever agree to having me around."

"Jared, be respectful," Alison repeated. Her heart was beating harder and faster. She realized she had no idea what she would do if Jared didn't back down—if he continued to defy her.

"Respectful, Ma, really? Don't you think Bobby is the person you should be saying that to, not me? He's the worst one yet, Ma. He's mean. He's stupid, too."

Bobby, Alison's latest boyfriend, had only been living with them in the trailer for two months. Bobby mostly ignored Jared. He was unlike Johnny, who had spent hours playing with Jared when he was younger. He wasn't even like Cole, who would watch sports with him, but what did it matter? Both of those men were long gone.

"Jared, Bobby loves me. He's a part of our family now."

"No, Ma, he doesn't love you, he loves having a place to stay, and you love the shit that he can score."

"Jared, stop this now!"

"You think I can't hear what goes on here at night! It's a small trailer. Just because my bedroom door is shut, I can still hear. He's mean to you, Ma. He calls you bad names. He doesn't respect you, and he treats me like I'm invisible."

"Jared," Alison sighed, "he is helping us with the rent, and we need help, you know that. You don't know him that well yet. You have to give it a little more time. Maybe you should try to talk to him. He might not know what to say to you."

"Yeah, right," Jared rolled his eyes again.

Just then, the trailer door opened, and Bobby burst in, carrying a case of beer and gripping a bottle of whiskey by its neck.

"Hey, woman," he said, smiling at Alison and walking around Jared.

"Hi, Bobby," Jared said, looking at his mother as he said the greeting.

"Oh, hey, kid," Bobby acknowledged. "Shouldn't you be at school or something?"

"It's Saturday," Jared said, turning on his heel, stomping to his bedroom, and slamming the door.

Alison shook her head.

"Maybe I should slap that kid around for you, huh, baby? That one is not very respectful."

Alison shook her head.

"He's a teenager, Bobby. They get moody, that's all. Jared is a good boy."

"Bout time for him to head out on his own soon, won't it be, baby? It would be great if we had the trailer all to ourselves."

"Bobby, he's only fifteen years old! He's not leaving home yet."

"Maybe he should stay with his grandmother more."

"Believe it or not, Jared and I were talking about that, but you know she's getting older. Taking care of my dad took a real toll on her. It's not a good time right now."

Bobby removed the bottle of whiskey from the paper bag, opened it, and took a large swig.

"Yeah, ok, as long as the kid stays out of my way. Hey, Peter and Sandra were at the liquor store. I invited them over for to-night. I thought a little party might be in order. What do you say?"

"I guess," Alison nodded reluctantly.

"Baby, why are you being such a downer? You like Sandra."

"I know, but I don't like to party so much in front of Jared. He's older. He understands now what is going on."

"And that is exactly why he should be spending more time with his grandmother. If not that, what about friends? Doesn't the kid have any? I was out of the house all the time when I was his age. What's wrong with him?"

"There's nothing wrong with him, Bobby."

"Yeah, well, the whole situation makes me tense."

"Sandra and Peter can come over," Alison acquiesced. "It will be fine. Jared will stay in his room."

"Yeah, maybe I'm tense, but you seem pretty stressed, too. Come on, let's have a little hit right now. Junk and whiskey — nothing better for re-lax-a-tion."

He drew out the word into four syllables and wiggled his eyebrows at Alison. She felt stressed, but Jared was only being a typical teenager. She had to let it go.

"Alright, alright," she said, smiling up at Bobby. "But let's do it in the bathroom—farther away from Jared's room."

"Baby, it's your trailer. You should be able to do what you want where you want, but if you want to stoke up in the bathroom, it's okay with me."

CHAPTER 57

THE LAST MONTH HAD BEEN AWFUL. Alison was feeling depressed and anxious and had come close to a full-blown panic attack three times in the previous week. She hated that she was using needles now regularly. Bobby had encouraged her to make what had been an occasional habit a regular part of her daily existence. It was terrible, and she knew it, but after the hit and for a shorter and shorter amount of time, well, that was the only time she felt better and normal. Jared was growing increasingly sullen, but he was at home less and less, which made Bobby happy. He was helping with some horses on a nearby farm. His friend had gotten him the job. Her mother looked worse each time Alison saw her. She was now easily looking twenty years older than her actual age. Her mother seemed so tired. She never asked how she and Jared were doing anymore. She was consumed with her own life. And Bobby, wow, Bobby, what a mess! He had lost his third job in as many months. It was a small area. Word would get around, and no one would want to hire him. He had a temper, but lately, the littlest thing seemed to set him off. He hadn't paid Alison rent for four months. She was buying all the food, too. Bless Jared, he was always giving her an extra twenty dollars. He couldn't be making that much with the horses, but he always shared what money he had. Bobby didn't mention how he wasn't paying for any of the expenses anymore. He always seemed to have enough money for booze, pills, and the smack, though. He always shared what he had with Alison, so that was something, she guessed.

Tonight, Bobby had come home in an awful mood. He hadn't had anything to say at dinner. He had only sat, staring at the meat pie and moving it around on his plate. During the meal, he had quaffed down what —three whiskeys? Four? Jared had made a beeline for his bedroom and firmly closed the door as soon as he had finished eating. Alison finished the dishes and joined Bobby on the couch, where he was moodily staring at the television.

"What's wrong, baby?" she said, gently touching his shoulder.

He jerked away from her touch.

"Bobby, I haven't done anything! Are you mad at me?"

"Maybe I'm tired of all this shit, especially this shithole of a town. Thinking it's about time to move on."

"What! You're leaving me! Why?"

"I didn't say I was leaving you; what are you, some kind of stupid! It's not you. It's this place and all the assholes in it. Come with me. Alison, we could even leave tonight—just up and leave it all behind. What do you say?"

"Bobby, be serious. I can't do that. I have Jared, and I can't leave my mother."

"Yeah, well, guess what? I knew you would be a total bitch about it."

"Bobby, no, I want to understand."

"Yeah, you can't understand, Alison. You're too stupid to see what is right in front of your face, you know that."

"I have no idea what you are even talking about. I thought we were fine. I don't want you to leave."

"Don't be needy, Alison. I hate that shit!"

"Bobby, I haven't asked anything of you for months, and you haven't paid me rent in almost six months now."

"Oh, so now it's all about money. You know I lost my job through no fault of my own, and now you're bitching and moaning, asking for money that you know I do not have. What a slut, Alison."

Alison was crying now, which seemed to infuriate Bobby even more.

"Bobby, I don't know what is wrong with you. I don't know what I've even done."

"Don't play stupid, Alison, even though you are."

"Please, Bobby," Alison reached out her hand to him. He slapped it away and stood up.

"I'm going to lie down, Alison. I feel like shit."

"Okay, baby, you rest."

"Okay baby, you rest," Bobby repeated the words back to her mockingly.

"You don't need to talk to me like that, Bobby."

"I'll talk to you however I want, you little druggie slut."

He gave her a push as he passed by. Alison lost her balance, and her hip hit the kitchen counter hard. The pain infuriated her, and she rushed at Bobby, pushing him in the chest.

"You don't push me! "You don't treat me like that," she yelled.

"Oh, yeah? Who says?" Bobby slapped her hard on the mouth. She punched his nose but missed as he turned his head. He grabbed her shoulders and shook her hard. Then he slapped her hard in the face. She saw stars and tried to bring her foot up to kick him, but he put his foot out, causing Alison to lose her balance and fall. He grabbed her shirt, pulling her back up, his hand out as if he intended to slap her again.

Suddenly, Alison heard a loud noise —a door slamming— and Jared launched himself onto Bobby's back.

"What the fuck?" Bobby muttered. "Get off me, you little fag!"

But Bobby, taller than Jared, was also scrawny and strung out. Jared might have outweighed him by twenty pounds.

Alison screamed, "Don't hurt him."

Bobby tried to shrug Jared off his back. Jared hung on until Bobby collapsed to his knees. Jared towered over Bobby with his fists clenched.

"Get out, get out of here now. I'll call the cops, you loser!"

Bobby stumbled to his feet. Jared gave him a push toward the door, and Bobby staggered.

"Get out and don't come back, you hear me," Jared said menacingly.

Bobby shook his head and crossed to the kitchen table, where what was left of his whiskey bottle sat.

"Yeah, I could fuck you up, little boy, if I wanted to, but it's not worth it. And her," he pointed at Alison, "she is definitely not worth it."

Bobby grabbed the whiskey bottle, his backpack, which was lying by the kitchen table, and an envelope of money—Alison's rent money, which had also been on the table. Bobby shook his head and slammed out of the trailer. Jared looked at Alison.

"Was that his money?" Jared questioned. "Was that his money, or was it yours, Ma?"

Jared looked as if he was ready to go after Bobby to retrieve the money.

"Jared, Jared, let him go, baby. Please. It doesn't matter. It's better that he's gone."

Jared looked carefully at his mother.

"Are you okay, Ma? Do you need a doctor or an ambulance?"

"No, honey, I'm fine. Of course, I am. I don't know what I would do without you, though!"

Jared shook his head and slammed the door as he retreated into his tiny bedroom.

CHAPTER 58

"OH, MY GOD, MA! That is not what is happening. He doesn't like me in that way," Jared said with disgust. Sixteen-year-old Jared rolled his eyes at his mother. Jared was six feet tall now, a sturdy, muscular boy with curly, dark black hair.

"It's just that this is the third time this week that Mr. Sullivan has driven you home in his truck."

"He's helping me, Ma! He says I need to take the SAT next year and that I must go to college. He says I have too much potential not to go."

Jared stood taller, seemingly proud of the compliment. Alison looked up at her son. He towered over her. She looked at his arms and noted that they were becoming increasingly muscular. This was probably due to his continued hard work on the horse farm. Jared had been working there for over two years now. *Longer than I have kept every job I ever had*, Alison thought ruefully.

"Jared, that's great," Alison said but simultaneously began shaking her head.

"I don't know, honey, how we would ever be able to afford a college education for you, though."

Jared interrupted with a frustrated sigh, "That's what I am talking to Mr. Sullivan about. Mr. Sullivan says that I can get scholarships, plus there are work-study programs and even loans. Mr. Sullivan says we can make it happen."

Alison sighed again. She didn't want to burst his bubble, but things didn't work out for people like them, and she knew that all too well.

"Honey, I just want you to be careful. Sometimes, people have ulterior motives. They aren't always what they seem to be or say what they mean. You've been alone with this teacher a lot lately."

Alison couldn't help but shiver as she remembered all those years ago and the rides that her teacher had offered her. She remembered the last ride she had accepted from Mr. Bryce in that snowstorm. It had been so cold, and she hadn't wanted to wait for her dad to pick her up after he got off work. Alison had stayed late at school, and the bus had already left fifteen minutes prior. Mr. Bryce's car had been warm and inviting. He had driven her home twice before, and everything had been fine. She realized something was wrong only after he had driven right past the trailer park entrance.

"I'll show you what it's like to be with a real man, not some boy," he had said as he pulled the car over into the small copse of trees. It was too late to get out, Alison thought.

"Ma, Ma, hello, are you even listening to me? Mr. Sullivan says I might even be able to get into an Ivy League college. He went to Yale, you know. He only moved back here to take care of his mother. He said he thinks I can become a lawyer if I want. I don't even know why I'm so interested in law, but it feels like it is what I was meant to do," Jared enthused.

"Just be careful, baby," Alison repeated.

Jared scowled at his mother angrily and said, "I'm getting out. I'm leaving all this behind. Watch me! I have work in half an hour. I have to get ready."

He stomped away.

CHAPTER 59

ERIC LOOKED AROUND HIS STUDY as he sat at his desk, finishing up his brief for Monday. He felt blessed as he glanced at the photos on his desk of Katrina and all four of his children, the youngest just seven years old. It was only two weeks before Christmas and would be another happy holiday. He had been given so much grace and was genuinely thankful for it. This would be the second Christmas without his mother, who had died suddenly of an undiagnosed heart ailment over two years ago now. He missed her, but he was so blessed to have Katrina, who was warm and loving. She did a great job with the kids. She even understood his periodic moodiness when something would trigger a memory of Paul. Eric rarely talked to Katrina about Paul. He remembered well the last time he had spoken to Brynn. She had said that she thought Paul was still alive, that he was out there somewhere. Eric didn't want to admit this, but he didn't believe Paul was alive. He felt sure that his baby boy—his first baby boy—had been killed years ago by some freak. He only hoped that he hadn't suffered too much. As he did every so often, he wondered how Brynn was doing. He had stopped calling her periodically to check in years ago. He wasn't sure if she even knew that his mother had died. He had moved on with his life. He was busy with work and his family; besides, he didn't want Katrina to think he still had feelings for Brynn, even though Katrina had been endlessly patient and understanding. The last time he checked on Brynn, she lived alone in that beach cottage. It seemed she was living a solitary existence. She had just broken up with a guy she had been engaged to; a significant amount of time had passed since then. Well, hopefully, she had someone else by now. Maybe she had even remarried, as he had. Just then, he heard a shout from the other room.

"Daddy, come see, Daddy!"

"Eric," he heard Katrina call, "the kids want to show you the Christmas tree."

Eric smiled. His family was waiting for him. He smiled and thanked God for all he now had. He knew too well that bad things could happen without warning, but he had been given a second chance, a whole new life.

"Be right there," he shouted, closing the legal brief folder and rising from the chair.

CHAPTER 60

SIX YEARS LATER

BRYNN WAS SCROLLING THROUGH FACEBOOK and Instagram again. It was an activity that she often engaged in late at night. She would usually start innocuously enough, looking for that new recipe she had heard discussed on TV or checking the latest news updates. Still, invariably, she would end up on Katrina's pages. Katrina, Eric's wife, was a very active serial poster on both mediums. Eric had remarried years ago, less than six months after Brynn had left. He had married so quickly that Brynn had always wondered when and for how long he had been seeing the woman. So long ago now, it hardly mattered, but still, Brynn often felt compelled to check to see what Eric was up to. They had four kids. The oldest son had just started attending Harvard. *Two girls and two boys*, Brynn thought, *a perfectly balanced family*. She continued to scroll through more pictures. Both girls were blonde like their mother and seemed eager to pose for the camera. Pictures of Eric were few and far between. He never liked having his picture taken, Brynn remembered, smiling. Wait, there he was! She quickly scrolled back and leaned toward the computer to get a better look at her ex-husband. "Finally, I got a picture of DAD!" the post above the picture said. "Hope the internet doesn't break!" Brynn picked up her coffee and took a large swig. She peered intently at Eric. He looked much the same, but his dark, curly hair now possessed streaks of gray and appeared to be thinning slightly on top. He was grinning with his arm around Katrina. Heavier than he used to be, Brynn mused, noticing a slight belly bump protruding under his polo shirt. She continued to stare at her ex-husband and futilely tried to enlarge the photo so she could see better. Eric did look older—something about him looked tired around the eyes. Brynn shook her head and stared down at her own hands and arms. *If he looks older, I must look older too,* she thought. She stared down at her stomach, but there was no bulge. Brynn weighed at least fifteen pounds less than she had when she was younger. She struggled to keep weight on. She could go days without eating, although she tried not to. She forced herself to eat regular meals, but still, she stayed painfully thin. Brynn sighed and thought back over her life. What must it be like to be married and surrounded by all those kids? His house must be loud and busy, with everyone coming and going. Brynn looked around her quiet, comfortable cottage. It was small but only two blocks from the beach. Walking the beach was her favorite thing, and she frequently did so for hours. The cottage was small but large enough for her. "Just enough room for Mr. Whiskers and me," she used to say, as her friends would frown at her and complain that she was too isolated, especially in the winter. Now, Mr. Whiskers was gone. He had been dead almost two years now. Brynn didn't mind being alone; it was certainly easier that way. She was infrequently in contact with most of her friends and liked it that way.

Brynn had never remarried. She had not dated or had a serious relationship in years now. Her last serious relationship was only three years after Paul had been taken. Brynn had passed through all the craziness of those first two years, hallucinating that she saw Paul, thinking every young boy she passed was Paul. She had cycled through myriad antidepressants and anti-anxiety drugs. She had seen several psychiatrists, and there had been that awful three-week stay in Barber, the mental hospital. But she had gotten better—or at least had gotten better at telling everyone what they wanted to hear, whether it was the truth or not. Eric was busy with his new, growing family, and Brynn met a kind, funny man standing in line behind her at the coffee shop one day. She had been so hesitant to date. She had met him only at the coffee shop for upward of six months. Kevin turned out to be endlessly patient with her anxieties and fears. When she eventually disclosed what had happened to Paul, tears immediately came to his eyes. He gripped her hand across the table.

"My God, I remember reading about that baby in the paper. I felt so bad for the parents! I can't believe that was you."

After that disclosure, Brynn and Kevin started dating in earnest. They had been very happy for a while, Brynn thought whimsically. She remembered when she told Kevin that she didn't want more children. She thought it would be too much, too hard, and would constantly remind her of Paul. Plus, she was stable on her medication now. She didn't want to risk going off and becoming unbalanced again. Brynn's hands had shaken as she had said these words to Kevin. She was so sure that he would dump her, so sure he would say, "Okay, that's it, goodbye!" She was sure he wanted a family. He would notice babies in stores and was the much-beloved uncle to all his brother's children. When Brynn had told him, though, he had only nodded and said, "I understand, Brynn, I do. It's whatever you want. I love you."

Her heart had soared at his words.

Now, Brynn snorted and took a sip of wine. She was an infrequent drinker these days, but somehow, she felt that this trip down memory lane had earned her a glass. Anyway, two months later, they had gotten engaged. Brynn thought that her life was beginning again. Maybe it wasn't all over for her yet. But then, at the engagement party, Brynn had gotten up to go to the bathroom but circled behind the table when she realized she had forgotten her purse. She had heard Kevin talking to a cousin.

"I thought you always wanted kids, man. Now I hear Brynn say that's not in the cards. I know she's been through a lot, but are you sure you're okay with that?"

Brynn had been behind them, but a wall jutting out hid her completely.

"Hey, it's hard for Brynn," Kevin said, "but someday. It's a slow process, but I know I can talk her into kids."

Brynn's heart had cracked into a million pieces, and it felt like it had fallen right onto the floor at her feet. She had asked Kevin if he was okay with never having children, and he repeatedly said he was. She felt tricked and lied to. Brynn had waited till the party was over, until all the guests were gone, and she had broken up with Kevin that night. She had walked out of the restaurant, and though he tried for several months, she never took his calls or saw him again. Brynn had decided right then that it was too hard to be around people, deal with their wants and needs, and parse out how they felt and what they actually wanted. It was too easy to be hurt when their needs did not jibe with your own. So, Brynn had chosen to be alone. It was safer. No worries about trying to please someone else. She had been alone for all these years and now not even a cat to worry about. It was so much safer this way. No one around to wound with casual words wielded either accidentally or intentionally.

CHAPTER 61

ALISON PULLED THE COAT TIGHTER around her body as she approached her mother's trailer. Gail was getting sicker each day. Alison knew it wouldn't be long before she could no longer care for herself. The cancer was spreading quickly, metastasizing, the doctor had said at their last appointment. Alison checked on her mother multiple times each day. She made food for her, too, although Alison could tell that Gail rarely ate what Alison had made. Betty stopped by Gail's trailer frequently, too.

"She'll need hospice soon," the doctor had said.

Alison knew that Gail wanted to stay home as long as possible, and Alison intended to make that happen. She also needed to save as much money as possible. How could they ever afford a funeral? Even without a service, a basic cremation was way out of Alison's and Gail's price range. Gail's voice on the phone sounded urgent when she called Alison and requested—no, demanded—that she come over immediately. Alison had been there two hours prior, helping her with her pills, making sure she had water nearby and heating up the soup. What could she need now, so soon after Alison had left?

"Mama?" Alison called.

"In here," a weak voice answered.

Alison burst into her mother's bedroom. Gail was sitting up in bed. Alison allowed herself a sigh of relief. Her mother didn't look nearly as bad as Alison had feared.

"What do you need, Mama? I just left. Did I forget something you needed?"

Gail shook her head, and Alison saw a hint of tears glisten in her mother's eyes. Alison perched on the edge of the bed.

"Are you in pain, Mama? Is it getting bad?" Alison questioned, grabbing her mother's hand.

Gail shook her head. "No, dear, but I need to talk to you. I have something that I need to tell you right now. It can't wait any longer."

"Okay," Alison said, wondering what could possibly be so urgent.

"Where's Jared? He's not here with you, is he?"

Alison's heart dropped. *Oh, no.* The doctor had said that it was possible her mother could become delusional as her condition worsened.

"No, Mama," Alison said, shaking her head. "Jared is not with me. He is away at school, you know that. He is miles away from here."

Her mother sighed. "Good, that's good. Alison, shut the door, please. I must tell you about Jared, and I can't risk anyone overhearing us."

"Mama, no one else is here. It's only you and I here in the trailer."

"Shut the door, please, Alison," her mother implored.

Alison got up, shut the door, and shook her head.

"Your dad will be so mad. If I tell you and Jared finds out, he will be very mad!"

"Mama, Daddy's been gone a long time now. You know that."

"Of course, I know that, Alison," her mother snapped, and her eyes blazed at her daughter.

Okay, so maybe she was becoming delusional. Or perhaps she was taking too many pain pills. They were strong; the doctor had even said so. Alison knew for a fact that they were potent because she had sampled several herself. She never took enough that her mother would run short or even notice, but they were strong and provided a nice buzz. Alison moved back and sat down on the bed once again. Gail inhaled a shuddering breath.

"I have to, Alison. I must tell you something about Jared, about where he came from. Who does Jared belong to, Alison?" Gail quizzed.

"Why, Mama, he's ours. He's always been ours."

"But where did he come from, Alison?"

"We told people that he belonged to my cousin in Ohio."

"Alison, do you have a cousin in Ohio?"

"No, Mama," Alison said hesitantly. "Mama, Jared is my baby boy and has been for a long time. I don't understand what you are saying. Jared is ours. We love him. We all loved him, even Daddy."

"Alison, where did your father and I get Jared from?"

Her mother was waiting for Alison to answer. Alison shuddered. "I don't know, Mama. That was a bad time, a dark time. I was so out of it. Remember all that awful medication the doctors put me on? I barely knew my name. I remember you and Daddy returned with a baby and told me he was my baby. Right after that, we went to Ohio for a few months. Daddy worked there, and you helped me take care of Jared."

"But Alison, you didn't answer my question: where did your father and I get Jared in the first place?"

Alison ran her hands over her face in frustration.

"I don't know, then. I guess I don't know where you got Jared."

"We got him at a store, Alison," her mother said solemnly.

Okay, this was great. Her mother truly was losing it. She was sitting here listening to absolute fiction!

"Mama, you can't buy babies from a store. Don't be ridiculous!"

She was going to take several pills from her mother's bottle before she left today. After this preposterous conversation, she was going to need them.

Gail shook her head.

"No, Alison, we didn't buy Jared at a store. We stole him from a store—we stole a baby from a store for you. You needed something to live for. It was all your dad's idea initially, but I followed it. Jared does not belong to us. He never did. He has a whole other family out there. What we did was so wrong, Alison, so very wrong."

CHAPTER 62

ALISON HAD WAITED until her mother was asleep before she left her trailer. She had called Betty and asked her to go over for the afternoon check-in on Gail. Alison would go back in the evening, but right now, she planned on taking all three of the pain pills she had nabbed from her mother's bottle and taking a rest this afternoon. It had been quite the disturbing story that her mother had related. But was it true? Had her mother hallucinated the whole thing? Hard to believe that her holier-than-thou father was a kidnapper, but Cecil had always doted on her. Alison knew he had always tried to give her everything she wanted. She didn't know what to think. There, she felt the pills begin to kick in. She wouldn't worry about the disturbing story right now. It could not possibly do any good to tell Jared. Jared rarely came by anymore anyway. He was drifting further and further away. She was glad he was doing so well in college and was happy he was taking an extra year to complete his double major, but she felt she was losing him. She was pretty sure—no, she was certain—that he was ashamed of her and where he had lived growing up. She knew in her bones that she was losing him. Tracey, her last boyfriend, had left over six months ago. It was only a matter of time before her mother was gone. If she mentioned this disturbing story to Jared, he would leave her, too. She couldn't do it. At least, not now. She had only been off the smack eight months. If everyone left her, she would go right back on, and she did not want to do that shit anymore. Better to keep quiet. For all she knew, the whole story was just a fever dream of a very sick, dying woman. It had all happened so long ago. As the days passed and Alison's mother got sicker, Alison became convinced that the whole story was made up. It must have come from a dream that her mother had. The story was just too implausible. It had to be untrue. Plus, she needed Jared in her life. How could she live without him? She couldn't risk losing her baby, not now, not yet. Eventually, she stopped thinking of the story that her mother had told.

CHAPTER 63

BRYNN HATED HOLIDAY SHOPPING. Even after all these years, seeing mothers and children in stores was still hard for her. She hadn't thought every child she saw might be Paul for years. Such delusions, such hope, had left her years ago. She snickered as she realized that if she were to search for Paul in every stranger's face, she would no longer be looking for a boy but a man. Paul would have turned twenty-three on his last birthday. How weird was that! Brynn would be spending most of this Christmas holiday alone. Nothing unusual about that for her. She preferred it that way, but the kind, older woman who had moved into the cottage next to Brynn's only two months ago invited her for Christmas tea or coffee, "whatever you prefer, dear."

Brynn could not refuse. The woman had confided that her husband had only recently passed and that her son lived in California and wouldn't be able to visit his mother till the new year.

"You know how it is. They get so busy with their own lives!"

I had a son, too, Brynn had wanted to say, but saying that would only precipitate questions, and then she would have to come out with the whole sordid story, so Brynn said nothing.

"Since we're both alone," Eve had said, "why don't we spend part of the day together? Neither one of us needs to be lonely."

Brynn had agreed, so now here she was just a few days before Christmas and shopping in an overcrowded store for some small present that her new neighbor might appreciate. She should bring cookies or some pastry to the visit, too. What better place to get everything than this big-box store? Brynn rounded the corner and stopped so abruptly that she almost dropped the tray of cookies that she had just picked up. It couldn't be—standing at the other end of the aisle were Eric and Katrina, who was instantly recognizable from her myriad Facebook and Instagram posts. Brynn had not seen Eric in years. How did this happen? But then, Brynn remembered. He lived nearby, and she had traveled outside her usual area to get to this store, which should have everything she needed. One-stop shopping. Maybe he hadn't seen her. Perhaps she could slink away. Too late! She saw his face light up with recognition and watched him whisper something to his wife, who also looked up to stare in Brynn's direction. Brynn smiled at them, hoping it looked more like a smile and less like a grimace. Now, the couple was advancing toward her as she took steps in their direction as well.

"What a surprise to see you here!" Eric said heartily.

Brynn nodded, noticing the extra gray in his hair and the fact that he had clearly gained a few pounds since his younger years.

"Brynn, I don't think you ever met my wife. This is Katrina," he said.

"How very nice to meet you. I've heard so much about you, Brynn!" the woman gushed.

Brynn stopped herself from saying, "I recognize you from your posts," because that would only make her look creepy and like a stalker. She also refrained from blurting out, "What have you heard about me? Has Eric shared that I used to be batshit crazy?"

"We're just trying to pick up the last-minute stocking stuffers for our kids. We have four kids. Crazy time of year!" Katrina was prattling on and on.

"Are you still in the cottage by the beach?" Eric inquired.

"I am. I love the beach," Brynn said quietly.

"Well, good for you, Brynn. What are you doing for the holiday?" Eric questioned.

If Brynn had only rapidly responded, lying and saying that she was spending it with a bunch of friends, but instead, she hesitated just long enough to see the sad look pass between the couple. *Way to make yourself look pathetic*, Brynn thought.

"Oh, I'm going to visit my neighbor for part of the day."

"Brynn," Eric hesitated, again looking at Katrina, "if you don't have anywhere to go, you are welcome to come and join us?"

He said this with a question mark at the end. *Way to check with your wife first, Eric*, Brynn thought. *In case your wife doesn't want some pathetic loser around her kids*. But Katrina began to nod vigorously, with a huge smile as if she was excited by the prospect of Brynn's possible presence.

"You sure can," Katrina said, reaching out to touch Brynn's arm. "We would love to have you."

She probably just wants to post it on Instagram, Brynn thought. *Look at me. Look how charitable I am. I even get along with my husband's ex!* Brynn had to get out of this, had to get out of here.

"Yeah, Eric, I'm fine, but thanks anyway. I'm busy with the neighbor, and then I have other things to do." Was there any way she could make herself sound less odd? Apparently not. "You're busy with your own family. You don't want me hanging around. You will have plenty of people at your house already."

"Brynn, what's one more?" Katrina enthused. "We have a lot of room. Please come."

I know you have plenty of room. I've seen that big house in your photos, Brynn thought.

"Thanks for the offer, but no, I'm sorry, I can't."

"Ok," Eric said, running his fingers through his hair as he always used to. *Maybe that's why he has less hair than he used to*, Brynn thought. This thought made her smile, and she almost laughed as they smiled back at her, unaware of what had triggered the facial expression.

"Brynn, if you need anything, know that I'm here. We're here for you."

"Family is family," Katrina added chirpily. Brynn nodded but walked quickly away without saying anything more.

CHAPTER 64

ALISON LOOKED UP from where she was lying on the couch. He had made it! She heard Jared's car in the driveway. She knew he wouldn't let her down. Now, the rent would be paid on time. There would be no more harassment from Mr. Green and, best of all, no late fees.

"Ma?" she heard Jared call as he burst into the trailer.

"Right here, son," Alison said as she sat up with a grimace while trying to smooth her hair down.

Jared reached into his pocket almost immediately and extracted an envelope. He held it up before laying it on the small kitchen table.

"It's all there, Ma."

"Thank you so much. I don't know what I would do without you."

"Yeah, Ma, can you just do me a favor, though? Next month, if you run out of money, please let me know before the very last minute. I have no problem helping you if I can, but I had to rush to get here, and I need to leave"—he looked at his watch—"in twenty minutes. I have a four o'clock class that I can't miss, and if the traffic gets bad, I'll barely make it back in time."

"I'm sorry, Jared, it's just that I thought I would have enough this month. I was going to work extra hours at the store, but" — Alison sighed— "it's just my stomach hurt so bad that I couldn't go in for two days. Do you have time for a quick sandwich? You must be hungry."

"Oh," Alison said, suddenly remembering that she had used the last of the bread last night and had also used up the cold cuts as well. "You could run and get us some bread and lunch meat, and we could eat together."

"Ma, I have no time," Jared said, mildly irritated. He dug in his pocket again, pulling out his wallet. "Here," he said, holding out two twenties and a ten to his mother. "Use this to buy yourself some food."

"Jared, I don't want to take more of your money."

"You need to eat, Ma. I'd give you more if I had it."

"No, son, no, I don't expect you to. Are you hungry, though?"

"I'm fine. I'll eat at the dining hall after class."

"Sit down," Alison said, patting the couch next to where she had been lying. "What have you been up to?"

Jared shrugged as he perched on the edge of the couch. "Seriously, Ma, I would stay longer if I could, but this class is important."

"Ok, ok, I understand. Just talk to me for a few minutes before you have to leave. I miss you so much."

Jared ran a hand across his face. "So, I'm doing this DNA test with my roommate, Randy. It just came out. You spit in a tube and send it to this company. They test your DNA and tell you about yourself. You can even find relatives that you didn't know you had. We both thought it would be cool to try. Randy's going to write a paper about it for his bio class."

Alison's heart quickened, and the knot in her stomach tightened. She frowned.

"Jared, that sounds silly and expensive."

"No, it's not that expensive, well, maybe a little, but we're just interested."

Alison found herself feeling angry without being sure why.

"What a waste of time and money, Jared! You already know who your relatives are."

"Do I, Ma? Are you sure?"

"Randy's girlfriend did the same test six months ago. She found a cousin that she talks to all the time now."

"Jared, you don't have any cousins. I'm an only child, and you are, too. You are being ridiculous!"

Jared looked at his mother, perplexed.

"Why are you so against this? What's the big deal? I'm paying for it myself, so why are you getting so upset?"

"It's foolish, Jared, it just is! It's—" Alison stopped speaking and cried out as she grasped her stomach.

"Ma, if your stomach hurts that bad, you need to get to the doctor."

"I'm fine, Jared. It will go away—it always does." Jared rolled his eyes.

"Yeah, Ma, but your stomach has been hurting for months now, and you just told me the pain is causing you to miss work. What if it is something serious?"

"It's not serious, Jared. It will get better."

"Jared, please do me a favor—don't waste your money on that DNA thing."

"Ma, what is it to you? It's not a big deal."

"Jared, I forbid it. You can't do it."

"You forbid it? What, are you turning into Grandpa now?"

"It's up to me. You don't even understand what it is. Although I can't imagine why you're afraid of the unknown."

"Jared, I don't want to argue with you. Just stop. Please don't do it."

"Ma, I make all my own money, and I have for years now. I give you money all the time. I give you whatever you need, even when I have to drive hours out of my way at the very last minute. Taking a DNA test doesn't hurt you at all."

"Jared, it's foolish."

"It's not foolish, and it's my decision. I should never have told you about it."

Jared rose from the couch.

"You have everything you need. There's all the rent money on the table. Here, take another twenty in case you need something else. I'm heading back now."

"Jared, wait, please."

Jared shook his head. "I have to go, Ma. I have a class at four. If I leave right now, I'll just make it back."

"Jared!" Alison implored, opening her mouth to say more, but Jared bent down, kissed the top of her head, and then bounded out the door.

Alison heard his car start up and listened until the engine noise faded. Her heart was beating so hard in her chest. For the first time in several years, she remembered the improbable story that her mother had told her only two weeks before she had passed.

Jared isn't ours; she heard her mother's voice saying in her head. *He has a whole other family out there.*

Alison grabbed at her stomach yet again as a searing, knife-like pain cut right through her. Damn it, the pain was getting worse. What was she going to do? Maybe she did need to see a doctor.

CHAPTER 65

JARED HAD NEVER HAD AN EASY LIFE. Money had always been hard to come by in his world. But here he was now, thriving in college and about to finish his senior year. He should have been a senior last year, but with the double major, it had taken him longer to get all the credits he needed. He had just turned twenty-two. He was tall with a bulky build and curly dark hair. He looked so unlike his mother with her pale skin and blonde hair. He was taller than anyone in the family. Gammy and Grandpa had been much shorter than Jared by the time he turned thirteen. He would stare at the picture of his father, who had died in Afghanistan, for hours when he became a teenager. Gammy said he must have gotten his height from his father, but in all the pictures Jared had seen, his father, also named Jared, was not nearly as tall as he was now. In fact, his father was the shortest in the photo they had in the living room. The photo with his arms around his fellow Marines. Jared sighed as he prepared to leave his dorm room. He was happy here. He was reluctant to make the hour drive back home and return to the small trailer where he had spent so much of his life. He knew he should keep in bet-ter touch with his mother, especially now that Gammy and

Grandpa were deceased. His grandfather had died of cancer many years ago, but Gammy had only been gone a few years. He knew his mother missed them both terribly. There was something so freeing about being out of the house, out of the small town that he had called home his entire life. It seemed to Jared that everyone there was so narrow-minded and judgmental. He felt different from everyone there. The few friends he had in high school had drifted away and moved on to bigger and better things—or on to a life of crime, he thought wryly, as he thought of his former best friend's disintegration into drug addiction and thievery as a way of life. His mother didn't ask Jared for much help, maybe with the rent every few months but she couldn't need more money so soon. He had visited her with the rent payment less than two weeks ago, so it had to be something else that she needed this time. When she had called last night and, in her raspy voice, requested that he come home for a visit, he felt compelled to comply.

"You don't need to stay long, son," she had said, sensing his reluctance.

"I just, I have something I need to tell you."

Maybe she wanted to apologize for her overreaction, in his opinion, during his last visit. He had mentioned that he was going to send in for one of those popular and ever-cheaper DNA tests. He had only said it in passing, making conversation, but his mother had reacted with uncharacteristic anger. She told him not to do it, that it was a waste of money, and that he was even foolish to consider it. Her reaction confused him, as she usually let him do whatever he wanted, so her vehemence had startled him.

His mother had battled depression since he was old enough to remember. She had also been a drug addict with an ever-worsening heroin addiction by the time Jared was seven or eight, somewhere around there. From the psychology classes that Jared had taken in college, he became convinced that his mother had self-medicated for years. Maybe if she had been able to treat her anxiety and depression effectively, she wouldn't have felt the need to drink and drug as she had for all those years. Alison had never had consistent health coverage or a stable job. Maybe if she had, everything could have been different for her and him. It didn't matter now. It did no good to look back and pine for the past, playing the "what might have been" game. He was out of the house and would never go back. He would be successful. He would care for his mother as best he could, but she had made her choices just as he was making his now. And his choices were going to be a damn lot better than hers had ever been. Gammy had helped out a lot with his needs when he was small, but as she had gotten older and Grandpa had gotten sicker, he had been left more on his own with his mother. By the time he was eight or nine, he had been essentially running the household. Sure, his mom helped some, but there were too many days, weeks, and months when he had been on his own, making his own food, washing his own clothes, and forging the signatures he needed for school trips. His mother hadn't been physically absent. She was there but not there. Gammy hadn't known it had been that bad, as Jared consistently covered for his mother, saying she was up and around, working when she wasn't, when she was in reality lying in bed. Jared had learned to cook out of necessity. Hey, he got hungry. So, he made food for himself and his mother.

Those years were filled with alcohol and pills, and finally, with the needles that his mother self-medicated with. She had only been sober—at least, he thought she had been sober—for the last two years. She looked a little weaker, a little smaller each time he saw her. Did she want to tell him she was sick? That was a distinct possibility.

CHAPTER 66

JARED RAN THE WORDS THROUGH HIS HEAD that his mother had shared with him on the visit repeatedly as he drove back to campus. She had been lying on the couch when he arrived, and though she had smiled at him happily as he entered the trailer, she had not tried to get up.

"Are you okay, Ma?" he immediately questioned, even though he knew the answer resounding in his gut.

"Oh, Jared," she had said, then stopped for a coughing fit.

"I love you so much. Your dad would have been so proud of you if he had lived. I'm sick, son. The doctor says I have liver failure and probably won't have that long."

"Ma, no!" Jared said immediately. "We'll get you to a good doctor. Maybe they can do a transplant or something."

His mother had wearily shaken her head.

"Son, no, I'm fine with it. Truly, I am. It's too late, and with my history, well, I would never be on the top of anyone's list for a transplant. I don't want to go through all that anyway. I just want to tell you something. There's something you need to know. Jared, I love you so very much. We all loved you. You made our lives. I don't know where I would be without you." She hesitated as if she had more to say. His mother had such a faraway look in her eyes.

Jared heard his heart thrum in his chest. Oh, God, no, she wasn't using again, was she?

"Ma," he said loudly to shake her from her reverie or whatever it was.

"Ma," he repeated loudly, "I'm listening."

Alison shook her head, and tears sprang to her eyes as she buried her head in her hands.

"What am I doing? I don't even know what I'm saying! I don't even know for sure! Don't do this, Alison. You can't!"

Jared looked at her, confused. It seemed now that she was not speaking to him but to herself.

"It's the medication, Jared. It's messing me up, but I'm in so much pain."

She rocked and grabbed for her stomach. Jared's heart sank. The medication! That was what Alison and the ever-rotating cast of boyfriends that had lived with them in the trailer had called the pills and the smack that they had regularly imbibed when he was a kid. Jared rose from the end of the couch where he had been sitting. He was trying not to be angry. He ran a hand through his curly dark hair.

"The medication?" he questioned, realizing his voice had come out louder than he meant. She was going to know how angry he was.

"The medication, Ma? Are you talking about something the doctor gave you, or are you back on that shit again? If you are using now as sick as you are..."

"No, Jared, no," Alison said, her voice rising as she attempted to sit up.

"Ma, I told you before I won't come around if you're using. I'll still give you money, or better yet, I'll buy your food for you, but I can't—I won't be subjected to what that shit does to you anymore."

"Jared, please, baby, I would never do that to you. I'm still clean, I swear. I swear on Grandpa's soul that I haven't used in two years. I haven't even had a drink in nine months. I'm on a lot of medication from the doctor. I'm in so much pain, Jared. I guess I deserve the pain. I get that. I do. But the pills I take them exactly as they are prescribed. No more—never any more than what I really need!"

Jared sighed and stood up. He wanted to believe her, but he thought she had stopped drinking more than nine months ago. He saw tears forming in her eyes.

"Ok, Ma, ok, calm down."

Jared sat back down. "Lie down, Ma, you don't look so good."

He noticed that her body was shaking, and her light skin had turned even whiter, so she looked positively cadaverous. Alison lay back down and took a deep breath.

"The last thing I want to do is fight with you. Remember the last time you were here? We argued over that damn DNA test, and I am so sorry we argued about it. Jared, we all loved you so much, but…"

"But what, Ma, what are you saying?" Jared questioned.

His mother shook her head and pointed to the pictures of his father on the end table.

"I wish you had known him. Jared was a good man. He would have known what to do about all this."

"All this what, Ma, about you being sick?"

"No, baby, about you."

"What about me, Ma?"

Alison got a faraway look in her eyes again. Jared stared at her. It was almost as if she wasn't aware of his presence. *My God,* he thought, *she is very sick. This is so bad.* He was going to have to prepare. Who was it that took care of dying people? Hospice, yeah, that was it. He was going to have to call her doctor and see if they had hospice around here.

Alison began to speak again. "It was a dark, dark time, Jared. Your father—I mean my husband—had died in the war, and I lost my…"

"Lost your what, Ma? You were pregnant with me, right?"

"Oh, Jared! I tried to commit suicide more than once. Did you know that?"

"No, Ma, no one ever told me that."

"Gammy and Grandpa didn't know what to do. They thought they were going to lose me. They were desperate. I was heavily medicated then, Jared. I don't even know all the details. I was so out of it for months. What I do know is that…" She hesitated.

"Gammy told me something truly disturbing right before she died. You, Jared, you," Alison stopped speaking yet again. She seemed to want to say something, but the words would not come out.

"What, Ma?" Jared said gently. "Just tell me."

"We loved you. We always will."

"I love you too, Ma. Look, I know you tried. I don't blame you for all the shit that went down."

Alison leaned back into the pillows propped behind her head. Her voice was becoming even slower and slurred. She was now speaking with her eyes closed. "From a store, I think, a store," she said so quietly that Jared leaned close to her to hear.

What she was saying made absolutely no sense!

"You saved my life, Jared. That I know, because I didn't want to live anymore. You gave me purpose."

Jared was feeling hot and cold at the same time. He didn't know what to do, what to say. Was it even safe for her to be here alone if she was hallucinating? What the hell was she trying to say?

"I wanted you to be mine, only mine. I needed you to be mine!"

Jared ran his fingers through his hair in agitation.

"Jared, Jared, please. I love you," his mother said, now half asleep.

"They must miss you so much."

"Ma, I'll come back on the weekend when I can stay longer. You rest now."

Alison nodded. "Okay, baby. Thank you for understanding. It will all work out. I'm sorry for what we did."

Jared would call Alison's doctor immediately this afternoon. He would ask about hospice and whether it was safe to leave her alone. He ran his hands through his curly hair. He covered the now-sleeping Alison with a blanket, shaking his head as he left the trailer. He would have stayed, but he had a final exam in less than two hours.

CHAPTER 67

ALISON WAS STILL BREATHING HEAVILY and feeling exhausted after forty minutes of rest. She leaned back in her brown easy chair. Getting the three boxes from the storage basement had been even more difficult than she imagined. Charlie, the young kid who did maintenance for the trailer park, had helped her locate the boxes and carried them back to the trailer for her. Now, here they sat on the threadbare carpet right at her feet. She didn't even have the energy to try to open them. Maybe if she took a little nap, she would feel better.

Alison stretched and looked at the clock on the wall. She had slept for two hours! She breathed in deeply to test if she was as winded as earlier, and thankfully, her breathing was much improved. Alison stood unsteadily and moved slowly to the kitchen to get a pair of scissors to cut the tape securing the boxes. Once the boxes were open, she began to rifle through them. She found herself smiling at the photos of Jared as a young child, even then with his thick, dark, curly hair cascading down. She looked at the tiny young boy who would grow up to be the large, handsome man he now was. In one picture, she held him in her arms, and you could tell she was struggling to hold him upright. Alison was so tiny, and he had been a sturdy baby with long legs. Here was a picture of Jared with the trophy he had won for first place at the science fair. Her mom and dad were standing next to him. Her father was beaming down at Jared. She almost heard her father's rough voice saying to Jared, "You're a smart one, huh, boy?" She opened the second box. There was that baseball trophy. She hadn't realized they still had the large, garish trophy. Jared hadn't particularly liked baseball, she remembered. The third box contained all her mother's photo albums. How many were there? It had to be at least ten. Gammy loves her photo albums; Alison remembered saying that to Jared when he was a boy and would grouse about having his picture taken by Gammy yet again. Alison realized that photos of Jared became sparser as he got older. Alison's addiction had been worsening by then, and her mother first was busy caring for her dad, and then she had become sick herself. Still, she had tried to photograph each aspect of Jared's life. She opened the last box and drew in a breath, seeing Jared looking impossibly handsome and dressed in a tux for his junior prom. He was standing next to his date, Cassie Winters. Alison hadn't even remembered that he had taken her to prom, but the memory had been rekindled because Cassie had called her yesterday. The girl was a hospice nurse now. She would be coming by for an intake interview for Alison in two days. Bless Jared. He had called the doctor and helped set up the whole hospice thing. Alison wanted to stay at home as long as possible, and with hospice coming, she would be able to do so. Alison sat back in the chair. She was tired again. Her breathing was becoming heavy once more, and her stomach was beginning to hurt. She wanted to get the task done now. Who knew how long she had? Maybe Cassie could help her move the boxes into Jared's bedroom and position them on his bed when she arrived. Alison moved slowly into her bedroom, carefully slipping the box containing the old newspaper out of her dresser drawer. Alison had only recently discovered the newspaper article. It was in the back of her closet at the bottom of a pile of books she had brought over from her mother's trailer after she died years ago. Alison had thought it was a large book, but on closer examination, it was one of those boxes that looked like a book. This one had a red cover and said *Moby Dick* on the spine. When you opened the book, however, you discovered it wasn't a book but a storage box for valuables, only meant to look like a book. Alison knew now that her mother must have placed the newspaper article in the faux book years ago. So, it had been on her mother's small bookshelf for years without anyone knowing the article existed. Did her mother want someone to find it? She had certainly hidden the article in plain sight. It was quite unlikely, however, that her father would have picked up a book that wasn't the Bible. He wasn't a reader. Alison hadn't been a reader either, but it wasn't out of the realm of possibility that she could have picked up the book when she was living at home with her parents. But she never had. She had other interests even then. Breathing heavily now, Alison trundled back to the living room and the boxes. She opened the fake *Moby Dick*, carefully removing the newspaper article and then tossing the book aside. She glanced at the damning article, not bothering to reread it. She knew what it said. It hurt her deeply to think of what they had done. The article was old and beginning to yellow. She placed it carefully in the third box. She started to place it on the very bottom but then shook her head and shifted the article so just the edge of it stuck up on the side. She didn't want Jared to miss the article. Bending over, she tucked the flaps of each box and, with her foot, pushed them into the order that she hoped Jared would open them. She lay back, exhausted. Now, she had to get someone to carry the three boxes and place them on Jared's bed. She wanted the box with the article in it to be the last one Jared would go through. Hopefully, after she was gone, he would look at them, almost in chronological order. She wanted him to recall their happy times when he was younger. Gammy and Grandpa had helped her care for Jared then, and her pain-in-the-ass father had always harped on them all going to church. She rolled her eyes even now as she always did then. But who knew? Those had been the good days. Gammy making her big Sunday dinners for all of them, and Grandpa teaching Jared how to pray. But then, her disease raged out of control. Her estrangement from her father was ever-deepening, and then he became sick and was gone. Alison believed that each of her boyfriends was the one who would save them and take them away from this godforsaken town. It had never happened, and the drugs had loomed ever larger in Alison's existence. They were the only thing, other than Jared, that made her feel better. All the wasted years! Jared grew angrier and angrier with each passing year as his awareness of what she did increased. The drugs had eclipsed everything, even Jared! Would she go to Hell when she died because of the pain she had caused Jared? Did she even believe in Hell? If she went there, surely her father would also be there for what he had done. She guessed her mother, too, but somehow Alison knew that her father had been the one who had implemented the idea. Her gentle, loving mother could never have devised such an idea on her own. Her father, on the other hand, was stubborn as a mule. Once he thought he was right and wanted something, no one could dissuade him. What they had done had to be what her father wanted. Alison shuddered as she picked the article up. She knew she wouldn't be able to reread the whole thing. She looked at the headline. *Allenburgh Couple Still Hopeful Missing Infant Will Be Found.* So, her parents had been kidnappers, and she had never known. She had been so upset after the loss of Jared and then their baby. She had been on such heavy antidepressants. She barely remembered being in Ohio with the baby. All she remembered was her father saying, "He's your baby," repeatedly. Playing with Jared had been the first time she had smiled in months. She hadn't known. How could she have possibly known? Maybe she could have stopped them or returned Jared if she had known all those years ago. Although, how could she have given him back? She couldn't imagine a life worth living without him. And her mother had tried to tell her the truth when she had been the one dying. Alison had been heavily into her addiction then, and she had dismissed her words as hallucination. The story was so very improbable. But now, she was sober and finally found the newspaper article two months ago. She knew it was true, and still, she had done nothing. Jared would forever hate her. How could he not? It would have been one thing to tell him immediately after finding the damning article; but to wait, made her complicit in her parents' evil. She had been considering writing Jared a letter to explain, but what would she say after all this time? What was her excuse for not telling him? It wasn't as if he was a young child needing protection. He was a man able to make his own decisions. That he was not theirs explained so much. He didn't look like any of them. He was so smart. She couldn't just leave him without his knowing the truth. The way it was now, he would be all alone in the world without any family when the reality was that there was a family out there for him. He had to know the truth. She had been a coward not to tell him. Her pathetic attempt to tell him had been too little, too late, and still, she had not gotten the words out so he could possibly understand. She was a coward now to not share the truth with him. She was afraid of the look of disgust that would become present in his eyes if she disclosed what she knew. He had been so mad at her in the past for using, but in the last two years since she had been somewhat sober, he had been kind and attentive to her. She couldn't destroy that in her last few days. She didn't have much longer. She was sure of that. She carefully repositioned the article in the box, ensuring it was under the photo albums, with only one edge sticking up. She stepped back, looking at the box. No, Jared couldn't miss the article if he opened the box, and surely, he would open the box. She would tell him that he needed to go through all the boxes after she died. She would tell him it was important to do so when he visited her this weekend. He would open the boxes. He would discover the article, and he would find his way home. She was sure of it. She picked up his baby picture from the first box, peering at it closely.

"I loved you so," she whispered fiercely to the picture. The picture had supposedly been taken on his birthday, May 23. But May 23 wasn't his birthday, was it?

"May 23 was the day they stole you," Alison whispered, shaking her head and wiping away the tears that had sprung forth from her eyes.

CHAPTER 68

"OH, SHIT," JARED SAID UNDER HIS BREATH as he entered the trailer and saw the young woman sitting there. He knew her! Cassie was his mother's hospice nurse! As he pulled into the driveway, he was happy to see a car there he did not recognize. He felt sure the car belonged to the hospice nurse and was pleased that they had been able to start so quickly. It was only a week after he had talked to his mother's doctor and explained her situation, and the doctor had approved hospice care for her. Jared shifted his backpack to his other shoulder awkwardly. It contained everything he would need to spend the entire week-end with his mother. He had been looking forward to talking to the nurse, asking exactly how to administer medication to his mother —maybe even have a chance to ask someone else about the confusing comments his mother had made to him. How normal was it for someone so sick to say strange things? But now the hospice nurse was Cassie? Cassie, really? His date to the junior prom. They had slept together following prom. It had been Jared's first time. They dated for several months after. Jared hadn't been disrespectful to her, and he hadn't used her, but he had broken it off because she began to talk about the kids they would have in the future and what their wedding would be like. Jared knew what he wanted, and it wasn't any of that. He wanted out. He was determined to escape this small town and its lack of opportunity. He was going to college. When he broke it off with Cassie, his teacher had even been helping him begin to apply to the Ivy League colleges. Well, that hadn't worked out, but Jared knew he was still leaving even if he ended up at the state college, which is precisely where he had gone. Cassie's talk of kids and weddings had scared him so. They always used protection, but still, he began to envision what could happen if she did wind up pregnant and how he would never get out. He had envisioned himself still living in the trailer and struggling to find work in an area rife with a lack of opportunity. He had broken it off with Cassie; she had been furious. She accused him of only using her for sex and of thinking that he was too good for her. She enlisted her other girlfriends, and they left nasty notes in and on his locker. She would call him up crying, late at night. There had been so many ugly scenes, and each one had only strengthened Jared's resolve that he needed to get the hell out of there. But now she was sitting right there in his own living room in his mother's brown armchair, smiling at him. She must have known who his mom was before she took the placement. He looked down, unsure of what to say, what to do. Cassie waved her hand at him and said gently, "It's ok, Jared. What happened between us was a long time ago." She stood.

"Obviously, I'm over you," she laughed gently and cradled her belly. He realized she was quite pregnant.

"I've been married for four years now. This is our second child. I married Henry Dawkins from two towns over. I have my LPN certificate, but I'm studying to become an RN. Henry is finishing college now, just like you. After this baby is born, I'll go back and finish, and then we are getting out of here."

"Jared," she said, and she hesitated. "I get it now. You didn't want to be tied down. You wanted to make something of yourself, and the opportunities are not here. I was so young and immature then. I'm sorry for the way I treated you after we broke up. Henry and I can't wait to get out of here, and I certainly will not raise my kids here. The drugs, the lack of opportunity, the ignorance, it's an awful place! You were so right, and you knew it back in high school. I knew who your mama was when I took this job. I hope you don't hold the past against me."

Jared felt his shoulders relax, and he finally set his backpack down.

"It's ok," he said, nodding. "Where is she? She must be sleeping."

"She is. The night nurse said she had a lot of pain last night and was awake most of the night. I got her to take her medication earlier, and she drifted right off. Are you here for the whole weekend?"

Jared nodded.

"The medication schedule is right there on the table. Jared, it is so much better if she takes the medication before the pain gets bad. She needs encouragement to do that, though. If she waits, the pain only gets worse, and the medication can't catch up. It's like a fire. If you catch it right away, you can put the fire out with just a little water, but if you wait until the whole house is on fire, it's harder, if not impossible, to put it out. Does that make sense?"

"It does," Jared affirmed.

"I think she is reluctant to take the meds because of her history. She says a lot that she doesn't want to disappoint you. Maybe it will help with you here. You can explain to her how she needs this medication. Using the medication she is taking now is not drug abuse. It's what her body needs."

"Ok, thanks, Cassie," Jared said, smiling at her.

She gently touched his shoulder.

"This is hard, Jared, very hard. Death is not easy for the person dying nor for their loved ones."

"What does she say about me? Does she talk a lot about me?"

"She loves to talk about you. She says how very proud she is of you. She says that you are brave and smart."

"Does she say anything that doesn't make sense? The last time I was here, she said confusing things. It was like she had something she wanted to tell me. I don't know!" Jared ran his hands through his hair in frustration.

"Jared, people as sick as your mama do hallucinate. She is lucid, though, most of the time. Earlier today, she said she was so happy you were coming for the weekend. Let's see, what else did she say, exactly," Cassie said, looking away as if she were trying to recall the conversation. "She said that you were smarter than she ever was. She said that you were smarter than all of them."

"Oh, she did say she wished that you knew and that she had known sooner. She was saying this right before she fell asleep."

"She wished that I knew what?" Jared said, exasperated, running his fingers through his hair once again.

"I don't know," Cassie said, frowning. "I asked her, but she didn't say. She said she wanted to tell me a secret and then said that you didn't belong here and that you never did. After saying that, she fell asleep," Cassie said, shrugging.

"What does that mean?" Jared questioned.

"I don't know, but hey, how many of us do belong here, right? If you want to get ahead in life, you have to get out of here. We know that, don't we, Jared?"

Jared nodded.

CHAPTER 69

"JARED, JARED," he heard a wispy voice call out.

Cassie had only left fifteen minutes ago. Damn, had he woken his mother moving around? He padded to her bedroom and opened the door. She saw him and smiled, attempting to sit up and rubbing at her eyes.

Jared frowned. Was it possible she had lost even more weight since he had seen her two weeks ago? She looked even tinier and paler than the last time he had been here.

"Jared!" she cried out, pleased to see him.

He entered the room and crossed to the bed.

"Hey, Ma," he said, smiling at her and willing himself not to cry at her diminished state.

"Are you staying the whole weekend, son?"

"Yeah, Ma, I am. I brought all my things."

"Yay," she called out, clapping her hands together like a young child.

His heart clenched.

"Sit down, talk to me," she said, patting the bed. He told her about his classes and shared a funny story about Randy, his roommate, getting locked out of the room in only a towel. He had hoped the story would make her laugh, and it did.

Then, suddenly, she turned serious and frowned.

"You know what I did this week?"

"No, Ma, what?"

"I went to the storage lockers with Charlie and got three boxes of pictures and old photo albums. Remember Gammy and her photo albums?"

Jared nodded.

"Anyway, I had Charlie help me, and we brought the boxes back here."

Jared frowned.

"That was a long walk, Ma. Why didn't you wait for me? I would have gone to get anything you wanted."

"I know, but I wanted them right away. I needed to make sure they were here before, well, you know," she stuttered, "before, before I left."

She means died, Jared thought, trying to keep the tears from his eyes and being unsuccessful in the effort.

"I want you to have these boxes, son. All the old photos are in there and other mementos of yours from school and other..." She hesitated again. "Things. The boxes are in your room now on the bed but please don't look at them yet. You weren't planning on sleeping in your old room, were you?"

"No, Ma, that bed is too small for me now. I was planning on bunking out on the couch."

Alison nodded.

"After I'm gone, Jared, I need you to look through the boxes."

"Okay, Ma, I'll keep them, sure."

She sat up in bed suddenly.

"Jared, after I leave, you must go through the boxes not just keep them and store them somewhere. Make sure you go through all the boxes, go through every single one! Please! Promise me!"

She was getting agitated, and then she grimaced in pain.

"Does something hurt, Ma? Are you in a lot of pain?"

Her skin was looking even paler if that was even possible.

"Yeah, a little," she said breathlessly.

He stood up to get the pill bottle.

"Jared!" she called with some urgency. "Promise me you'll go through those boxes, all of them!"

"Yeah, okay, Mom, sure. Look, right now, you need a pill, and I need to go get them."

"Promise me, Jared! Say it! Promise me now!"

"Yeah, Ma, I'll save the boxes," he said, shaking his head as he exited the room. What was the big deal with a bunch of old pictures? He didn't like to think much about the past, but he would save them if it meant that much to her.

CHAPTER 70

ALISON STRUGGLED TO BREATHE. The hospital bed was so uncomfortable. Every inch of her body hurt. Alison was aware of what was happening and that she was in the hospital now. She knew she didn't have much longer. She felt trapped in her body, and she wanted out! She heard the constant beep and whir of the monitors surrounding her. She knew what she should have done. It had become all too clear to her now that it was too late. He might not understand. She should have told him the truth. Saying nothing was no better than lying to him as they all had done for so long. He deserved to know the truth! She needed to write Jared a note! *Please! Please! I need paper and a pen!* A paper and a pen now! Her vision was fuzzy for some reason, but she knew two nurses were standing near her bed in the hospital room. Why wouldn't they listen to her? Why were they just standing there? Why wouldn't they help her? Why had she waited so long? She was running out of time quickly.

"She seems agitated," the young nurse whispered to her older colleague.

"She does," the older woman agreed. "The doctor said we could increase her pain meds. It won't hurt her now. She seems like she wants something."

The young nurse bent very close to Alison.

"Can I do something for you, honey?"

In Alison's mind, her words were coming out strong and clear, but the nurses heard, "Mm, pa, pa pe, pp, Jah, Jar!"

"I don't know what you want, dear," the nurse said, looking over at her colleague, who shrugged in reply.

Alison struggled to sit up without achieving the posture. She tried to speak again. She urgently enunciated, "Jare, Jare, d, d."

"Oh, your son! I think she wants her son. We called him," the older nurse said, rubbing Alison's shoulder. "He's on his way here."

No! No! Why wouldn't they help her? She needed to write the note now. Why did her head hurt so bad? With herculean effort, Alison shook her head back and forth.

"No! No!" she said in a voice as loud as she could possibly make it.

"Need paapaa, pnn, pnn."

Alison lifted her arm and mimed writing.

"Does she want to write something down?" the young nurse exclaimed as if she had just solved a puzzle.

"Maybe," the older nurse shrugged. "It certainly can't hurt. Susan, get a notepad and pen from the nurse's station."

Alison thought she saw the younger woman walk out of the room. She was running out of time. She knew it.

"Hurry," she said urgently, yet the words came out as "hoo-hoo."

"Try to calm down, sweetie," the older nurse soothed. "The medication will take effect soon."

No, no, no! The meds would make her go to sleep. She wouldn't be able to write the note. Jared wouldn't know the truth. The young nurse walked back into the room carrying a small notepad and a pen.

"Do you want to write something down, Alison?" she inquired.

Alison grabbed for the pen and paper hungrily, urgently.

Why wouldn't her fingers work? She wrote, *Jared, I love you. I didn't know until Gammy died. I didn't know,* she wrote, followed by three exclamation points. She handed the note back to the nurse and laid back against the pillow. She was so exhausted, and now she was getting so very sleepy.

"She's calming down now."

The older nurse nodded.

"What does the note say? It looks like gibberish, basically. It says Jare, Jar, that's all I can make out."

"Her son's name is Jared. Maybe give it to him when he gets here. Maybe it will mean something to him."

CHAPTER 71

JARED LOOKED AT THE NOTE AGAIN. It looked like hiero-glyphics, but it was definitely Alison's familiar scrawl. The nurses were right, though. He was sure that the note was meant for him. He shifted uncomfortably in the green upholstered chair and looked at his mother, lying silently in the hospital bed. She was heavily medicated due to the pain. She had been nonrespon-sive since he had entered the room. Even when he kissed her and stroked her forehead, she had not responded. He looked down at the note. The writing was dark as if she had pressed the pen into the paper with all her might. *Jar*—yes, that had to be him. He peered closely at the note. Alison had always written in a jagged form that, to strangers, would look like scribbling. He was usu-ally good at deciphering her writing. *Didn't know*, he finally made out those two words. Then, *didn't know* again, followed by excla-mation points. The next line was something undecipherable about Gammy. He sighed and stuffed the note in his pocket. A nurse, followed by a young doctor, entered the room. They lifted the sheet and looked at Alison's feet and legs. The nurse crossed over to Jared and patted him on the shoulder.

"It won't be long now," she said solemnly.

Jared nodded sadly as tears began to fill his eyes.

CHAPTER 72

JARED SHIVERED AND PULLED ON HIS JACKET, zipping it up. The key was stuck in the lock of the trailer door. He looked down, seeing the slight bend at the bottom of the storm door where Bobby had kicked it all those years ago. Jared wiggled the key firmly and heard the lock finally click over. He pushed the door open the rest of the way and entered the trailer he had shared with his mother for all those years. He hadn't been by in months. The trailer made him sad. He could still see his mother lying in her bed the last time he had been there. She had passed away in the hospital two months after that visit. Jared was all alone in the world now. Gammy and Grandpa had been deceased for many years. Alison's own death was approaching the six-month mark. He had thrown himself into finishing school after his mother's passing. Finals had been coming up in six weeks at the time of her death, and he had been finishing his senior thesis. He hadn't been back home in all that time. What was the point, really? No one here to see, to visit. As he finished his finals, Harold, the trailer park owner, had called him. A generally unpleasant man, he proved no different, saying without preamble,

"Jared, you're a hard one to reach. You owe three months' back rent. I know your mom has passed, but business is business."

"I'll pay it," Jared sighed. "Send me the amount."

"Look, Jared, if you aren't interested in moving back here, I can find someone else to lease the trailer. I've already had a couple of people call saying they need a place to stay."

"Yeah, yeah, do that," Jared said, not wanting to deal with the issue. Two months later, Harold called and said the trailer had been leased. He told Jared if he wanted anything from inside, he would need to get it this weekend. Jared didn't want anything, not that they had ever had anything of monetary value, but he knew he should collect the few photo albums that Gammy had made years ago. Plus, there were some other mementos that his mother had saved. He remembered now how adamant she had been about him keeping the boxes. He wasn't sure what was in the boxes. There were probably awards from school and that one baseball trophy from the only year he had ever played baseball in the community league. These things he guessed he should keep. Maybe he could show the old pictures to his kid one day.

It was cold in here. As he walked further into the trailer, he wrinkled up his nose. What was that smell? It must be rotting food. Had no one cleaned out the refrigerator? Who wanted to live here with the trailer in this condition? Someone as drugged out as his mother had been in the past. He entered the kitchen. He opened the refrigerator. It was practically empty, but the smell was coming from inside it. He opened the crisper drawer and discovered a head of lettuce; well, that was what it used to be. Now, it looked more like some science experiment about the effects of mold. He found a garbage bag, picked up the noxious clump, and dropped it inside. He would put it in the dumpster when he left. He randomly opened the cupboard. A large box of Cheerios sat inside with a large hole gnawed in the side. Rodents, ugh, he was going to get his things and get the hell out. He found several boxes stacked on his bed. They contained all of Gammy's photo albums, certificates from school, and the baseball trophy he remembered. He wondered why they were all out on the bed like that. Had his mother been going through things before she died? He opened one of the photo albums. Once he started to look, it was hard to stop. He saw pictures from the aquarium, where he had gone with his mother, Cole, and best friend Jackson years ago. Here was a picture of him standing in front of the trailer the year before he had started working at the horse farm. He knew it was the year before because he stared at a tall, pudgy boy staring awkwardly at the ground. Those had been hard years. Jared had been teased unmercifully at school. "Hey, fatso. Of course, he likes sea creatures. He's a whale himself."

He could still hear the taunts of his classmates so clearly in his mind. But soon after this picture was taken, he started working at the horse farm. He flipped a page of the photo album. Yes, there it was. He remembered this picture. He was proudly leading a horse out of the barn. That job had saved him in so many ways. It had gotten him out of the trailer when his mother's addiction had been raging. Mr. Anderson, the owner of the horse farm, had told him that his father was an alcoholic when he was a kid. He understood Jared. He had been a hell of a role model when Jared needed someone more than ever. The work had been hard and physical, but Jared hadn't cared. He had been happy to be away from his mother and the rotating cast of boyfriends that entered and exited their trailer regularly. Also, the longer Jared worked on the horse farm, the more his physique changed. He began to fill out and build muscles from hauling and lifting. By high school, he had developed into a large, muscular young man. With his cascade of dark, black curls and over six feet tall, girls became attracted to him. He dated some and lost his virginity after junior prom, but seeing his mother cycle through lover after lover for years left a bad taste in his mouth. He wanted out. He didn't want to be tied down. He wanted a good life far from here, and that was what he had focused on. Also, while almost the whole high school class seemed to want to party, Jared was decidedly uninterested in drinking and drugs. He had seen way too much of that with his mother. No thanks! So many memories came flooding back. He picked up an even older album. There was Gammy and Grandpa years ago. Here was a photo of Gammy holding a baby and Grandpa smiling so widely it looked like his face might break. *The baby must be Mom*, Jared thought. He flipped a page and saw a picture of Alison as a young woman. It must have been her high school graduation, as she wore a graduation robe and a mortarboard. He peered at the photo more closely. His mom was young and thin, and he could see a light in her eyes. That light had gone out so long ago. He flipped another page. Alison was standing with her arms around a young man in a uniform. Jared stared at the picture of Jared, the father he never knew. The father who had died before he was even born. Jared peered intently at his father. Grandpa had always said that Jared looked just like him. As Jared got older, he became aware that he was taller and larger than all his family. Gammy, Grandpa, and Alison were fairly tiny people, all with lighter, straight hair. His friend Jackson had even asked him, "Are you adopted? Because you don't look like your mom or grandpa at all."

But Grandpa had always maintained, "You get your height from your dad, boy."

Jared continued to look at several more pictures of Jared, his dad. The man had straight hair; many shades lighter than Jared's own dark, curly mop.

"He is much smaller than I am," Jared said aloud.

He had seen these pictures before and had never seen the resemblance that his grandfather proclaimed. *Don't see the resemblance, never did,* Jared thought, shaking his head. As Jared got older, other than a few photos taken by Mr. Anderson at the horse farm, family photos became nonexistent. Alison would have been too high to photograph her son. First, Grandpa and then Gammy became too sick to continue taking pictures and making albums. He had reached the very bottom of the third and last box. He understood why there were no photos of him as he got older, but now that he had gone through all the albums, he did wonder why there were no newborn photos of him. There were photos of Alison pregnant but none of her holding him as a newborn. The pictures of him started at about nine months of age. Why nothing before? Weird! Jared was about to return all the albums to the boxes when he noticed that some newspaper article was folded up and stuck under the flap at the bottom of the box. He pulled it out carefully and started to read. Suddenly, he felt hot, then cold! What? What was he reading about? He carefully unfolded the paper. A headline blared: "Baby Paul Still Missing." He began to read the short article: "There are no new developments in the missing child case of the nine-month-old boy abducted from Allenburgh." Jared stared at a blurry picture of a baby that resembled him with dark, curly black hair. He continued reading: "The police say the search is still active even with no new leads. Baby Paul Branson was abducted from the Total Foods Store in Allenburgh on May 23." May 23 was his birthday! Is that why Gammy had saved this article for all these years? Because some missing kid had the same birthday as him? Jared continued reading the article. "His parents, Eric and Brynn Branson, say they still hold out hope that their missing child will soon be found." Jared turned the page carefully and stared at a photo of a couple holding hands and looking sad. *My God, that man looks like me,* Jared thought, looking at the man's stocky build and cascade of curls. Jared ran his hands through his hair. *Why had Gammy kept this article? Why was it hidden away at the very bottom of the box? Why does this random guy resemble me so much?* His baby pictures all started at the age of this baby, this Baby Paul. *What the hell?*

CHAPTER 73

JARED LOOKED UP AND STARED out the trailer window, remembering his confusing conversation with his mother. It was the time before the last time he would see her alive. It was one of the last semi-coherent conversations they had.

"They must miss you," she had said.

It had all been so weird. Her words had made no sense to him, and as he began questioning her, she fell asleep. The conversation had deeply confused him. He had even called his old roommate's father, who was a doctor, to question him. He had shared that his mother had said disturbing things to him without stating what they were, that she had told him strange things about his past that didn't seem likely to be true. Randy's father had told him that with Alison so sick and on substantial painkillers, it was highly probable that she might hallucinate. Randy's father stated that she could have seen something on TV and became confused about whether it was real or not. Jared had put the confusing conversation out of his mind, not having the time or the inclination to process words that made no sense.

But now this! What did it all mean? Were Alison's words true? Had she been trying to tell him something? He picked up an old photograph of his mother and stared deeply into her face as if the picture might begin to talk and give him the desired answers. He picked the newspaper article back up and turned to the photo of the young parents of the missing baby. He stared at the father, Eric. There was no doubt that he looked like this man. He picked Alison's picture back up. "Mom," he said aloud, "or whoever you are."

He looked back down at the newspaper article. He read the final paragraph: "If you have any information, please contact the Allenburgh police on Old Main Road." Jared looked at the date of the paper. The paper was yellowing and was over twenty years old. Suddenly, Jared knew what he needed to do. He would load the boxes in his car, and then take a trip. He was driving to Allenburgh. His GPS stated that it was only two and a half hours away. Jared stood up and ran from the trailer, hurtling back to his car as fast as his legs would take him.

He was going to Allenburgh now—right now.

CHAPTER 74

"AL," THE RECEPTIONIST CALLED OUT, "There's a man out front who wants to speak to an officer. Butch and Don just left on a call. Can you help him?"

Al rolled his eyes. When random people showed up, it was usually to complain about something. Usually, a neighbor or some other minutiae. Invariably, they were old. *Sometimes*, he thought, *they just want something to do—someone to talk to.*

"Yeah, ok, be right there," he called out, straightening his tie. He walked out to the public area, surprised to see a large man in his twenties standing there. Not an old person who wanted to complain about the neighbor's dog. The young man looked mildly upset as he ran his hands through his curly hair.

"Sir, I'm Detective Al Grover. Is there something I can help you with?"

The young man nodded and held up a yellowing newspaper that looked ready to fall to pieces.

"Have you heard about this case? A Baby Paul was kidnapped in this town from a grocery store?" the young man questioned.

Al took the newspaper, handling it carefully as he looked at the date. He whistled. This paper was from over twenty years ago. He had been a young cop then, just beginning his career. He read the first few lines of the newspaper article. He remembered this case. He hadn't worked on it, and the detectives on it had long since retired.

"Yeah, I think I might," he said, looking back at the young man.

The man sighed and ran his hands through his hair one more time.

"I might be him; I don't know, but I might be Baby Paul."

"What! How old are you?"

"I'm twenty-two, almost twenty-three."

Ok, so the age was right.

"My mother started to tell me something confusing right before she died. I thought she was hallucinating, but I just found this newspaper earlier this morning. I took a DNA test last year, and my mother got very upset about it. I couldn't figure out why, but maybe now I know."

The young man was frustrated and confused. He grabbed the paper from Al's hand and flipped it to the second page.

"Look, look," he said, pointing to the picture of the parents of the missing child.

"Do I look like that guy? Do I look like the father? He's named Eric, I guess."

Al looked at the picture and then studied the young man before replying. He whistled and said, "You do—you look almost exactly like that guy."

He gestured behind the front desk.

"Come on back. I want to take some information from you and pull some old files."

The young man nodded.

CHAPTER 75

BRYNN GLANCED DOWN AT THE RINGING PHONE. She didn't recognize the number, and normally she would not answer, but strangely she heard a voice in her head say, *do it, pick up the phone.* She sighed and said, "Hello," in a somewhat grumpy voice to discourage interaction. She braced herself to hear some fast-talking telemarketer try to convince her that her windows or roof needed to be replaced immediately, but instead, she heard a polite male voice rumble, "Mrs. Branson? I am trying to reach Mrs. Brynn Branson?"

"That's me," Brynn replied.

"Mrs. Branson, my name is Detective Al Grover. I believe you used to live here in Allenburgh with your husband."

She heard papers shuffle. "A Mr. Eric Branson?"

Oh, God, had something happened to Eric? She certainly hoped not.

"Yes, I did, but that was over twenty years ago. Eric and I have been divorced for many years. He is remarried."

"Yes, yes, I have that right here," the detective affirmed. "Ma'am, we had something strange happen a few days ago. We did some investigation to make sure it wasn't a scam, but so far, everything we have been told is checking out."

"I have no idea what you are talking about," Brynn said, beginning to feel aggravated and hoping that this man was who he said he was.

"Anyway, we have just called your ex-husband, and he is on his way here now. We want to do a DNA test on him."

Brynn interrupted, "Wait, wait, I don't understand. Is Eric in some type of trouble?"

"No, ma'am, not at all. We need you to come in for a DNA test as well."

"What! Why! What are you talking about?"

"I don't want you to get overexcited until everything is confirmed, but it is possible, actually likely, that we have found your son."

"My son!" Brynn gulped. "You mean you found his body? Is that what you mean?"

"No, ma'am, if it all checks out, your son is very much alive."

"But he would be twenty-three years old now."

"Yes, ma'am, that's right. Is it possible for you to come to the station for the DNA test? As I said, your ex-husband is already on the way, and your son—at this point, your purported son—is here as well. We want to sort out this case as soon as possible. As I said, the initial information we obtained from the young man all checks out."

"Wait, Paul, my baby, is there at the police station at Allenburgh?"

"Yes, ma'am."

The detective continued talking, but Brynn dropped the phone in her bag, grabbed her car keys, and sprinted out the cottage door. If the traffic were good, it would take her at least thirty minutes to get there.

CHAPTER 76

BRYNN PARKED IN THE POLICE STATION LOT. She cast her eyes around, looking for Eric. There were many cars, and she had no idea what Eric was driving these days. She saw no one. She clicked her car door closed with the key fob. Her heart was beating so hard in her chest. She hesitated right before she pulled the door open. She rehearsed the phone call she had with the detective once again in her mind. On the drive here, she had thought more than once that she hoped she hadn't hallucinated the whole conversation. A call actually had occurred; she had checked her call log more than once, and yes, the call was listed right there. Brynn had been off all medication for years now and rarely drank alcohol. She wasn't depressed. She wasn't anxious and no longer thought obsessively about Paul. She couldn't be losing it after all this time, could she? Seeing Eric would confirm that the story was real, that this wasn't just a figment of her imagination. She looked around the parking lot again. No one. She made a large intake of breath and opened the door. She approached the window where a receptionist sat behind a large piece of plexiglass. The receptionist was looking down and seemingly unaware of Brynn's presence. Just then, the door opened. Brynn looked over and felt relief washing over her. Eric! There he was! So, it wasn't all a dream. But then Brynn let out a gasp. Wait a minute, the man was not Eric. He was much too young. This man, with his dark, curly hair, stocky build, and trace of a beard, looked like the Eric Brynn had lived with and loved all those years ago. Brynn closed her eyes, wondering if the man was a mirage. She had seen Eric and Katrina in the store two months ago. Eric was now losing his hair and had a definite middle-aged paunch. She opened her eyes, shaking her head.

The young man seemed to notice her for the first time. He eyed her carefully before slowly walking toward her. Brynn felt all kinds of feelings in her body; her heart beat even faster, and her stomach did a series of somersaults. Her body was telling her something. She knew, she just knew! The young man looked at her carefully. He put up his hand and ran it through his mop of curly hair as Eric had always done. "Do I know you?" he inquired carefully. You seem very familiar to me," the young man rumbled in a deep voice.

Brynn began to cry.

"Oh, Paulie, Paulie, my baby," Brynn cried out. "You're home, you're finally home!"

The door opened again, and Eric entered. He stopped short as he saw the young man and Brynn.

"What the actual hell!" he said in amazement. Just then, the door behind the receptionist opened, and the detective walked out.

"Guess you've all already met," he said. "Come on back, all of you. We have some things to figure out."

CHAPTER 77

JARED SIGHED AND PULLED THE CHEAP, threadbare towel tighter around his waist. This hotel sucked! The water had come out of the showerhead in a dribble. All the corners looked dirty, and a half-chewed piece of pizza had been on the floor next to the bed. He had picked it up quickly with a handful of Kleenex and placed it in the small trash container. He was loath to investigate it further. Did he really want to know? Both his mother and his father—his mother and father! —had offered to let him stay at their houses. Apparently, his mother lived alone in a small beach cottage about thirty minutes from Allenburgh. His father had remarried and had four kids. He had brothers and sisters! He hadn't wanted to stay with either of them. It was too much to process. Everything had checked out. The timeline that Jared knew matched perfectly with the kidnapping of Paul. The initial DNA tests had been submitted and should be back tomorrow afternoon. This would confirm that he was related to Eric and Brynn. Although, there was absolutely no denying that he closely resembled Eric Branson. Jared hadn't felt comfortable staying with strangers, which was what they were, even if they were related. He needed time alone. He should have picked a different hotel. There had to be a less crappy choice. He would sleep here tonight. Maybe get up early, get coffee, and try to find a better hotel before returning to the police station. Suddenly, Jared remembered the box he had thrown in the back of the car. Detective Grover had the newspaper article, but there was more in that box. Suddenly, he felt compelled to rifle through the remaining items in that box. He hurriedly put on his jeans and grabbed a T-shirt. He rushed to the car, grabbed the box, and brought it back into the hotel room. He perched on the edge of the bed. The pictures he had already looked at were lying in disarray on top. He removed them from the box. He also pulled that clunky, heavy softball trophy out of the box as well. He hesitated, with his hand hovering over the box. He was having a flashback as he remembered the exact moment he had pulled the newspaper article out of the box. He still could see the article clearly in his mind. He could replicate the heat and the cold that had washed over his body as he tried to read and understand what it all meant. He shook his head in an attempt to clear it. He reached into the box and pulled out the certificate he had received for winning that essay contest in his sophomore year of college. So that was it. The box was now empty. He peered into it. He smelled the familiar smell of his mother's trailer—or maybe he imagined it. He picked up the box. He prepared to place it on the floor and then scoop the mementos and photos into it, but as he did so—wait! Was something else stuck under the flap of the box at the very bottom? The article had been half hidden under the flap. He picked the box up, bringing it close to his face. Yes, a small white piece of paper was jammed under the flap at the bottom. He pulled at the paper. It was stuck tightly. What the hell! Had his mother—err,

Alison—glued something to the bottom? He gave another careful tug. He didn't want to rip whatever it was. It wasn't dislodging. He lifted the flap and saw a piece of tape. She had taped this piece of paper to the bottom inner flap. Why? Jared began to carefully peel off the tape. At first, only small strands pulled free, but then, all at once, he was able to extricate a much larger piece of the tape. The paper was loose now. He pulled it carefully out of the box, turning it over. It was a half sheet of white printer paper. There was his mother's familiar scrawled handwriting. He began to read: "I love you so much, Jared!!!" Three exclamation points, he noted.

"I must tell you. We all loved you. You made our lives. Your grandparents kept the secret from you and took it to their graves, but I can't. It was a dark time, Jared. I was so messed up, more messed up than I knew. You aren't ours. Grandpa and Gammy kidnapped you when you were a baby. They stole you from a store. I don't know the details. They thought I was going to kill myself, so they brought you home to me. Gammy told me two weeks before she passed. You know how messed up I was then, so I put it out of my mind. It was a sin that I didn't tell you. I found this newspaper article hidden in Gammy's stuff after she died. I tried to pretend that maybe she hallucinated what she told me, but I think I knew it was true, and I just wanted you to be mine, only mine. You have a family out there somewhere. I hope the newspaper article will help you find them. I truly didn't know where you had come from when they gave you to me as a baby. During all those years while you were growing up, I was convinced that you were mine, and I guess I convinced myself that Jared was your father. I wanted that to be true. Sorry will never be enough, so I won't say it. I hope you can find answers. I hope you have the best life and maybe one day you might be able to forgive me. I will never forgive myself. I love you."

He peered down at the note. She had started to sign it "Mom," but then had scratched it out and written "Alison." So, it was true, no doubts now. This was it! This half-page of scrawled confession was all that he would ever know. Why? Because his mother had been sad! How had they been able to pull it off? So many unknowns. Jared shook his head. He would show this note to Detective Grover and Brynn and Eric tomorrow morning. Brynn and Eric! He looked up and took in his own reflection in the adjacent mirror. "Mom and Dad," he whispered, running his hands through his hair.

CHAPTER 78

BRYNN SMILED AS SHE PULLED into the circular driveway of Eric and Katrina's house. There was the sports car that Eric drove. She parked directly behind it. The car was so small, and Eric was so large. *How did he even fit in it? All about the status,* Brynn thought. She didn't see Katrina's van as she stepped out of the car. She hoped she was home. Katrina was consistently warm and friendly to Brynn. She made her feel she belonged here, even in this improbable situation. She might feel uncomfortable if she was alone with Eric. He, too, seemed slightly uncomfortable around her. Oh, well, the kids were probably home. They were a talkative, lively bunch. They would make her feel comfortable even without Katrina there. She knocked on the door, and it opened immediately. Had he been standing behind it, watching her walk up the driveway?

"Hi, Brynn," Eric said, gesturing for her to enter and then looking down.

Brynn stepped into the entryway. The house was very quiet.

"Where is everyone?" Brynn questioned. "The kids? Paul?"

"Oh, they'll be right back. They all ran to the store with Katrina to pick up a few things for our dinner."

"Paul, uh, Jared, man, I don't know what to call him! He was going to stay and wait for you, but Carrie insisted that he come with them." Eric smiled.

"I think Carrie has a little crush on Paul. She hangs all over him and always wants his attention."

Brynn nodded. "Paul seems to love all the attention, too. I think he loves having brothers and sisters."

Eric nodded. "Thanks for coming tonight, Brynn. Jare, Paul really wanted you here. I'm not sure why. I don't want you to feel awkward. I know the situation is a little strange."

Brynn nodded.

"It's fine. I would do anything for Paul. And Katrina doesn't seem to mind when I am around."

"She doesn't mind, Brynn, not at all, ever. Family means a great deal to Katrina, and she completely accepts you as family. You are always welcome here."

"How is Paul? Is he doing okay? He has been through so much."

"He is, Brynn. He is doing quite well. He really likes the therapist he is seeing and is starting to open up a little more. He talks more to Katrina than me but is sharing more about his past with her. It was rough for him, Brynn, very rough."

"Oh, okay," Brynn nodded, gulping.

"Oh, Brynn," Eric said, "don't feel bad. I don't think he is trying to keep things from you or from me. I think he is trying to protect you, so you don't feel bad."

"Katrina actually said that he feels guilty for what he put us through. That he knows we suffered for years."

"Oh, no, it's not his fault!" Brynn said immediately. "Poor baby!"

Even now that he towered over her, she would always see Paul as her baby.

"I know why he talks to Katrina," Eric said and stopped.

"Well, Katrina is warm and easy to talk to. I understand that," Brynn said.

"No, Brynn, it's more," he said, running his hands through his thinning hair. He sighed and continued. "Katrina had a very tough life growing up. I think she and Jare—Paul relate to each other."

Brynn nodded again with a quizzical look, unsure of what Eric was talking about.

"Look, Brynn, it's not my story to tell. I'm sure Katrina will tell you if you ask, though. She's not ashamed of her past at all. She's done a lot of therapy to heal. Katrina basically grew up in a cult. Her family was very religious, and they followed that weird guy, Daniel Lewison, all over the country. You might have heard about him on the news. He committed suicide several years ago."

"Maybe, yeah, I think so," Brynn said.

"Anyway, that nut led them and his other followers down a terrible path. There was drug use. They did sexual stuff with the kids, including Katrina."

"Oh, no," Brynn said, drawing in a breath and shaking her head.

"So, yeah, I think Paul and Katrina relate to each other. The misuse of religion, the drug use."

Brynn looked down, thinking of Katrina. Her mind flashed to all the snarky comments she had made in her own head about Katrina as she had looked at all those Facebook and Instagram photos over the years. All those positive, sunny posts. So, Katrina wasn't what she seemed. She wasn't obliviously optimistic and trying to show how much more she had than others. She wasn't lording her best life over everyone who had less. Maybe she was just that grateful for all she had because she knew true lack—knew what abuse was. *It is so easy to judge others, so convinced we know all about them when what we know is nothing at all. Everyone suffers,* Brynn thought. *Just because it doesn't show doesn't mean it isn't there.*

"She'll tell you about it if you ask," Eric repeated. "I don't want to tell her story, though. It's her journey, not mine."

"I will ask her," Brynn said with resolve. "I want to know, Eric. I will talk to both Katrina and Paul. Maybe, somehow, I can help."

"That's great, Brynn," Eric said, smiling at her.

Outside, a car door slammed. Eric looked out the window at the side of the door.

"Hey, my crew is back," he said cheerfully.

CHAPTER 79

INSTEAD OF CLOSING HER EYES AND PRAYING with Katrina, Eric, their four kids, and Paul, Brynn looked at the others seated around the dining table. How improbable this all was! Paul was back, and he was now staying with Katrina, Eric, and their kids. Eric had confided in Brynn that Paul wanted to go to law school, although he had thought that was just a dream since he had no money.

"We're going to make it happen," Eric told Brynn. He made excellent grades in college."

Then, Eric's face turned deadly serious.

"I'll do anything I can to help Paul. He had such a hard upbringing, Brynn. He finally told me that his mother—I mean the woman who raised him—was a heroin addict."

Brynn drew in a breath. "I didn't know that. He tells me so little."

"I know. I think he is trying to protect you. Please don't feel rejected, Brynn. I think he believes he is supposed to protect you. I think he thinks that's what you have to do. It seems that he cared for that woman, the one who raised him, since he was just a boy."

Brynn shook her head.

"He's going to therapy regularly. I think it's helping him too."

The prayer was done, and the food was now being passed around. Paul—or Jared, or, to Eric's daughter, 'hey you,' as she called him—cleared his throat.

"Mom," he said, looking at Brynn, "I requested that you join us for dinner tonight because I have something to tell everyone. I have a surprise."

Katrina nodded. *She already knows what it is*, Brynn thought, looking at her.

"It's a good surprise," Katrina confirmed.

"Well, I've been seeing my counselor for several months now, and I have more work to do, but there is one thing I'm ready to do right now."

Eric and Brynn looked at each other quizzically.

"I want to change my name legally. James, my counselor, says I need my own identity. I don't want to be Jared anymore. I'm named after a man I never met and am not related to. With all due respect, Dad, I don't want to be Paul anymore either. I know I was named after your grandfather, but if I use Paul, I will be 'Baby Paul,' the missing boy. You know what happened at the registry last week, with that clerk yelling out, "I know you, you're Baby Paul. I read your story in the paper."

I don't want that."

Brynn and Eric nodded.

"I understand, son," Eric affirmed.

"Anyway, James and I came up with a new name for me."

"It's good," Katrina said.

"Ok, what is it?" Eric asked anxiously.

"I'm going to be—well, I already am—Brendon Branson."

"I like it, son. It has a real ring to it," Eric enthused.

"Oh," Brynn inhaled and tried to hold back tears. "After me? You're changing your name to be like mine?"

"Yeah, Mom, if it's ok with you."

"Oh, son, of course it's ok with me."

"Ok, but there's more. Here's my whole name."

Brendon took a dramatic pause.

"Brendon Eric-Allen Branson," he said with a smile.

"I want to acknowledge both my parents and the 'Allen'—well, I hope you both understand, but it's in honor of the woman who raised me, Alison. She had her problems, but with James's help, I am coming to see that she really loved me. She tried her best even though she messed up repeatedly. And she didn't kidnap me. She didn't even know what had happened for years and years."

"That's a fine idea, son. It's an honor."

Brendon sighed in relief. Katrina touched his arm.

"See, I told you everyone would be fine with it."

"Hey, kid," Brendon said, pointing his knife at Carrie, Eric's youngest daughter.

"Did you hear, kid? I'm Brendon. No more calling me 'hey you'!"

Carrie giggled.

"Hey you, Brendon," she said.

THE END